JUST KILL ME

ALSO BY ADAM SELZER

Play Me Backwards

JUST KILL ME

ADAM SELZER

SIMON & SCHUSTER BFYR

NEW YORK LONDON TORONTO SYDNEY NEW DELHI

An imprint of Simon & Schuster Children's Publishing Division
1230 Avenue of the Americas, New York, New York 10020

SIMON & SCHUSTER BFYR is a trademark of Simon & Schuster, Inc.
For information about special discounts for bulk purchases,
please contact Simon & Schuster Special Sales at 1-866-506-1949 or
business@simonandschuster.com.
The Simon & Schuster Speakers Bureau can bring authors to your live event.
For more information or to book an event, contact the Simon & Schuster Speakers
Bureau at 1-866-248-3049 or visit our website at www.simonspeakers.com.
Also available in a SIMON & SCHUSTER BFYR hardcover edition
Cover design by Chloë Foglia
Interior design by Hilary Zarycky
The text for this book was set in Bembo Std.
Manufactured in the United States of America
First SIMON & SCHUSTER BFYR paperback edition August 2017
2 4 6 8 10 9 7 5 3
The Library of Congress has cataloged the hardcover edition as follows:
Names: Selzer, Adam, author.
Title: Just kill me / Adam Selzer.
Description: New York : Simon & Schuster Books for Young Readers, [2016] |
Summary: After taking a summer job with a Chicago ghost tour company, eighteen-year-old Megan is interrogated for murder, when the reports of "real" ghost sightings increase along with the number of missing tourists.
Identifiers: LCCN 2015038791 | ISBN 9781481434942 (hc) |
ISBN 9781481434966 (eBook)
Subjects: | CYAC: Death—Fiction. | Ghosts—Fiction. | Murder—Fiction.
| Tour guides (Persons)—Fiction. | Lesbians—Fiction. |
Summer Employment—Fiction. | Chicago (Ill.)—Fiction.
Classification: LCC PZ7.S4652 Ju 2016 | DDC [Fic]—dc23
LC record available at https://lccn.loc.gov/2015038791
ISBN 978-1-4814-3495-9 (pbk)

ACKNOWLEDGMENTS

Thanks to everyone at S&S, in order of appearance: Dani Young, Justin Chanda, Liz Kossnar (hey Liz, get the new Grimes album), and Alison Velea (who had to fact-check me on all the historical swearing). And to Adrienne Rosado, my agent, who does impossible things.

In Chicago: thanks to Ronni and Aidan, to the crews at The Wormhole, UPS at Grand and Ogden, Chi-Town Eatery (R.I.P), and Sip Coffee. To Angie at Bestway, Ray Johnson, Dale Kaczmarek, Amelia Cotter, the Newberry Library, the Harold Washington Library, Augie at Centuries and Sleuths, Jen Hathy, Patti Vasquez, Craig Collins, and Michael Glover Smith.

From all over, Frank Redfield, Stiffs Incorporated, Caitlyn Doughty, Bess Lovejoy, Atlas Obscura, Amy Vincent, Ryan and Sooj, Tanner, the real Punk Rock James, and Seth (my first partner in ghostly crime).

From: Megan

To: Zoey Baby

Date: Wednesday, 5:12 p.m.

Subject: Something wicked this way comes. . . .

When you were little and watching Disney movies, did you ever sort of wish that the villains would win? I totally did. They had cooler outfits, much better castles, and all the best songs.

For a while I believed that if I watched the same movie a thousand times, just once the ending would be different, and the prince and princess would end up in the dungeon while the villain took over the world. And every time I watched one of those movies, part of me always hoped that this would be the time.

God, I sound like a psycho, don't I? LOL.

Anyway, off to my job tryout. Wish me luck!

Megan

Chapter One

"In this life I have already been declared dead. It wasn't so bad."
—ROGER EBERT

The Blue Line "L" train rolls toward downtown Chicago, and I point my face at my phone so it doesn't look like I'm staring at the two weirdos sitting across from me. Even though I am.

"My old roommate . . . now he was a rat bastard," says Comb-Over Al. "One time he borrowed my boat without even asking, you know. My boat!"

In the seat beside him, Stanley the Stinger grunts.

Comb-Over Al, as I've named him, has dyed the last few hairs on his head so freaking dark that it's like he used India ink, and his furry gut is hanging out from beneath a stained white T-shirt. Beside him is this wrinkly old guy in a pinstriped suit and matching hat. I assume he's a retired hit man and decide to call him Stanley the Stinger. In a movie, he'd be the guy you called to get things done. Comb-Over Al would be his bumbling assistant who eventually screws the whole thing up.

"He's lucky he didn't screw me out of one more dime,"

Al continues, spittle spraying from his mouth. "Because he worked down at the funeral home, ya know. And he'd talk when he got home. I mean, the jag-off would talk, ya know. And I remember every date, every stiff, every amount! Fuck."

Stanley the Stinger grunts again.

Life must have been weird down at Comb-Over Al's place. I imagine him sitting on a cracked leather couch, eating sardines out of a can and watching bowling on television when his roommate blows in, saying, "Boy oh boy! I will always remember this, July seventeenth, as the day I stole $47.50 out of the pockets of the corpse of Hank Jamrag. Now I'm gonna take your boat across the lake to Gary, Indiana, to spend it!"

There is no better people-watching on the planet than on the Blue Line, which starts in Forest Park, where I live, and goes East through downtown Chicago before looping back west to the airport. The Red, Orange, and Brown Line trains have better views out the window, and the Green Line has more entertaining panhandlers, but the Blue Line is the weirdest. I have no idea why, but almost every time I ride it, the other passengers are a regular carnival of grotesques, ghouls, and freaks of nature.

I seriously don't know how people who live in small towns without public transportation cope.

Comb-Over Al and Stanley the Stinger get off at the Pulaski stop, presumably to go break somebody's thumbs, and the train rumbles on while my phone buzzes with enough messages that I feel rather popular for a minute or so.

ADAM SELZER

Zoey, my long-distance girlfriend, sends me a text to wish me luck at the job interview I'm heading into town for. Then Cynthia, my former babysitter (and possible future employer), sends me one to make sure I'm on my way. Mom asks if I'll be home for dinner. I send a smiley face with its tongue out to Zoey, a "yep" to Cyn, and nothing to Mom.

I get along with Mom fine, but she'd flip out if she knew what I was doing tonight.

Our house is a two-story Victorian in Forest Park, a suburb close enough to Chicago that it's basically still the city. The second floor is an apartment just about like any other, with cat-scratched furniture in the living room, Taco Bell wrappers on the floor, and prints from the Frank Lloyd Wright museum on the wall. But the first floor is the funeral parlor my mother owns. In the basement we have all the prep spaces.

Having lived above a funeral home all my life, I have reason to doubt Comb-Over Al's story about his roommate. I'm pretty sure we never had any corpses brought in who had cash in their pockets. Al's roommate probably worked in a morgue or something, and Al just didn't know the difference.

The train goes underground when it comes to the Loop, the main downtown area. When I get off at the Clark and Lake stop and make my way upstairs and outside, I'm right in the middle of a dense forest of gothic towers, art deco skyscrapers, and glass hotels. The heart of the city. French-fry grease permeates the air and mingles with the aroma of freshly-baked brownies from the Blommer's factory, which you can smell all over downtown.

Panhandlers panhandle. A guy plays passable jazz on a saxophone. Some drugged-up freak with a beard smacks his own ass like a prince whose villain put him under a "spank yourself" spell.

Chicago is roasting in the summer and freezing in the winter. It costs a buttload to live here, it's run by criminals, and you see a lot of rats at night. But still. It's Chicago. You either love it or you move out to one of those strip-mall towns in the outer suburbs and wait to die.

The fact that my house was a funeral parlor made it hard for Mom to keep babysitters for me when I was a kid. Mostly they just came to watch me upstairs while Mom worked below, but as soon as they saw a coffin, or followed me down when I went to check out a particularly rowdy funeral, they'd freak out and bolt. It was like they'd gotten clear into high school without ever being confronted with mortality before.

The one sitter who lasted a whole summer was named Cynthia Fargon.

Cyn was like a teenage version of Ursula the Sea Witch from *The Little Mermaid*. She had the same body type, and her smile was always an evil smile. I was sort of smitten with her. She was seventeen or eighteen when I was eleven, but she swore in front of me like I was a fellow teenager, and I really appreciated that.

The funeral stuff didn't bug her a bit. Even going into the basement prep room with me didn't give her the creeps. She gave me some tips when Mom let me help with putting makeup on the bodies, which I loved doing even though it wasn't entirely legal.

Cyn was also the one who introduced me to the joys of looking up rude words in the online *Oxford English Dictionary* (*OED*), which has the complete history of just about every word ever; the print edition is about forty volumes long with tiny type. One time we both got in trouble when everyone at a funeral downstairs heard us laughing at the term "gingerbread-office," a sixteenth-century slang word for "bathroom" that we thought was hilarious.

Some of my other favorite words we found that year were:

podex (slang for "butt," first recorded in 1601)
fore-buttocks ("boobs," first recorded in 1727)
milky way ("boobs," 1622)
suck-egg ("a silly person," 1640)
mustard-token ("worthless person," 1600)

I was sort of disappointed when Mom decided I was old enough not to need a sitter the next summer. I wasn't exactly a social butterfly, and Cyn was just about the best friend I'd ever had. A friend who I knew wouldn't freak out if she came over.

Now, seven years later, Cyn and her friend Ricardo have started a ghost tour company—one of those outfits that takes people around town, tells them scary stories, and lets them look for ghosts. She contacted me out of the blue and told me that being a funeral-home kid with some theater experience made me a perfect candidate to be a ghost-tour guide, so I'm going into the city now to meet Ricardo and ride along on a tour. But I don't think there's any chance I'll end up with the job. My mother's potential customers would probably go apeshit if they knew that someone in the house worked in the ghost business, and anyway, I don't believe in ghosts.

The real reason I'm going is that I'm dying to hang out with Cynthia again

I've kept up with Cyn, off and on, over the years. Now and then we've texted back and forth about what we were doing, and whether the lack of raunchy historical slang terms for "sanitary napkin" in the *OED* was a sign of sexism or respect. But the last time I actually saw her was more than two years ago, when she came to a play I was in, and even then I only saw her for a second.

When I see her waiting for me on Clark Street, it's the first time I've seen her without her hair dyed black—it's more of a lunch-sack brown, which I guess is her natural color, and it's even longer than it used to be. I don't think I like it as much. Her skin seemed almost alabaster white next to black hair, but now it just looks like the color of a pale bus-station hot dog that you only eat half of.

ADAM SELZER

I look different too, of course. Last time she saw me I was dressed as an old lady for a role in *Arsenic and Old Lace*. And the time before that I was just a kid.

"Holy shit!" Cyn says with a laugh, as I approach. When we hug, she runs her fingers through the red section of my hair that hangs just below my shoulders, beneath the dark brown.

"So, you're all graduated and everything?" she asks.

"Yep. Last month."

"College?"

"Doing a couple of years at junior college to get the boring stuff out of the way cheap," I say. "Did you finish your archaeology degree?"

She nods. "Not exactly using it, though. Just driving an excursion van at a nursing home by day, and the tour bus at night. And for this I have racked up six figures in student loans."

"Ouch."

"Seriously, if you can find something better to do than college, do it. I don't know if working for us would make you enough of a living, but you never know. We're working on some initiatives that could make this ghost tour thing a lot more lucrative."

When you cross the Chicago River downtown, you're out of the Loop proper and into a neighborhood called River North, which is mostly tourist traps. The Rock and Roll McDonald's, a two-story cash cow on Clark Street, looms large before us. In the blocks approaching it, happy tourists in

Ohio State University T-shirts walk five abreast. A guy with a giant nose tries to sell necklaces that I assume were stolen by orphans. A dude with a clipboard and some pencils offers to draw people's portraits. A guy in a frog suit poses for photos outside of the Rainforest Cafe across the street.

"All tourist crap around here," says Cyn. "And at night it turns into douchebag central. The McDonald's isn't really a McDonald's so much as a place for nightclub refugees to pee. It's also the city's designated tour-bus parking spot, though, so here we are."

A motley assortment of buses are queued up along the road. First we pass a black bus that says AL CAPONE TOURS on the front, then two sleek motor coaches that say DARKSIDE CHICAGO TOURS: GHOSTS, GANGSTERS, AND GHOULS. Then comes a double-decker sightseeing bus, and a rickety old school bus painted midnight blue with the words MYSTERIOUS CHICAGO: AUTHENTIC GHOST TOURS in yellow vinyl lettering. It brings up the rear of the group like it's the Littlest Tour Bus trying to tag along with the big kids.

Standing in front of it is a young guy who looks like Houdini, only with darker skin and more facial hair: Ricardo. He's talking with a couple of curious tourists in University of Georgia hats.

"We drive people around to murder sites, disaster sites, body dumps . . . all sorts of places that are supposed to be haunted," he says. "We tell you the stories, then you get off

ADAM SELZER

the bus and see if any ghosts show up. It's really the best way to discover the city. If you're here on vacation, it's the thing you'll remember the most about your trip a year from now. Guaranteed."

"Do y'all, like, have people jumping out from behind bushes and stuff?" asks the woman.

"Nothing of the kind! We are the *authentic* ghost-tour company. See, I got my start working for those other guys, and I can tell you right now, their stories aren't anywhere close to accurate. We tell the truth here. It's all meticulously researched."

"How do you tell the truth on a ghost tour?" asks the guy. "Just tell people that ghosts aren't real?"

Now Ricardo folds his clipboard up in his arms and gives the guy a very, very serious look. "Sir," he says, "every time someone says 'I don't believe in ghosts,' there is a little ghost somewhere that falls down dead."

"Uh, Rick?" says Cyn. "They're already dead."

"True," says Ricardo, lightening right up. "So no harm, no foul, I guess. What do you say, folks?"

"Y'all are hilarious," says the woman. "Maybe tomorrow night."

And they walk away to take selfies in front of a bronze statue of Ronald McDonald.

"Hey," says Cyn. "Did you notice she called you 'y'all' when there's only one of you?"

He nods. "In the south, the plural form is 'all y'all.' 'Y'all' is singular."

"Nice," says Cyn. "Because we are large, we contain multitudes."

"Don't call me large," says Ricardo. Then he looks at me and asks, "This your new recruit?"

"Yeah. Megan Henske," says Cyn, as she puts her hand on my shoulder. "Megan, meet Ricardo Torre."

"What's up?" I ask.

He looks me up and down, like he's checking to see if I have good birthing hips or something, then says, "What are you, like, eleven?"

"Eighteen," I say.

"Rick, be nice," says Cyn. "She's got a good head on her shoulders. And she's lived in a funeral home all her life, so you know she's death-positive."

"Yeah," I say. "I'm a black-diaper baby."

"I'm just fucking with you." He laughs, waving a hand. "Much love. You look great. You know much about Chicago history?"

"Enough," I say. "And I could learn more."

"She's good at researching things," says Cyn. "She and I used to play on the *OED* all the time. She knows what a gingerbread-office is."

"And a thunder-mug," I add.

Rick looks at Cyn, then at me, and asks, "What is it?"

"A chamber pot."

He nods thoughtfully, then says, "What about ghosts? You know much about ghosts?"

"Well, I hate to make one fall down dead, but I don't really believe in them."

He seems to loosen up when I say that; he stops leaning forward and lets his shoulders fall back.

"That's actually good," he says. "We tried out a couple of people who were hardcore believers, and it didn't go well. We had this one guy who kept waving holy water around and saying he was helping ghosts 'cross over.' I was like, 'Dude, you're an adult.'"

"Not to mention you kind of need ghosts to stick around, not cross over, right?" I ask.

"Exactly!" He points at me and nods to Cyn, like he's saying, *Well done, scout.*

"Ghosts are real, though," says Cyn. "Rick and I used to know one back home in Magwitch Park. She didn't look nearly spooky enough to be a tour attraction, though. Just like a regular person."

"And her being real doesn't mean every ghost story is real," says Rick. "One percent, tops. For all I know she's the only one."

"So you never see ghosts on the tours?"

"We see some weird stuff. I couldn't swear they were really dead people in front of a panel of scientists. But some weird stuff."

A few more tourists walk up and start asking Rick a question, and Cyn leads me away.

"Come on," she says. "Let me show you the bus."

The seats in the Mysterious Chicago bus are half ducttape, and two of the windows are cracked, but the ceiling is really cool—they've painted a giant map of the city with markers, showing famous disaster sites, the dens of various antique serial killers, and old neighborhood names like "Little Hell" and "Satan's Mile." A few of the landmarks are jokes, like "South Side: Birthplace of Bad, Bad Leroy Brown" and "Rick and Cynthia's Apartment."

I wipe a smear from a window with my sleeve. "So, are you and Rick . . . you know?"

She glances at the back of his head through the window in a way that makes me think he's her unrequited love, but she says, "Sometimes we are, sometimes we aren't. Sometimes we aren't but we still sleep together. It's complicated."

"Got it."

"What about you? You seeing anyone?"

"Not exactly seeing, but I have a long-distance thing with a girl in Arizona."

Just as I say that, as if by telepathy, Zoey sends me another "good luck" text and a drawing of me dressed as a Disney villain, summoning lighting and thunder from the balcony of my castle.

I would have preferred a picture of *her*, but she's really

paranoid about that sort of thing. She's never sent a photo, or done a voice chat, or anything like that.

Which, of course, means that there's a pretty good chance that she's not who she says she is. Maybe she's really a guy. My hunch is that she's transgender and afraid to tell me, even though I've told her again and again that I'll be okay with anything she is. All things being equal, I think I like girls the best, but you know how you automatically go for chocolate over vanilla most of the time, except sometimes it's a choice between a smooth, creamy vanilla made with real vanilla beans and some crummy dollar-store chocolate that tastes like chalk, and then you're like, "well, I guess vanilla this time?" And sometimes there's strawberry, too, and that just fucks the whole thing up? It's like that.

All I care about is that Zoey *gets* me. She loves my fan-fic stories instead of being freaked out by them—even the darker stuff that I worry is going to make her run off screaming. And if I follow in Mom's footsteps as a funeral-home owner, that won't scare her off either. From previous crushes and aborted attempts at relationships, I've learned that people putting up with your weirdness is important.

And really, really hard to find.

Long-distance invisible girlfriends might be all I ever get.

While I answer Zoey's message, I look at the pictures that are set up in the space above the bus windows and below the map on the ceiling. They're shots of what I guess are supposed to be ghosts—odd shadows and blurry, vaguely humanoid forms glowing in alleys, stairwells, and dead-end streets.

"You get these shots on the tours?"

"Most of them. We only get a picture that I'm really impressed with every now and then. Even with most of these, we know what they really are, and we're pretty up front about it. That shot that looks like a guy in a hooded robe on the staircase is really just a reflection of Rick's ear."

I can think of good explanations for most of the pictures without much effort. The rest could just be outright fakes, but that doesn't seem like Rick and Cyn's style. And I appreciate that. I'd been thinking I'd have to tell people that pictures of their flash bouncing off of windows are actually "spirits" on this job. If I don't, the gig is a lot more attractive to me.

I take an empty seat up front as customers start checking in. When the bus is about a third full, Cyn gets in the driver's seat and tests the microphone.

"So, what do you guys wanna see?" she asks.

"Ghosts?" someone asks, like they aren't quite sure.

"Ghosts!" says Cyn. "Perfect. Now, who brought someone we can murder?"

People chuckle, but not enthusiastically. They all seem like they're tired from a long day at Navy Pier and the Hard Rock Cafe, or whatever tourist places they've been to.

One girl holds up three fingers, *Hunger Games*–style, and says, "I volunteer as tribute."

ADAM SELZER

"You can't volunteer *yourself* as a victim," says Cyn. "That makes it a suicide, not a murder. We've gotta control these variables. That's science. Look it up." Then she sits down and ties her hair into a low ponytail.

While we wait for the last couple of people with reservations to arrive, Rick comes onboard, takes the mic, and starts warming the crowd up, making friends with everyone.

"Did you all see this in the news?" he asks, holding up one of those free weekly papers. "Someone broke into President James Garfield's tomb in Cleveland and stole a dozen commemorative spoons. Spoons! Who gets buried with spoons? And who busts into a tomb and steals a bunch of spoons?"

"Maybe they aren't really spoons," I suggest.

"What else would they be?"

He puts the mic in front of me, and I take it.

"Maybe some stormy night, an old woman showed up at the White House and offered President Garfield one single rose for shelter," I say. "And when he sent her away, she turned his staff into flatware, so whoever stole them was just, like, rescuing them. And now the cops will never find the spoons, because they're human again."

Ricardo's face breaks into a grin. "Okay. You, I like," he says.

Score.

A minute later the last parties show up, and it's time to get going. Rick introduces Cyn as "'Switchblade' Cynthia Fargon, my roommate, my oldest friend, and the best damn driver in the city." Then he says "All right, you guys wanna go see something scary, or what?"

"Yeah!" people shout.

"All right, Cyn. We're gonna start out at the men's room of the Greyhound station."

"Got it."

"After that, we're going to your house."

"It's your house too, doinkus," says Cyn. "Screw your courage to the sticking place, team."

And he navigates us out from behind the DarkSide buses, down Clark Street, and toward the Loop. The guy in the frog suit at Rainforest Cafe waves as we pass.

Chapter Two

As we head toward the first haunted stop of the tour, Ricardo points out some sites of interest along the way. Just south of the Rainforest Cafe is a spot where a brothel owner named Tillie Wolf was stabbed in the face with a sharpened umbrella stick in 1898. The next block has the spot where a gangster named Hoops-a-Daisy Connors was shot through the eye and the groin one unlucky evening in 1929.

Then he points out the fire station that was built over the site of the old prison where they used to hang people, and tells the story of a guy they tried to bring back to life with electricity after they hanged him in 1882, just to see if they could.

"And all of this is to give you fair warning," he says, "that this is gonna be an inspiring and uplifting tour for everyone tonight. We're gonna talk about puppies and ponies and horsies and kitties and rainbows and flowers and sunshine and unicorns."

Everyone laughs, and he laughs too. "Actually, this is a ghost tour, which means we're talking death, disease, destruction, dismay, decapitation, defenestration, decomposition, decay, and Donald Trump. So, fasten your seat belts, and if you're in the first three rows, you may get slimed."

I've made up my mind about the job before we even cross the river into the Loop.

If I don't get this gig, I will never forgive myself.

The first stop turns out to be the site of the Iroquois Theatre, where a fire in 1903 killed about six hundred people. The robber barons who built it cut every corner they could in order to get it open in time for the holidays, and the whole place was a death trap. We cruise slowly past the newer theater that stands on the site now, then around the corner to the alley that runs behind it.

"A lot of people, like our competition, say they didn't even build fire escapes," says Rick. "They did build them, but the problem was that they were completely useless. They were only built to hold a few people at a time, so when there was a stampede, most of the people got shoved over the railings and fell down to the alley. This alley. Right here. The next day the *Chicago Tribune* called it 'the Alley of Death and Mutilation.'"

Stay classy, *Chicago Tribune*.

A few people squirm, and Rick starts telling ghost stories about the site. "Employees at the new theater on the grounds," he says, "talk about a ghostly little girl who makes her presence known by flushing a toilet backstage and giggling."

"You should be careful of that one," says one passenger. "On *Ghost Encounters* they say that ghosts who sound like little girls are actually demons trying to trick you."

Cyn turns around and says, "That's because the guys on that show are drugged-up misogynist pigs."

"Dude," says Ricardo, "if some demon's idea of evil shenanigans is just flushing the toilet now and then, I can live with it. It's wasting water, but still."

People laugh, and Rick goes into a whole talk about other old theaters in the city with haunted bathrooms. Apparently there are quite a few.

"If I were on *Ghost Encounters*," he says, "I'd probably say, 'Old theaters in Chicago are vortexes for phantom poopers, bro. And they never hear the sound of them washing their hands!'"

My phone buzzes in my purse, presumably either with texts from Mom or Zoey, since no one else ever really messages me, but I don't check. I'm not going to take out my phone and risk looking unprofessional. I want this job.

After getting back on topic and telling stories about ghosts in the Alley of Death and Mutilation, Rick takes us off the bus and lets everyone walk around looking for them. It doesn't seem very spooky to me; it's bright, clean, and only smells vaguely of stale urine (which is pretty good for a downtown alley). A tag on the wall says, BOB SAGET SELLS DRUGS HERE.

That's Cyn's handiwork, I assume.

Back when she was my sitter, her hobby was using a pencil to tag walls around Forest Park with fake gang names, like the Butt Onions. She let me act as lookout a couple of times. She'd tag a wall, then walk away casually while I ran off down the road, laughing and shrieking. I was the kind of kid who never had the nerve to do anything that would get me sent to the principal's office, so being an accessory to tagging a wall—in pencil—felt like I was really living on the edge. Like I was really living like a villain.

As people wander the alley, taking pictures, Rick comes up beside me.

"So, this is what we do," he says. "We tell people stories from history, then let them wander around to see if any ghosts show up. Firsthand ghost sightings are pretty hard to find, but I try my best to stick to primary sources. Out here it's mostly stuff I hear from employees on smoke breaks."

"I'm glad you aren't just making stuff up. I think even the guides on the architecture tours make half their stories up."

"They do. Most of them are actors. And you do have to put on a good show, even if you stick to the facts. Cyn said you had some theater experience?"

"Couple of plays in high school. I was one of the sweet old ladies who kill people in *Arsenic and Old Lace*."

Rick holds up a hand. "High five."

I explore the alley a bit myself, getting a feel for the place and trying to imagine what it was like with dead bodies strewn all around. Most of the people on the tour are having a morbid sort of fun with the whole thing. It would seem like an odd place to take selfies, but they're not taking shots of themselves at the former site of a pile of bodies, they're taking shots of themselves going ghost hunting. There's a difference.

Still, I hear one lady say, "I just think this guy is too flippant about death."

I can see where she's coming from, but you *have* to be flippant about death. I mean, when you laugh at death, it loses a bit of its power over you.

Not that it doesn't have all the power it needs.

There are more gruesome stories about the spots we drive by after getting back on the bus. An actor leaving his skull to a nearby theater so he could play Yorick in *Hamlet*. A barber shoving his girlfriend's chopped-up body in a barrel and mailing her to New York. The wreck of a homemade submarine containing a dead guy and a dead dog being dredged out of the river in 1915. When Rick mentions the dog, people say "awww."

"There it is," says Cyn. "There's always an 'awwww' right there."

"Every time," says Rick. "I've talked about the grisly deaths of more than seven hundred people so far, but I mention one dead dog, and that's what gets them."

One woman gets really defensive. "Well, the dog didn't do anything wrong!"

Yeah. Unlike those kids who had the nerve to go into a theater without making sure it was following all the fire codes. Those little bastards deserved it. Obviously.

Cyn veers around the curve of Wacker Drive, toward Lake Street, which runs underneath the Green Line "L" tracks.

"All right," says Rick. "Now, in 1934, a woman named Mary Bregovy went out drinking and driving with a couple of guys she'd met at the Goldblatt's department store. They ended up crashing into the 'L' track support beam right here in front of us, and she died right on the sidewalk. Excuse me."

He opens the door and shouts, "She died right on this spot!" at a couple of women who are standing there with Old Navy bags. Everyone laughs, including the women, who wave as Rick shuts the door and turns back toward us.

"A few days later," he goes on, "she was buried at Resurrection Cemetery and became one of the most popular candidates for the true identity of Resurrection Mary, the most famous ghost in Chicago."

Everyone who grows up around here knows the Resurrection Mary story: people pick up a girl on the south side, offer her a ride, and she disappears as they drive past Resurrection Cemetery. Rick tells the basic story, then explains that vanishing hitchhiker legends are pretty common, but it's usually something you hear about happening to a friend of a friend of the cousin of the guy standing next to you in line at Garrett's Popcorn. With Mary, there are some firsthand accounts.

Construction on Lake Street slows us down to a standstill before we get to the next point of interest, and Rick has to fill time. He covers a few other theories about who Mary might be the ghost of, and talks about a couple of the known sightings. But traffic still isn't moving.

"Why don't you tell them about your plan for how to kidnap Resurrection Mary, Rick?" asks Cyn.

"Not that. I was in middle school when I thought of that. *Middle school.*"

"I think Megan needs to hear a bit of Ricardo History 101."

"Yes, I do!" I call out.

Rick grits his teeth and inhales, then sighs, shakes his head, and chuckles a bit.

"Okey dokey," he says. "Look. Cyn and I have been friends since we were kids out in Magwitch Park, and one of the reasons we became friends is that we both loved Resurrection Mary. We had both read everything written about her. Which, at the time, was mostly bull."

"But we didn't know that then," says Cyn. "Now hurry up and tell them your plan for kidnapping her."

"All right, all right," he says. "Here's how you kidnap Resurrection Mary. All you have to do is pick her up, then turn around and *don't drive past Resurrection Cemetery.*"

A few people chuckle, and Cyn grabs for the microphone, holding it with one hand while she steers with another. She obviously loves teasing Rick.

"Now," she says, "I told him that Mary was too smart for that, and she'd just jump out of the car at a light or something. But Ricardo here said he was going to distract her by making out with her in the backseat while his friend Willie drove. Willie was thirteen."

"He could drive when he was ten," says Rick.

"And, keep in mind," Cyn goes on, "that Resurrection Mary is supposed to be at least eighteen or nineteen years old. Some accounts say early twenties. Tell them what you planned to do to get her to make out with your slick thirteen-year-old self, Rick."

Rick hangs down his head in shame, though he's clearly having a hard time not laughing, and says, "I said I'd seduce her by whispering some Spanish in her ear."

"But the trouble is," Cyn goes on, "that while Ricardo here is of Puerto Rican and Cuban descent, he is a fourth-generation American who doesn't really know much Spanish. And I called him on that. So, tell the nice people what you told me you'd whisper in her ear, Mr. Smooth-Talking Kidnapper Tour Guide."

He takes another deep breath, then smiles, takes back the microphone, and uses a sexy voice to whisper, *"Sí, yo soy el baño loco, por favor."*

"Which means . . . ," Cyn prods.

"It means, 'Yes, I am the crazy bathroom, please.'"

Everyone laughs. Cyn hardest of all.

"Hey," says Rick. "Resurrection Mary would have died way before they started teaching Spanish in school. How would she know? Tell me it doesn't sound suave."

"You are the crazy bathroom, Ricardo," says Cyn.

He makes a pretending-to-be-hurt face, then says, "What about you? Why don't you tell them all how you used to claim to be part headless."

She snatches the mic. "My great, great, great, great-something grandmother was beheaded in France," she says proudly. "So I'm part headless. Simple as that."

"That's not how genetics works," says Rick.

"Don't mock my heritage, doinkus."

Rick takes back the mic and says, "Hashtag: white people."

Cyn wriggles the bus through the last of the construction traffic, and we head down Des Plaines Street, past the site of the Haymarket Massacre, winding our way to the next stop as the two of them make fun of each other, laughing and socking each other in the arm. It's off topic, mostly, but they're having a good time, so the customers are too. Sometimes the two of them aren't even laughing at anything, just looking at each other and giggling at some private joke. Anyone on the bus who can't tell they're sleeping together is an idiot.

The next place we pull up to is Hull House, an old brick

mansion on South Halsted Street. I can imagine it looking pretty creepy in the dark, but right now, in the daylight, it really just looks like a regular old house that's been turned into a museum. According to Rick, it was already supposed to be haunted in 1889 when a woman named Jane Addams moved in, turned it into a settlement house, and basically invented American social work here.

A DarkSide Chicago Tours bus is parked right in front of us, and Rick keeps looking over his shoulder to check on it while he talks, like he thinks a group of hit men are going to come out of the emergency exit and blow him away. But he doesn't miss a beat in telling the story of Hull House.

"Now, if you look at the bedroom on the right-hand side of the second floor, that was the one that the early staff here called the Haunted Room," he says. "No one ever got a good night's sleep there. And Jane wasn't a big believer in ghosts, but she loved ghost stories, so she had to try it out. She and her partner, Mary, spent exactly one night in there."

He doesn't elaborate on what he means by "partner," but it's easy enough to guess.

"Jane woke up hearing a rustling sound," he goes on. "So she said, 'Mary, is that you?' But Mary was still in bed next to her. So she looked down at the foot of the bed and saw a woman in an old-fashioned dress. Jane tried to turn on a gas-light to get a better look, but the woman was gone, just like a breath into the wind. She never decided that what she'd seen was really a ghost, but I don't think she ever spent another night in that room, and the woman in the dress was seen off and on throughout her life, and even up to now. People report sightings of her on the tours from time to time."

Not a bad story.

He shows us a few pictures that have been taken on the grounds and talks about the ghosts people say they've seen on tours, but he doesn't have enough to say to keep us all on the bus until the DarkSide Tours group is done. They're still roaming the grounds when we get out of the bus to explore ourselves.

In the courtyard next to the house, the DarkSide guide, an older man in a cowboy hat with a long beard and a curly mustache, is pointing to a cement patch on the ground and saying, "Yes, that's the spot where Jane buried the devil baby. They covered it up with cement so it couldn't crawl back out."

Rick, who is standing next to me, groans.

"Devil baby?" I ask.

Rick shakes his head.

"That was a rumor that went around in 1913. Some of the old women in the neighborhood started saying that a Catholic married an atheist or something, and God punished her by giving her a baby with horns, hooves, and a tail, and she ended up dropping it off on the doorstep here. Some of your less scrupulous tour guides swear it was all true, and that Jane Addams buried it alive."

"Hey," I say. "My atheist mom married a Catholic, and I didn't come out like a devil baby."

He looks my head over very carefully. "That's debatable, padawan," he says. Then he tilts his head toward the garden and says, "The old guy out there is Edward Tweed, my old boss from when I worked for DarkSide. He's been running these tours for forty years now. Back in the old days people couldn't fact-check him on their phones, so he could just make up any old shit and get away with it."

"People fact-check you on their phones?"

"Oh, never. But I'm always afraid they will, and then I'll look like a first-class ding-dong if I'm making stuff up. I keep an iPad full of primary sources, just in case."

The two of us watch as Tweed makes a speech about how the courtyard is also an Indian burial ground, and that Potawatomi came to the grounds to do a Ghost Dance to curse all white people after the Fort Dearborn Massacre in 1812. Rick says he doesn't know where to begin explaining what's wrong with that. And that the cement patch is just the base of a bird bath that used to be there.

But Tweed's customers are entranced.

And he has a lot more of them than Rick and Cyn do. He winks at Rick, and Rick gives him a rueful wave.

I immediately hate Edward Tweed, and resolve to write a story in which Madam Mim from *The Sword in the Stone* turns him into a toad.

After a quick ride on the interstate up to the north side of the city, the Mysterious Chicago bus pulls into a little dead-end street with an overgrown vacant lot.

"Here, where the vacant lot now sits," Rick says, "H. H. Holmes, a multi-murderer from the 1890s, owned a building that he said was a glass-bending factory, but was more likely used for cremations. There's no proof that he did anything sinister in the factory, but he sure as hell wasn't bending any glass there. And there's a pretty short list of things a known murderer would be doing with a hundred-and-fifty-foot-long furnace."

It looks like a good place for a body dump to me. The weeds have grown as high as my head. A couple of gnarled old trees stretch up past the electrical lines toward the sky.

"We started coming here just as a historical curiosity," says Rick. "People were always asking for H. H. Holmes stops after the book *Devil in the White City* came out and made him a star all over again. But his famous 'murder castle' is long gone, the site is too far from downtown for most tours, and frankly the stories about it are way exaggerated. So we started taking people out here now and then if anyone asked about him, and so much weird stuff happened that we added it to our standard route. One night we came out here and there were three hawks with dead doves in their mouths."

"Another night there were chickens," adds Cyn. "Like, six chickens, just randomly crossing the road."

"And here you thought that chickens only crossed the road in jokes," says Rick. "But those are just environmental oddities. We also had sightings of a full-body apparition here, a woman in a black dress who appears and then disappears. One night we even thought we hit her with the bus."

"Worst night ever," says Cyn.

"It was snowing, the windows were fogged, and when we were backing up, we hit something," says Rick. "I thought it was a tree or someone's car, but then these two customers in the back started saying 'No, there was a woman back there.'"

"But there was nothing," says Cyn. "I ran out and checked. No car anywhere near us. No tree. No footprints in the snow."

"And right after that," Rick goes on, "we started getting pictures of shadowy, humanesque figures. Hard to say if they're the ghosts of Holmes's victims or maybe someone who died here more recently, but there's *something* out here. There's also a floodlight that sometimes turns on and off when I say the name of one of the victims."

Everyone wants him to try it, and Rick acts like he's afraid to. But he consents, faces a floodlight attached to an old house at the back of the lot, and says, "Emily Van Tassel."

Nothing happens. The light stays off.

"Well, there you go," he says. "Now you can tell I'm not just faking you out, or that would have worked."

"It used to work," Cyn insists. "But they disconnected the

ADAM SELZER

light altogether now. Even a ghost can't get a disconnected light to come on."

It seems to me that anyone who can come back from the dead ought to be able to plug a light back in, so I don't change my mind about ghosts being real, but the dead-end street does look pretty ominous, even in the glaring summer daylight. The curling weeds look like they're beckoning us all to our doom. There's something about the place that just doesn't feel . . . right. When I step off the bus, the hair stands up on the back of my neck. The breeze seems like it's cooler than it ought to be, and everywhere I look there are little touches that make this space seem eerier than your average dead-end street. There's even some sort of blood red sap oozing from a tall Tim Burton–style tree at the edge of the lot.

While we're walking around, Rick tells me that Holmes didn't kill anywhere near two hundred people, like the stories I've read about him like to say, but he did probably kill a dozen or so, which is plenty. Just knowing he was here, that I'm standing where he stood, is sort of chilling.

As we're heading back to the bus, I think I see a shadow that shouldn't be there dart across the ground, like someone just ran by.

Power of suggestion, I guess.

"Hey, Rick?" I ask. "How many ghosts does it take to screw in a lightbulb?"

"How many?"

I shrug. "Well, more than just Emily Van Tassel, apparently."

He laughs. "Yeah, from what I've observed here, unscrewed lightbulbs are their kryptonite. Who knew?"

I have *got* to get this job. But I have no idea how I'm going to sell it to my mother.

I'm not just a black-diaper baby, I'm a *third-generation* black-diaper baby. Mom grew up in the very funeral home we live in now, and took over the business when her dad died, right before I was born. According to her, Grandpa was the most upright citizen this side of a 1950s sitcom. He got a haircut every two weeks, didn't take a single drink of booze in his entire life, and never swore or wore casual clothing in public. He probably ate really boring breakfast cereals. Plain Shredded Wheat would be my guess. With no bananas added.

That's what people expect from funeral parlor directors. Even though Mom can swear with the best of them and listens to classic rock while she works in the basement, she makes her boyfriends sneak in the back, and even goes to a church service now and then just to keep up appearances. She drinks once in a while, but never in public in Forest Park.

She didn't stop me from getting a lip ring or dying the bottom half of my hair bright red, and doesn't require me to keep quiet about liking girls or anything, but I can picture her saying that having her daughter work in the ghost industry is just taking things too far. And I can understand that. Having a ghostbusting daughter living upstairs wouldn't do wonders for the funeral home's reputation.

But I'll find a way to make it work.

This would be a *history* job, not a ghost job. Maybe I can sell it like that.

From the empty lot, we drive clear down Fullerton Avenue and then turn back onto Clark Street, going past the site of the Saint Valentine's Day Massacre (where Al Capone's gang shot a bunch of guys from a rival gang in 1929) and into Lincoln Park.

I already know that Lincoln Park was a cemetery once, but the customers who live in town all seem surprised when Rick tells them that.

"We can't really go into cemeteries on these tours," says Rick. "They close for business at about four o'clock here, and they don't allow buses even during the day. But we can make an exception for the one we're going through now. Up until the Great Chicago Fire in 1871, this space was called City Cemetery. It was very progressive of the city to put aside a space like this to bury the dead. Before that, people who died in cities were usually buried in churchyards. Now, how deep is a grave supposed to be, everyone?"

"Six feet," people mutter.

Rick looks right at me. "Hey, black-diaper baby: is that accurate?"

I shake my head. "Five feet is closer to the industry standard," I say. "And I think the state law just says it has to be at least eighteen inches."

"Right," says Rick. "But in those old churchyards, they didn't even always get that much. They ran out of space quickly, so they just stacked the coffins on top of each other."

"If you go online," I add, eager to show my worth, "you can find an old book called *Gatherings from Grave Yards*, all about the condition of London churchyards in the 1840s. It's awesome. They were nasty."

"'Nasty' barely begins to describe it," says Rick.

"Slubberly. Stercorous. Dungish."

He smiles as I list *OED* synonyms, but I worry that I'm overdoing it, so I shut up and motion for him to go back to talking. "Anyway, they thought they'd think ahead here in Chicago, and set aside a place way out in the outskirts where they wouldn't run out of space and no one would have to smell it. First place they tried was about two blocks north of where we picked you up, but the city grew out to that space almost immediately, so they kept moving people further north. Eventually they put aside this hundred acres right here."

It's a gorgeous park now. Looking at all the dog walkers and designer strollers roaming through the grounds, it's hard to imagine it as a cemetery.

"Obviously, this space wasn't on the outskirts for long, and eventually the city put in the order to close City Cemetery and move all the bodies. And there are tombstones and statues all over Graceland and Rosehill cemeteries that we know were originally out here. But sometimes those tombstones were all they actually moved. They still dig up bodies in Lincoln Park just about every time they dig. And now, if you'll all hold your breath in amazement, Switchblade Cynthia will execute a U-turn. In a bus with no power steering."

People chuckle, and as she waits for an opening in the traffic, Rick does his impression of a movie trailer. "In a world . . . where there are no rules . . . one woman . . . will challenge the laws . . . of traffic. Because when you can't believe in anything . . . you can still believe . . . in Cyn."

Cyn pulls off a perfect U-turn, to rapturous applause.

"That was totally legal right there," she says. "As long as I don't get caught."

She pulls the bus over on the street behind the Chicago History Museum, which sits at the south end of the park, and Rick starts telling ghost stories about the grounds. According to him, the early cops who patrolled Lincoln Park had all kinds of ghost stories about it—not just because it used to be a graveyard, either. In the 1890s the *Tribune* said that there had been enough murders and suicides in the park to furnish a ghost for every dark nook and cranny.

"Now, there is at least one reminder of what this place used to be," he says. He points to a little stone structure out in the middle of the grass between the museum and the road. "That little building is the tomb of Ira Couch and his family, which they never moved. You guys want to check it out?"

Naturally, everyone does, so Rick calls out, "Cemetery safari!" And we follow him across the grass.

"I've driven by this a thousand times," says one guy as we trudge through the park. "Never realized it was a tomb."

"Yeah," says Rick. "We get that a lot. If people notice it, they just think it's a tool shed or something. But it's a tomb."

Mom has pointed out the tomb in the park to me when we drove by a couple of times, but I've never gone to check it out up close. It's about the size of a one-car garage, with the family name COUCH in raised sans-serif letters in the stone above a black metal door. A little spiked fence, about waist high, surrounds it.

"It says 'Couch' because it's a resting place," says Rick. "Ho ho ho."

"Is he still in there?" I ask.

"Tough call," Rick says. "It was built to hold thirteen people, and the general consensus is that it's about half full. Or, you know, half empty. But there are a lot of different stories."

"Can't they open it up and see?" someone asks.

"Observe," says Rick.

And he hops over the fence and yanks on the door. It doesn't budge.

"See? It's welded shut or something. And there's no key-hole, no hinges, no latch. Just a metal slab that isn't going any-where. The handle is just a decoration."

"You think he might have any James Garfield commemorative spoons in there?" I ask.

"One can only hope. You can't expect zombie Ira Couch to eat brains with his fingers. Dude ran a very classy hotel. Abe Lincoln stayed there. So did John Wilkes Booth, for that matter. Right on the grounds where the Alley of Death and Mutilation is now."

I look down and notice a bug crawling under a crack between the metal door and the stone floor beneath it. When we're walking back to the bus, I ask Rick if he knows about the crack.

"Don't tell me my ass is showing again."

"No, under the door. There's a crack."

He stops in his tracks, then runs back to the fence around the tomb and looks down. When he sees that there's a small gap between the door and the stone, his face lights up like a kid who found his Easter basket, and he runs all the way back to the bus, where he breaks the news to Cyn. Her face lights up too.

"Well," he says to me, "you wanna come back here and go tomb snooping after the tour?"

"What kind of girl do you think I am?" I ask. "Of course I wanna go tomb snooping."

Cyn gives me a thumbs-up.

I'm pretty sure this job is mine if I want it.

Chapter Three

After Rick and Cyn get the passengers back to the Rock and Roll McDonald's and wrap up the tour, they split the tips, and we start making our tomb-snooping plans.

"Okay," says Cyn, putting her archaeology degree to use for once, "the first thing to know about tomb snooping is that it might feel kind of awkward at first, like you're invading Mr. Couch's privacy. Peeking in a tomb is like peeking in a bathroom."

"Decomposing: the final bodily function," I say.

"What's the second thing to know about tomb snooping?" asks Rick.

"That it's awesome as fuck."

We all high-five.

I don't feel awkward at all about peeking into a tomb. You lose a lot of fear about invading the privacy of the dead when you've seen what goes on in embalming rooms. Mom kept me out of the actual embalmings when I was really little, but I started helping with makeup and dressing when I was ten, and I've seen a full-on embalming or two by now. Not enough to be used to what goes on in them, exactly, but enough that what little I might see in a one-hundred-fifty-year-old burial vault is small potatoes. In other words, "goose-wing" (first recorded 1377), "snotter" (1689), or "flap-dragon" (1700).

Rick runs across the street to the Walgreens to spend his tips on tomb-snooping supplies, which I never would have guessed you could buy there, and I run into the McDonald's to pee and finally check my phone, which has continued to buzz in my purse throughout the tour.

Mostly it's hearts from Zoey.

But there are about ten from Mom:

MOTHER DEAREST:

Where are you?

Mom and I are close enough that she isn't used to me not answering her texts right away. Even now, I'm not wild about lying to her. But I'm sure as hell not going to tell her I'm out ghostbusting and tomb snooping with plans to make a career out of it. This is going to take some lying.

I tell her I was watching a movie with Kacey, a girl I work with at the grocery store where I'm a part-time bagger. Then I send Zoey some goofy-face bathroom-mirror selfies and look up words for "tomb" on the online *OED* on my phone before I go back outside.

Some good synonyms for tomb include "croft" (Old English), "lair-stow" (first recorded in AD 1000), and "the worm's kitchen" (1500).

Back onboard, Cyn is alone, waiting on Rick to come back.

"What did you think of the tour?" she asks.

"It was a blast," I say. "Rick's a hell of a tour guide."

"Rick is going to be a *star*," says Cyn. "It's adorable how excited he gets about this stuff."

"I get the impression that right now is one of the times when you're together?"

"Right now it's kind of ambiguous, relationship-wise."

"Got it."

"We drive each other nuts, but we're way too mixed up in each other's lives at this point not to be together. We have a history. That kind of shit. But there're some possible business developments and stuff coming up, and we're not sure if presenting ourselves as a couple would make things better or worse."

Rick bounds back onto the bus from the Walgreens with a couple of cheap Chicago souvenir T-shirts and a roll of clear packing tape.

"What're the shirts for?" I ask.

"Nothing. I just wanted the wire hangers they came on."

"That's some smart shopping, Rick," says Cyn. "There's about ten places we could go and just buy hangers."

"But I want to do it now."

He removes the shirts from the hangers and tosses them into a Rubbermaid bin at the front of the bus where they keep tools and cleaning supplies. Then he bends the wires into an L shape and tapes his phone to one end, so he can slide it under the door, prop it upright, and take pictures.

"Behold," he says, holding it up like a proud kindergartner who just made a bird feeder out of a pinecone. "The Tomb Snooper 500."

Awesome.

Then he pulls up a picture on his phone of a graveyard at night, with little white balls of light all over, and shows it to me.

"Pop quiz, padawan," he says. "This is the official start of your training. You know what they call these things?"

"Orbs, right?" I say. "People show us pictures of them at the funeral home sometimes and say it's someone's soul."

Rick rolls his eyes. "Right. And I don't ever want you to bring them up on tours. They're a cheap parlor trick. And as far as we can tell, Edward Tweed from DarkSide invented the idea that they're ghosts."

"They're usually dust," says Cyn. "Or a problem with a cheap lens."

"If people show up and they've already heard of them and make a big deal out of getting them in pictures, I just sort of let them go ahead and have fun with it," says Rick. "But if anyone asks you if they're for real, just say they're ghost farts, not ghosts."

"Got it."

I like that he's talking as though I already have the job. Finding the crack under the door of the tomb must have really ingratiated me to him.

"You know," says Cyn, "in a roundabout way, they *are* ghosts."

"What kind of roundabout way?" Ricardo asks.

"Well, there's nothing new under the sun. The atoms that make up those dust particles were probably bonded to molecules that were part of a human being once. So they're sort of ghosts. In a way."

"Yeah, but in that same way, they're also beetle shit," says Ricardo. "Fuck orbs. Let's go get some food."

Cyn drives us back up north, toward Lincoln Park and the Couch family mausoleum. It won't be dark for a while yet, so we head into a nearby diner Rick recommends, where Cyn spots me ten bucks from the tips to get a dipped Italian beef sandwich and a Sprite. I'm a bit hard up for cash right now—I dented up the hearse a couple of months ago, and what little I make working at the grocery store is eaten up paying Mom back for the damages. It'd be nice to make enough to have some spending money for once.

"God, I can't wait to snoop that tomb," Rick says. "Even Marjorie Stone probably didn't know what was in there."

"She probably never even tried to find out," says Cyn. "She would've found a way in. You know it."

"But she didn't," says Rick. "And now we will, motherfucker!"

He holds up a hand for a high five, and I don't leave him hanging, even though I have no idea what he's talking about.

"Who's Marjorie Stone?" I ask.

They look at each other, then back at me.

"Kind of a long story," says Rick. "I assumed Cyn told you all about her when you were a babysitting charge."

"Not that I recall."

"I'd just moved to Forest Park back then," says Cyn. "I was sort of trying to forget her."

"Fair enough," says Rick. "So, Marjorie Kay Stone was this old woman in Magwitch Park. You ever go out there?"

"Nope."

"No reason why you should. It's a dump."

"It's one of those old Route 66 towns off I-55 past the edge of suburbia," says Cyn. "We were kids together there. And we met Marjorie after Ricardo tried to bury his dead hamster in her backyard. What was the hamster called?"

"Sonja," Rick says, putting his fist to his chest in salute. "I wanted her to be someplace classy where no dogs would dig her up. That backyard had all these statues, bushes shaped like dolphins. Even a little pond. Classy as fuck."

"Got it."

"She was a retired professional thing-finder," Rick says. "Ran an outfit called Finders of Magwitch Park. If some collector wanted a rare old ring, or a painting that went missing in World War II, or if a movie director wanted some hard-to-find prop, she'd find it."

"And this was before the internet," says Cyn. "It took some real talent to find rare things back then."

"The internet kind of put her out of business," says Rick. "And made her into a bitter old psycho. Working with the old people at the home is a breeze compared to her."

The two of them swap anecdotes about Marjorie Kay Stone for a bit while I eat my sandwich. She sounds like quite a piece of work.

"There were wine stains all over that house from Marjorie getting pissed off and throwing glasses at the wall," says Rick. "Including the bathroom. Which means that now and then she'd be drinking wine on the toilet, and get so mad she threw the glass at the wall."

"Thank you for that image," says Cyn. "Now I'm gonna have to hope there's a rotting body in the Couch tomb so I have something more pleasant to picture than Marjorie drinking while she pees."

"New topic," says Rick. "What are we gonna find in the Couch Tomb."

"There's probably nothing to see by now, even if it was

totally full and they never moved anyone," I say. "Even the coffins have got to be dust by now."

"Not necessarily," says Cyn. "That was a seven-thousand-dollar tomb in 1850s money. There's a pretty good chance they would have sprung to put him in a Fisk Metallic Burial Case."

"Let us hope and pray," says Rick.

"Are those the really ornate metal coffins with the window over the face?" I ask.

Cyn smiles. "See? I told you she knew her shit."

"Nice," says Rick. "Yeah, those are the ones. They found one buried in Lincoln Park in the 1990s, just over where the parking lot is now, so Ira might be in one, and might even still be in halfway decent shape. Anyone else is probably dust, though."

"You ever see that one movie version of *Romeo and Juliet*," I ask, "where they bring Juliet into the tomb and everyone's just rotting on open slabs, like they wouldn't have turned to dust years ago?"

"Is that the version from the seventies?" asks Ricardo. "The one where you see his butt?"

"And her boob for a second."

We high-five again.

I have never high-fived so much in one night.

I take another bite of my dinner and feel like I've arrived in my element for the first time. Like my life is finally beginning.

I almost fit in with the theater group at school, and with the other kids when Mom goes to funeral director conventions, but not like this. I can't think of another time when I felt so at ease talking to two people. Being able to make references to rotting corpses without worrying that I'll freak them out is like a load off my shoulders. Maybe I could even tell them about the stories I write, and what goes on in them. I feel like I could.

This is awesome.

The city is awesome.

The Italian beef sandwich I am eating is awesome—the spices are just right and they dipped it in the gravy just enough.

The way Cyn is eating the chicken-and-rice soup with her fingers is awesome.

The yuppies walking past the window with their kids on leashes and their dogs roaming free are awesome. In their own way. I guess.

And the fact that I'm hanging out on something like equal terms with my former babysitter is awesome. I've been clicking the "I'm an adult" buttons on fan-fic boards since I was thirteen, but this is the first night that I really feel like one of the grown-ups.

We want to wait to "tomb snoop" until it's totally dark out, so after we park the bus on the road by the museum, we settle in to wait. When I think about it, I realize that it's the longest day of the year. Solstice.

Cyn goes to the gas station across the street to get some oil for the bus while Rick and I relax on the duct-taped seats. I pull out my phone and send Zoey a text saying I'm going "tomb snooping," and she texts back, "Don't you dare get sucked into the netherworld, baby," followed by a heart.

Rick reads it over my shoulder. "Boyfriend?" he asks.

"Girlfriend," I say. "But we're long distance and I haven't seen a picture of her, so . . ."

"So it might be a boyfriend."

I shrug. "I could live with it either way."

"What if she's fifty, though?"

"That'd be harder."

"And what if she's twelve?"

Now I put the phone in my lap and feel a bit sick.

"Shit, I hope not," I say. "Or I'm in real trouble."

"You been sexting with her?"

"Maybe a little."

"Or a lot?"

Some blood rushes to my face.

"I don't show my face in those shots," I say, "but I'm also sending her fan-fic about the Evil Queen from *Snow White* in her witch disguise hooking up with the Emperor from *Return of the Jedi*. And some of them aren't exactly suitable for twelve-year-olds."

He cracks up and asks to see some, but I shake my head. No one but Zoey ever reads my stuff and knows it's by me—

everyone else who sees it doesn't know anything about me except my screen name.

And now I'm a bit afraid to send her anything else.

God. You always worry that some pervert is gonna lure you someplace when you meet them online. I guess I never stopped to think that maybe *I* could be the pervert.

There's no way Zoey is twelve. She talks about bands like Dresden Dolls and Rasputina that most twelve-year-olds wouldn't know. I guess *I* knew them when I was that age, but only because Cynthia had introduced them to me. Anyway, Zoey's too damned proficient and creative when it comes to cybersex not to have at least been reading erotica for years.

Still, I know that at least to some extent, being with her at all is a bad idea. It's like Ginny Weasley writing in Tom Riddle's old diary because it wrote back, until it turned out to be Voldemort talking to her. I'm trusting someone without being able to see where she keeps her brain.

But Zoey understands me. The stuff in my stories doesn't scare her. She gets all my references; I never have to explain that Chernobog is the demon thing in *Fantasia* or that Grimhilde is the Evil Queen's name in *Snow White*, according to early marketing materials, though it's not completely canon.

And she thinks I'm awesome.

It's hard to let go of someone who keeps telling you that you're awesome.

Especially when you spend your work life bagging groceries for people who seem to think you're a muckworm (*OED* word for "a worthless person," first recorded in 1649), dogbolt (1465), or pettitoe (1599).

After a long day of abuse from customers, I need someone to tell me how pretty I am, how good my stories are, and call me adorable pet names while we fool around via text. No one else is lining up to do it. But at least I have Zoey. She's all I have, and all I need.

And while we wait for the sun to be down, I actually talk about all of this stuff with Rick and Cyn. About Zoey, about my stories, the unusual turn-ons and wirings in my brain that meant that every crush I ever had was doomed to lead nowhere. This is stuff I've almost never said out loud before. When I have, they seemed freaked out and I had to say I was just kidding.

Sometimes it even freaks *me* out. Sometimes I give myself the creeps. Sometimes I think I frame my stories around Disney villains and stuff just to give them a veneer of humor and silliness to take the edge off.

But Rick and Cyn don't make fun of me. They don't seem to think I'm a nut. They even talk a bit about the stuff they're into themselves. It's pretty soft-core, but it's obvious that I can be myself with these two, and it's so liberating to talk to someone about this stuff that I almost want to cry.

I don't want to monopolize the whole conversation by talking about myself and Zoey, like the two of them are my therapists, so I ask about the ghost Cyn said they knew back in Magwitch Park. They say she lived at Marjorie Kay Stone's house.

"Marjorie had been hired to find a real ghost who could act in a movie," Cyn says. "It was one of the few things she couldn't find."

"She should've tried your plan to kidnap Resurrection Mary," I say.

"Yeah, she was way ahead of us on that," says Rick. "She said she *found* Mary, but it turned out that she couldn't act for beans."

I'm not sure how to take all this. I mean, Rick and Cyn seem like reasonable people who don't believe every dumb ghost story they hear, but they're both pretty casual about saying they knew a ghost personally when they were kids.

It was probably some girl who *identified* as a ghost. Maybe she only ever wanted to be referred to in the past tense or something. I've seen people identify as stranger things online.

I guess believing in ghosts sort of comes down to the matter of what counts as one and what doesn't. When I pull out my phone to check, I see that the *OED* lists over one hundred and fifty definitions of the word "ghost."

There has to be at least one I can believe in.

Leaves rustle in the trees around the tomb.

A girl in yoga pants walks past without even looking at it.

Up in the sky, above the lake, there are a couple of clouds that look like the Headless Horseman chasing a mailman. I hope he catches him.

The shadows grow longer, then just melt into the darkness as the sun goes down. At ten o'clock, we decide it's finally dark enough.

Go time.

Cyn grins at me. "Now, when you go back to Forest Park, you'll be Megan Henske: Grave Robber."

"Hey, we're not robbing anything," I say. "Unless it turns out he was buried with some commemorative spoons."

"Speak for yourself, padawan," says Rick. "If there's anything jewel-encrusted, I'm having it."

We start marching through the park like we're in one of those slow-walk scenes they always have in superhero movies, and I feel a lot like I did back in the old days, when I was helping Cyn with her petty vandalism. Like we should be singing a villain song as we go. Like a cloud of bats should be following in our wake.

Rick and I give up on walking and just run like wild children toward the tomb.

Cyn doesn't run. She just walks, in the same casual stroll she used when she left the scene of a wall tagging. When I look back she's striding along, staring straight ahead, not picking up her pace. Like a queen who's just ordered the guy kneeling in front of her to be beheaded on the spot, and has more interesting things to do than stick around to watch the axe fall, or even turn her head when she hears the thud.

Rick hops the short fence around the crypt, shimmies the Tomb Snooper 500 under the crack beneath the metal door, and moves the wire hanger around, trying to get the phone to point in the right direction. A camera app with an interval timer takes a photo every two seconds. Flashes come from under the crack, giving me ideas for a story where the Emperor and the Evil Queen (in her old hag disguise) do it in this very tomb. I love writing about those two. They're an adorable couple. They have the same taste in black hooded robes.

Cyn picks up a stick from the ground, swishes and flicks it like a Harry Potter wand, and says, "Alohamora," the unlocking charm. It doesn't work, obviously, so she swishes and flicks it at Rick's upturned ass and says, "Coitus."

"I'm working here!" said Rick.

These are my people, all right.

The first time Rick pulls the phone out, the pictures are nothing but dark blurs.

He adjusts some settings and tries again. This time, he says, "Eureka!" and holds up the phone for us to see.

It turns out that what's behind the door of the Couch tomb is . . . another door.

Seriously.

Behind the door is a sort of foyer backed by a larger, slightly more ornate-looking stone door.

ADAM SELZER

And orbs. Lots of those. It's dusty in there.

"Damn it," says Rick. "Kind of a metaphor for life, isn't it? There's always another door."

"Any space beneath that door?" I ask.

"Doesn't look like it."

"Even if there was, we'd need a bigger tomb snooper," says Cyn. "The Tomb Snooper Five Hundred and One."

"Okay," says Rick. "Well, we've passed level one. Now we get back to the drawing board and work on level two. Still, how long has it been since anyone saw the inside door? We fucking rule!"

Cyn pats me on the back. "Welcome to the profession," she says. "Rolling with the rotters."

Rick and Cyn drive the bus to the Blue Line stop at Halsted and I-290, right near Hull House, so I can take the train back home to Forest Park.

"All right," Rick says. "Start researching all the stories you heard tonight, and be ready to tell the Resurrection Mary story next time you come on the tour."

"You can get the *Chicago Tribune* archives online through the same library portal you use for the *OED*," says Cyn. "A few years of some other local papers' archives, too."

"Thanks for giving me the opportunity," I say. "I won't let you down."

This may be the most sincere promise I have ever made.

I will learn everything. I will be the best tour guide ever. They will never regret hiring me.

On the train ride home, I start poking around on the *Oxford English Dictionary* online using my phone and find a fantastic word from 1785: "murdermonger." A word for one who deals in murders, or in murder stories.

That's what I am now. A murdermonger in training.

Awesome.

Chapter Four

From: Megan
To: Ricardo Torre, Cynthia Fargon
Date: Thursday, 12:15 a.m.
Subject: Articles

Reading up like crazy on all the stories in the newspaper archives.

The devil baby was definitely a real rumor that everyone got all excited about; Jane Addams wrote a whole book about it. But she said it was just an urban legend that had no basis in fact. Even if someone had brought a "devil baby" to Hull House, I assume they would have taken it to the hospital, not buried it alive! Jane Addams would never have buried a baby alive, and fuck anyone who says she would.

Also, I found a whole physician's report on the

guy they tried to bring back to life after they hanged him. They got his heart beating again but his neck was broken.

From: Megan
To: Ricardo Torre, Cynthia Fargon
Date: Thursday, 12:45 a.m.
Subject: More Articles

Found a few articles about that Marjorie Kay Stone woman, too. Have you seen this one from the 1960s describing her "Finders of Magwitch Park" business? Not that I doubted you guys, but she sounds like a real trip. It talks about her finding a monkey who could play Monopoly in a commercial. Fun job.

From: Ricardo Torre
To: Cynthia Fargon, Megan
Date: Thursday, 1:15 a.m.
Subject: Monkey

I could totally teach a monkey to play Monopoly. You just have to lay down the law. You say, "Listen, Monkey. Getting $500 for landing on Free Parking is a house rule, not a real rule, and we play the real rules here." If he doesn't play right, no bananas.

Thursday, 1:22 a.m.
From: Cynthia Fargon
To: Ricardo Torre, Megan
Subject: Re: Monkey

Doinkus.

ZOEY BABY:

Congrats on the job! You will be awesome.

MEG:

YAY!

MEG:

I'm a murdermonger now. Mom's gonna kill me.

ZOEY BABY:

Murdermonger?

MEG:

OED word for a person who deals in murder stories.

ZOEY BABY:

Hehe. Look up "ghost."

MEG:

The "ghost" entry is huge! Earliest English use is from "Old English Text #178" in the year 800: "To ymbhycggannae . . . hust his 'gasta' . . . seter deothrage doemid uueorth[a]e."

ZOEY BABY:
Bork bork bork.

MEG:
HEHE! Well, autocorrect hates me now.

MEG:
Here's a pic of the inside of the tomb. Rick just sent it to me, so you are the first outside Chicago to see it in decades.

MEG:
Would that be enough to get you to send one of you? Even just, like, a silhouette, so I know what to picture when we're . . . you know . . .

ZOEY BABY:
Hmmm . . . *blush* I just get so nervous about that stuff. . . .

MEG:

It's okay. No pressure.

MEG:

Here's another of me. Enjoy, baby.

ZOEY BABY:

mmmmmmmmmmmmm nighty night, my little murdermonger.

MEGAN:

Swoon.

From: Megan
To: Cynthia Fargon, Ricardo Torre
Date: Thursday, 2:30 a.m.
Subject: Re: More Articles

Digging up articles on the Couch tomb now.
There's a 1911 one in the Chicago Examiner
where a Chicago city official says he went inside
in 1901 and it was empty. But in the same article,
Ira's grandson says the bodies were never moved,
and that he thinks there are at least eight people
in there, including two of his own brothers. Dude
ought to know where his own brothers were.

From: Megan
To: Cynthia Fargon, Ricardo Torre
Date: Thursday, 4:45 am
Subject: Script for my Res Mary story

See attached file. This look okay? Found a few things on Mary Bregovy in the archives. Even if the ghost is real, it can't be her—the stories were already a few years old when she died. But people <u>have</u> been saying the ghost was her for years, so I can see why you'd use her as an intro. None of the others died right on the tour route!

From: Ricardo Torre
To: Cynthia Fargon, Megan
Date: Thursday, 6:00 a.m.
Subject: Re: Script for my Res Mary story

Jesus, Megan, go to sleep! Seriously!
But—great job. You're a natural, my little padawan!
On the Couch tomb: the guy who says it was empty in that article is a Chicago city official. Might as well listen to Edward Tweed.
On Mary: Your script looks good, but it might be too long. For stories we tell while we're moving, not parked, you want a very basic, short version

of the story for nights when traffic isn't too heavy, then a bunch of extra things to add in case you have to stretch it out. For that story, my basic outline is:

1. In 1934 Mary Bregovy died RIGHT ON THIS SPOT!

2. She's a popular candidate for the true identity of Resurrection Mary, our most famous local ghost.

3. People pick her up, then she disappears outside of Resurrection Cemetery.

4. Similar to other vanishing hitchhiker legends, but we have firsthand accounts. So there. Na-na na-na boo-bug, stick your head in a thunder-mug.

Then, if you need to fill space:

—Other possible Marys at Resurrection Cemetery (there are at least 70 from the right time period) (I always try to point out that no one's sure Mary Bregovy is really her, because she's totally NOT the ghost, the story was at least three years old when she died. But she was the girl they focused on when the story was on Unsolved Mysteries and she died right on the tour route, so.)

—Note that there's no reliable sighting in which the ghost even says her name, so we might just be calling her Resurrection Mary because it has a better ring than, say, Resurrection Ethel.

—Specific sightings

—How those specific sightings differ from the standard "vanishing hitchhiker" urban legend

—Other local vanishing hitchhikers (there's a hitchhiking flapper who disappears at Waldheim Cemetery, out by you)

—My plan to kidnap her (if you absolutely must)

We're working the early shift at the home today. Off by 2 p.m. Wanna come meet us at Graceland Cemetery? We'll do some training stuff. You can also sit in on the stand-up class I'm taking at Second City tonight if you want to. Being a tour guide is a similar skill set.

Now GO TO SLEEP!

—Ricardo

Chapter Five

The last three letters in my bowl of alphabet cereal the next morning are D, I, and E. Die.

"I'm calling in sick at the grocery store," I say.

"You're going to work," says Mom. "Don't listen to your cereal."

"If the youth of today stop listening to their breakfast cereal, this country is done for," I say. "You say so all the time."

"I've never said that."

"I heard you say it while you were embalming some punk who didn't listen to *his* cereal just last month."

"Not funny."

"Look, how is this not an omen?"

Mom looks down at my cereal. There is no denying that it says "die."

"It's German," she insists. "It means 'the.'"

"They make this stuff in Michigan," I say. "Why would it be speaking in German?"

"It's trying to say '*the* only way you'll work off the damage you did to the hearse is by going to work.'"

"In German?"

"In German."

"There aren't enough letters in a full bowl to say that all in German."

"You owe me money. Go to work."

I know I'm fighting a losing battle, but at least I've made my stand. I gather the last three letters—D-I-E—up in my spoon and gobble them down. In a symbolic way, I'm conquering death.

I'm not quite ready to tell Mom about the new job yet. And anyway, I'm not sure when I'll start getting paid, or how many tours I'll get to run. For now, I have to keep bagging groceries to pay off the damage I did backing her hearse into a cement pillar in a parking lot. A cement pillar which frankly had no business being there, for the record.

But during my whole walk to work, I'm messing with my phone, trying to get the *Tribune* archives to load on it.

I'm hooked.

There is no way to be good at bagging groceries. Everyone has their own weird way they want their stuff arranged, and they all expect you to be able to guess their preferences. Even the most hardened skeptics in the ghost-hunting business probably think their baggers have psychic powers.

Plus, the porta-potty blue of the uniforms is really, really not my shade. And they let me get away with the two-tone hair, as long as I tie it back, but I have to wear a Band-Aid over my lip ring, which is supposed to make me look more respectable to the old people but probably just makes them think I have herpes or something.

Trying to do the job on one hour of sleep is torture.

The line of registers beep and ding. The clang of the grocery carts sounds like the gurneys that carry bodies through my basement.

"You're doing it wrong," one old lady whines. "Eggs get their own bag. You just put a bag of rice on top of them!"

The previous old lady was mad that I didn't put enough things in with her eggs to stop them from bouncing around in her car.

I've never gotten used to this, having people complain about me right in front of me. I see their scowling, disapproving faces when I close my eyes at night. Sometimes I think of good ways to respond to their complaints, but I never actually say them. Even in my sleep.

One old woman today is such a freaking bat that I find myself imagining shoving her into the trunk of her car and just letting her roast inside of it. As she drives away, I wander around to the side of the store, where the break area is. Kacey—who is sort of my "work wife"—is taking a smoke break, and I take a seat across from her and pull out my phone to look up new disparaging words for "old person" in the *OED*. You're only really supposed to go to the break area if you need a cigarette, but the *OED* is my version of smoking, in a way. My addiction. It calms me down and relieves me of stress.

"'Grave-porer,'" I say. "First recorded in 1582."

"What's that mean?"

"An annoying old person. Also, 'mumpsimus,' 1573; 'huddle-duddle,' 1599; and 'crusty cum-twang,' same year."

"You just made that one up."

I hand her the phone and let her see for herself. Most of those terms were coined by Thomas Nashe, who was sort of an Elizabethan insult comic and pornographer. He comes up in the *OED* a lot if you're looking up naughty words.

You can't go around using most of these antique swear words in casual conversation without looking like a nut, but it's nice to know they're there.

The morning drags on. I can't wait to get to the graveyard.

When I finally get off work, I sleep through most of the Blue Line ride into the city, except for a part when some lady across from me is telling a little kid how to pray to the archangel Michael if he ever gets chased by witches. You don't want to sleep through a scene like that.

Rick and Cyn are waiting for me by the cemetery gates, holding hands. Cyn takes one of my hands, so all three of us walk into the cemetery like we're off to see the Wizard of Oz. I nearly start whistling. Rick actually does.

Graceland is a gorgeous cemetery. It looks like it should be autumn in there, even though it's June and hot as hell. There are statues everywhere among the beautiful trees. Not a bad place to get planted. There's lots of interesting company—architects, film critics, boxers, robber barons. Charles Dickens's no-good brother Augie is in here someplace, too. You know that guy's got some stories.

Rick starts pointing out notable graves right away. We walk up to this really spooky statue that looked like a grim reaper or something, and he shows me a decaying stone nearby that marks the grave of John Kinzie, an early settler who killed another early settler, Jean La Lime, in a drunken brawl. This is his fourth grave—they kept moving Kinzie's body when the earliest cemeteries closed down. Or at least they said they did. They might have left him in Lincoln Park, for all we know. Or even down by the Water Tower.

The guy he killed stayed buried in one place longer than he did, but in 1891 they accidentally dug up La Lime during construction and gave his bones to the Chicago Historical Society. I'm sure they must have been thrilled.

After Rick explains all this, he says, "Now tell that story back to me, like we were on a tour."

And I do. I repeat the story, then he helps me refine it, and tells me how to figure out which parts are important, which parts I would only throw in if I had time, and where the "gasp" lines are, the factoids that'll make people's jaws drop if I tell them just right. This one isn't a story he tells on the regular route, but it's good practice, and the spot where they dug up La Lime is close enough to the usual route—two blocks south of the gallows site—that we can use it as an alternate tour stop if we can't access all the usual ones some night.

When we're done with that exercise, the three of us head north on the path and end up at a massive family plot with a giant statue of a bored-looking guy on a throne, staring down at a reflecting pool, some benches, and a bunch of small stone markers.

"This," says Rick, "is the grave of Marshall Field, the department store guy, and his family."

"The reflecting pool is full of the tears of his workers," says Cynthia.

"With benches, so Field could enjoy the company of the sort of weirdos who hang out in cemeteries," I say.

"Ironic," says Rick, "because he hated weirdos."

Rick tells me some stories about how Field had helped get a group of anarchists hanged, and the mystery of whether his son's death was really an accident, like Mr. Field insisted, or if he was killed in a brothel, like everyone else believed.

Cyn walks up to the grave of Marshall himself and shouts "You stole all your good ideas from Harry Selfridge!"

"Dare you to piss in the reflecting pool," says Rick.

Eventually we end up on Burnham Island, a tiny wooded isle in the middle of the cemetery lake. It's sort of eerie here.

Rick loves it. "It looks like the spot where a guy in a folk ballad would take his pregnant girlfriend to murder her."

"Might make it more haunted," says Cyn.

She opens her backpack, pulls out some sandwiches and drinks, and sets us up for a graveyard-island picnic next to a boulder marking the burial place of Daniel Burnham, an architect.

The sandwiches are made with mayonnaise and look like they've been in the bag long enough to turn. But Rick tears into his, and Cyn looks at me expectantly, so I take a bite of mine and smile. It's terrible and possibly poison. But I don't want to hurt her feelings. I nibble the edges and put the rest in my purse when she isn't looking.

"So, you definitely want the job?" asks Rick.

"Hell yeah."

He nods. "We'll do your real initiation after the next tour," he says. "You make it through that, you're one of us."

"One of us. One of us," Cyn chants.

Right after the picnic, we get off the island and roam through the cemetery, past a bunch of mausoleums with the same basic aesthetic as the Couch tomb, and Cyn shows me how to see inside some of them. A couple of them aren't locked as tight as they should be, and no one cares since the whole family has died out and no one maintains them anymore. "Good places to stash some valuables if you ever need to," she says. "No one's ever gonna look."

Good to know.

I pull the sandwich from my purse, shudder at the thought of eating any more of it, and when Cyn's and Rick's backs are turned, I slide it into one of the tombs to rot away, never to be seen again.

We do a few more training exercises, but then we notice the tomb of the "Fuchs" family. Things get a little middle school from there. I think you can only spend so long in a graveyard before you notice that half of the gravestones look like dicks, and then names like "Johnson" and "Fanny" on the stones start to be hilarious.

Maybe some people can see that sort of thing and not chuckle.

But not Cyn. Certainly not Rick. And not me.

These are my people.

For dinner we go to the nursing home where Rick and Cyn work their day jobs. Part of the deal for them is that they get to eat for free in the cafeteria when they want to, which saves them a few bucks on groceries.

It's cute how popular Rick and Cyn are with the residents. We're invited to sit at nearly every table, and end up with a woman who can't be less than a hundred and fifty years old. She has a nurse with her to work her silverware and stuff, since she's too frail to feed herself.

"They keep wanting me to give a talk on local ghost lore for the residents," says Rick, as we sit down at the round table with our cafeteria trays. "But I'm afraid that'd be like giving a talk on career day at high school. Like, 'This could be YOU in a couple of years!'"

I snort, and the old lady sitting with us laughs a little bit herself. This only encourages Rick.

"Have you thought about what you'll be when you get out of here?" he goes on, in the kind of voice people use to impersonate salesmen. "Consider a career in the ghastly arts! You don't have to settle for being an orb; with the right training, you could be a poltergeist, a full-body apparition, or even a phantom foul-mouth! You have so much potential!"

"Phantom foul-mouth?" I ask.

"Yeah," says Cyn. "Ghosts who swear at people. There are a few of those in town. And there'll be one more when I kick it."

"Me too," says the old woman at our table. "That's what I want to be. One of those."

"Megan," Rick says, "this is Mrs. Gunderson. She'll haunt the crap out of everyone when she goes."

"Hi," I say.

Cyn starts to take a bite of an apple, but Mrs. Gunderson taps on the table and gives her a look. "We pray before we eat, young lady."

Cyn nods, puts down the apple, and gives me a "play along" look. I nod back, and Mrs. Gunderson puts her hands together and says, "Dear Lord, please hurry up and take me, because I am ready to go. This place smells and I do nothing but ache all day long. I can't see or move, but my brain is still sharp enough to know how miserable I am. Please bring me into your loving arms soon. In Jesus' name we pray. Amen."

Then she smiles at me sweetly as the nurse starts spoon-feeding applesauce to her.

"Oh, Mrs. Gunderson," says Cyn. "You're so silly."

When we finish eating, Rick and Cyn lead me outside.

"Is she always like that?" I ask. "Praying to die?"

"Every day," says Rick. "It's all she talks about. She's in a lot of pain. Lots of those people are."

"That really sucks," I say.

"Don't worry," says Cyn. "We're taking care of her."

At Second City, the comedy school where Rick is taking classes, we follow him up a maze of escalators and down a series of halls into a bare-walled room with nondescript carpet, fluorescent lights, and exposed pipes. While he chats with the lanky, gray-haired teacher, and the other students look at their phones, Cyn and I hang in the back by a stack of disused music stands. I send Zoey the pictures I took of the hallways, which have photos of all the famous comedians who got their training here: Tina Fey, Steve Carrell, Stephen Colbert, three out of four original ghostbusters. Everyone, really. I always like to impress Zoey with big-city name-dropping. She lives in some small town in Arizona.

"How's Zoey?" asks Cyn, reading over my shoulder.

"Okay, I guess," I say.

"Still no picture?"

I shake my head.

"I'm gonna set you up with a friend of mine," says Cyn.

"No thanks."

"Seriously. I'll have her come on the tour. She's about your age. Big into ghosts. And you can see what she looks like and be sure she's not twelve and all."

I lean back in the chair. "The reason Zoey won't send a picture is an anxiety disorder. What kind of asshole would I be if I broke things off because of her mental health?"

"You're not being unreasonable. There are safety issues. Not to mention physical ones."

I shrug. "I can deal."

"Have you ever at least kissed anyone in person?"

I don't answer for a second, then say, "I almost kissed the girl who played the other old lady in *Arsenic and Old Lace,* but she got freaked out when I tried."

"Not into girls?"

"I thought she was."

"Were you both still dressed as old ladies at the time?"

I pause, then nod. Cyn can't help but chuckle. I don't blame her. I chuckle too.

I was still sort of reeling from that particular misadventure when I first starting e-mailing back and forth with Zoey. If I hadn't had Zoey, I'd probably still be seeing that girl's heavily made-up face looking horrified every time I closed my eyes.

"You don't have to die a virgin for someone who won't even meet up with you," says Cyn.

"I don't feel like I am one."

"Just from cybersex?"

I shrug. "I think it counts. Virginity's a social construct anyway."

I sort of wish I really thought that more than I do.

And I do at least want to kiss someone. Soon.

Maybe I can be in another play where I get to kiss a costar.

We watch a few students stumble their way through stand-up routines, then Rick comes up and absolutely blows the others off the stage with a routine about an uncle of his whose hobby was buying new insurance plans.

"Seriously, folks," he says. "Every time I see the guy, he's got some new policy that he's all amped up about. He'll show up to Thanksgiving and be like, 'All I got to do is pay ten bucks a month, and they'll give me fifty grand if I lose one lousy limb!' Then at Christmas he'll have some new plan that costs fifteen bucks a month, but they'll give him half a million for a severed arm. I learned long division by him making me figure out how many months he'd have to pay before he lost money by losing a leg!"

He milks certain words perfectly, wringing all the laughs he can out of them. The class roars with laughter.

"See?" Cyn whispers. "Star."

She's right. Rick is head and shoulders above everyone else we've seen in the class.

"I'm totally serious," he goes on. "One day Uncle Carlos is going to be a very rich man. With no arms and no legs. We can hang him on the wall and call him Art. Throw him in front of the door, call him Matt."

It's a third-grade joke, but even the teacher is cracking up.

"Or toss him in the pool, and BOOM! Bob's your uncle!"

Now the class explodes.

Cyn has heard the routine a million times, but she smiles proudly when the class laughs. "That's my crazy bathroom," she whispers.

Between the teacher's notes and what Rick tells me on the way home, I can see that it's all in the delivery. It isn't just that the things he's saying are funny (they only sort of *are*), it's how he says them. Waiting until just the right second, when the laughter from one joke is just dying down, to throw out the next line. One change in word choice can make or break a joke. An extra syllable can screw up the rhythm.

And the same goes for ghost stories—one word, one pause, can be the difference in a gasp line working or falling flat.

Back home, I spend all night practicing in front of the mirror, just quietly enough that Mom can't hear me. I refine my stories a word at a time.

And I forget all about how Rick had said something back at the cemetery about an "initiation" after my next tour.

Chapter Six

Two days later, when I next come on a tour, I am a Resurrection Mary expert. I've learned my way around genealogy sites and found death records for lots of girls named Mary who ended up at Resurrection. I've pulled their obits from the *Tribune*. I've found academic articles about the urban myth of the vanishing hitchhiker from the 1940s. I am totally ready to tell the story on a tour.

On the Blue Line train into the city I sit across from a guy who seems to think he's a werewolf or something. He writhes and grunts and howls and licks his fingers as though they were claws, and he rambles something about cross-breeding gorillas with hippos. Everyone just goes about their business reading their books like nothing unusual is going on, because it's the Blue Line, after all, and he's not biting anyone or anything.

When I get to Clark Street, the necklace guy and the portrait guy are plying their trades again. A costumed guide from

Al Capone Tours lets a little kid pretend to shoot him for a *charming* photo his family can take home.

Edward Tweed is running two buses for DarkSide Chicago tours tonight. He's standing in front of one of them, and next to him is a scruffy red-haired guy in a threadbare brown sport coat that must be sweaty as hell in the heat, plus a fedora that has seen better days. He looks like the kind of guy who gets kicked out of pool halls.

Tweed tips his cowboy hat at me, and the other guy gives me a two-finger salute.

I meet up with Rick and Cyn by their bus, and Rick tells me the other guy is Aaron Saltis, Tweed's protégé. "He's younger than he looks," says Rick. "Actor. Nice guy, but he really needs to fact-check Tweed. Now and then we bump into him in the alley, and he's always saying a serial killer in the 1970s used to pick people up there. Pure BS."

The pure BS is clearly popular; Tweed's thirty-seven-passenger buses both look full, and our one smaller one is only half full. It feels half empty.

The customers we have are mostly tourists with kids, including a woman who shows up with a tiny accessory dog and insists that she has to take it along. I think that pets are officially against the rules, but she's with a party of five, and Rick and Cyn aren't doing well enough to turn away a party that large. And anyway, it fits in her purse.

Rick introduces me to the passengers as "part of the team,"

and I feel like people are giving me skeptical looks, like I'm too young to have this job and have no business being here. Maybe they think I'm Cyn's sister or something. I'll have to make myself look a bit older. I don't usually wear much makeup—I sort of associate it with dead people—but I know some tricks.

As we start, Rick says, "Now, this neighborhood isn't all that spooky these days, except that occasionally we do have this guy in a frog suit standing outside of Rainforest Cafe, and that guy scares the bajeezus out of me." When people chuckle, he says, "Yeah, you guys laugh, but I have to go through life without a bajeezus now." He pauses for another chuckle, waits until just the right time, then adds "Boom! You all just got privilege-checked."

While he points out all the murder sites, hanging sites, and disaster sites between the Rock and Roll McDonald's and the Alley of Death and Mutilation, I'm obsessively going over the Resurrection Mary story in my head, thinking of all the ways I can change it if I have to, like if there's some miracle and all the lights are green and I have to leave out a lot. I am nervous as hell. I've done a few plays and all, but I've always been in a zombie outfit, or an old lady costume. I've never just been, like, myself.

But I can do this.

After the alley stop, as we cruise onto Wacker Drive, Rick says, "Now, to tell you about a girl who died here in 1934, here's our

ADAM SELZER

own Miss Megan Henske, Mistress of Darkness and Shadows."

Mistress of Darkness and Shadows. That's me. Hell yeah.

I feel a surge of confidence for a second as I take the mic, but just as I'm about to talk, I hear some lady a few rows back saying, "Is she supposed to be scary?" to the guy she's with, like she'd expected me to show up in costume or something.

I try to ignore her or picture her in her underwear. Neither helps. I swear that even the dog is giving me a skeptical look as I take my place at the front of the bus, like even a chihuahua knows I have no right to be working this job. I forget just about everything I was planning to say and try to improvise.

Badly.

"So, uh, here at the 'L' tracks," I say, "this girl Mary Bregovy died in 1934. Some people say she's Resurrection Mary, a famous Chicago ghost. But there's an academic article that lists a sighting from three years before that, so . . ."

And then I freeze. For what seems like an hour. In grocery-store-hell time, which is infinitely slower than normal time. My knees start to shake, my vision goes blurry. I'm a trembling mess.

The silence sounds like a vacuum about to suck me back to Forest Park.

But just as the bus is getting to the spot where Mary Bregovy died, and I'm half-wishing I were her, a miracle happens.

Outside of the bus, a rail-thin woman is standing on the corner wearing a fur coat that's probably six sizes too big for her frame, and orders of magnitude too warm for the weather.

"Hey, look!" I say. "Special bonus tonight. On your right, it's Cruella De Vil, from *101 Dalmations!*"

All twelve passengers burst out laughing, and Rick nearly chokes on his Red Bull. When he swallows and opens his mouth, he's cracking up.

"That's got to be a ghost, right, folks?" I ask. "Why would a living person be wearing fur in this weather?"

"Why would ghosts wear clothes at all?" asks a guy in the third row. "Your pants don't have a soul."

"Well, maybe yours don't, sir," I say. "They must not have any good vintage stores where you live."

Rick laughs and says, "Just because you're dead doesn't mean you want your bits and pieces showing, man." Then he pats me on the back, retrieves the mic, and says, "A lot of people don't really think ghosts are peoples' souls or spirits, exactly. Some people think it's more scientific, like some sort of leftover energy. Some people call it a 'psychic imprint.'"

"Or a 'residual haunting,'" says Cyn.

"Right. As opposed to an 'intelligent haunting' that floats around and knows where it's going. And they're not always even from dead people—just something left over from a really intense emotion. Theoretically."

For a moment I think back to the Summer I spent living in my dad's apartment, back when I was nine. I thought it was haunted because of the moaning noises I heard in the next apartment over on the other side of my bedroom wall at night. I knew "the facts of life," but I hadn't yet figured out that sometimes people had sex when they weren't trying to have a baby, so it didn't occur to me that the eighty-year-old couple next door, the Weyhers, might have been doing it.

And the last time I stayed there, over spring break, I heard those sounds again. Even though the apartment has been empty for months, since Mrs. Weyher died. Maybe I was hearing some sort of psychic echo of her getting it on. I guess I could get behind that sort of ghost.

Go, ghost of Mrs. Weyher, go.

From there on, I relax a bit. Disney villains have saved my ass. I never do finish the Mary story, but Rick lets me tell some of the Hull House story myself, and then a bit about H. H. Holmes at the body dump.

There's a little parking area and a "senior living" apartment complex on the site of the old garage where the Saint Valentine's Day Massacre happened. The old people don't like buses to stop there, so it's usually just a drive-by, but tonight Cyn slows the bus to a stop as Rick finishes the story.

"Okay," Rick says. "Remember what I was saying earlier about psychic imprints?"

We all nod.

"Well, there's supposedly one right here at the massacre site. There was a German Shepherd named Highball who was tied to the axle of one of the trucks in the garage during the massacre. Even though he wasn't shot, he was apparently so scared that he left some sort of energy behind. For years, people said that dogs would freak out if they walked by this fence. Wanna try an experiment, since we have a dog with us tonight?"

The woman with the dog gets up and takes it outside to see what happens. The dog hops through the fence, trots right over to the spot where Rick said the bodies fell, and poops.

"Well, there you have it," says Rick. "It scared the shit out of the dog."

We all have a good laugh, the dog runs straight back to the woman, and the tour goes on.

The tips are good, and Rick and Cyn cut me in, even though I barely did anything.

"Total props for that Cruella joke," says Rick. "That was really thinking on your feet."

"I was screwing up the story before," I say. "I don't even know what I would have done if she hadn't shown up."

"No worries. You proved you can handle stuff as it comes up, and that's huge. And if we get any reviews from tonight they'll be good. So you're in the clear."

I take a deep breath and resolve not to check Yelp or whatever. I never read reviews of the fan fic I post online. I did once, and it took me weeks to get over the bad comments. I hadn't stopped to think that I could get reviews of tours, too. But I don't have to read them, I guess.

"Hey," says Cyn. "Weird night to have all that psychic-imprint stuff come up, huh?"

"I know, right?" says Rick. "It's like there's something in the air. Cosmic."

They both look right at me, grinning like they're about to let me through a door into a surprise party.

"What's up?" I ask.

"Your initiation," says Cyn. "One. Of. Us. One. Of. Us."

Rick switches to a more serious tone. "Megan, do you support assisted suicide for chronic patients?"

I nod. "Of course."

"All right," he says. "Let's head up to the north side, then. We're gonna see if we can create our own psychic imprint, and you get to help."

Chapter Seven

"Y ou, uh, aren't going to kill me, right?" I ask.

Rick laughs. "Nah," he says. "You're not an elderly chronic patient. People would ask questions if you died. Too much trouble, besides the ethical stuff."

"They'd probably assume Zoey did it, though," says Cyn, as she loops the bus around onto Dearborn Street and heads north. "Tell her about the brain punch, Ricardo."

"Right," Rick says. "The brain punch."

"Brain punch?" I ask.

"Brain punch. It's a Marjorie Kay Stone thing."

"Ah."

"Did you ever stop to wonder why we knew so much about her and her house?" asks Cyn.

"Not really. I guess I figured, you know, small town. Everyone knows everyone?"

"Magwitch Park isn't that small," says Cyn.

"We were kind of her slaves for a while," says Rick. "She

had, like, six thousand handwritten memoir pages, and she hated computers too much to type them herself. After she caught me burying my hamster in her yard, she sort of blackmailed us into doing it for her."

"Try *ten* thousand pages," says Cyn.

"Maybe twenty," says Rick. "Unless it was thirty. Unnumbered, and not in order. There were pages just scattered all over her house. We probably never even found half of them."

"God, that was hell," says Cyn. "Pages in every nook and cranny, and that house had thousands of nooks and crannies."

"Nooks and crannies and psychotic grannies," Rick says. "Rust and must and cobwebs. Dust and bones and skeletons."

"She had six of those," says Cyn. "Skeletons. First time Rick saw them he about peed himself."

"I did not," says Rick. "Point is, we had to type the pages into this ancient computer she had. We did find a bunch of consecutive ones about the time when she was hired to find a ghost that could be in a movie, and in the middle of them she talked about how someone taught her that most of what people call ghosts are just 'psychic imprints' from people who died in just a certain way, and in just the right frame of mind."

"It's all to do with dying super quick when you don't quite have time to react to it," says Cyn. "So the reaction is sort of cut off and hangs in the air. It's all scientific, not supernatural."

"I guess that sounds logical," I say.

"You don't even have to kill them, necessarily," says Rick.

"Like Highball the dog didn't die, but he still left something behind."

"Only that apparently didn't work," I say.

"It might have worked at the time," says Rick. "It's just long gone now. Those imprints, or whatever you call them, don't last forever. Couple years, tops. Eventually they dissipate into the environment. That's just the basic laws of thermodynamics."

"Listen to him, talking like he knows anything about the laws of thermodynamics," Cyn teases.

"I do too," he insists. "And if Highball had been shot, he might have left some stronger imprint that would have lasted longer. Same if it was a little girl—they're biologically more likely to leave an imprint behind, which is part of why every fucking haunted spot in the world is supposed to have a ghostly little girl floating around."

"Gun shots and baseball bats to the head will usually do the trick, if the victim is in the right frame of mind," Cyn says, "but there's this technique Marjorie called 'a punch in the brain.' It replicates the effect without the mess. It's a really quick operation. Painless."

"And no one's gonna suspect foul play," says Rick. "Not that this is foul, exactly."

I nod along, not sure if they're serious or what. Like, they're talking about how to make someone into a ghost in the same kind of tone you'd use to tell someone how to make a Denver omelette.

It's probably a hazing prank.

I try to play it cool and set my face into a smirk that I hope makes it look like I'm on to them, but playing along.

"Point is," says Cyn, "if you kill a person just right, you can get them to leave something behind, and people might pick up on it and perceive it as a ghost. And if we're going to beat Edward Tweed out, or even stay in business, we've got to get more ghost sightings."

"And you know I hate making stuff up or lying," says Rick, "but these imprints are close enough that I won't feel bad if people see one in Lincoln Park and think it's a ghost from City Cemetery or something. So tonight we're going to punch someone in the brain."

"Mrs. Gunderson, down at the nursing home," Cyn adds. "That poor old woman. Her whole family's gone. All her friends are gone. She's got nerve problems, so she can't even wipe her own ass anymore, and she's never gotten used to needing help with it, like most of them have."

"You know how she prayed to die at dinner? She does that at every meal," says Rick. "Breaks your freaking heart. So we're gonna help, and she is super excited."

I nod and freeze my lips in a sort of half-smirk, still trying to look like I'm just playing along. We're on Lake Shore Drive now, and the waves are coming in so hard and strong that Lake Michigan looks like the ocean. There was a hurricane on the east coast, and we're getting the tail winds.

Honestly, it wouldn't bother me that much if they were going to help Mrs. Gunderson slip quietly and painlessly out of the world. She's old and decrepit and sad. She has some chronic illness, though I'm not sure which one, and seems to want it all to be over with. I've heard Mom talk about people like this that she meets to plan final arrangements with, people who are just holding on because their family won't let them go, or because the doctors want to keep billing someone for taking care of them. People who are already dead, really, but still breathing.

Cyn pulls the bus off of Lake Shore Drive and into the north side of the city, past playgrounds and townhouses and trendy restaurants, while I try to figure out what to do and how I should be responding. I worry a little that if this is a prank and I say that it sounds like a good idea out loud, I'll fuck everything up. Maybe they'll think I'm a sociopath. Maybe they'll even call the cops.

I try to look busy. I take out my phone and start looking up words for "kill" and "dead" in the *OED*.

"You know," I say while I scan through synonyms, "I'm pretty sure my dad's old next-door neighbor once left behind a psychic imprint by having really good sex. Have you ever thought of, like, rigging one up like that?"

"Yeah, Rick?" asks Cyn. "Ever thought of giving it to someone so well they left a ghost behind?"

"Well, I might ask you the same question," says Rick. "But

I think people really have to die to leave anything behind that people might notice on a tour. Sit tight, and we'll all go kill Mrs. Gunderson."

I am so glad to have the *OED* on my phone so I can look distracted instead of actually having to react to this. Because I'm totally unsure how. Reading off synonyms seems safe. Helpful if they really want me to be helping, but casual and funny enough to seem like I might just be playing along. And, of course, it's a good way to relieve my own stress while I figure out which one of those I'm supposed to be.

"'Kill' is sort of a negative term," I say. "Maybe we should use something else. 'Forfere,' 'swelt,' 'occise,' or 'dislive.' There's a bunch of them here."

"Whatever makes you more comfortable," says Cyn.

"Here's one," I say. "'Ghosted.' Synonym for 'dead' from 1834. We could say we're going to 'ghost' her."

"Like, as in a verb?" asks Cyn. "You can't verb the word 'ghost.'"

"You can too," says Rick. "Or you could in 1834."

"'Fine," says Cyn. "We're 'ghosting' her."

"That does sound better than 'punching her in the brain,'" Rick admits.

"Don't the old ladies in *Arsenic and Old Lace* have a word for killing people?" asks Cyn.

"Not really a word," I said, "but they say it's 'one of their charities.'"

"Yeah," says Cyn. "That's exactly what this is. One of our charities. Ghosting elderly chronic patients."

As we're pulling into the nursing home, Zoey sends a picture of a cartoon butt.

This could escalate quickly.

The nursing home cafeteria is empty of people now, the tables full of half-finished jigsaw puzzles and stuff. It smells like moldy oranges and Lysol, and the only person there is a forty-something woman sitting behind a reception desk.

"Hi, Cynthia!" says the woman.

"Hey, Shanita," says Cyn. "We promised Mrs. Gunderson a moonlit stroll in the park tonight."

"Oh, she'll love that. Just sign in, and you can go get her."

Rick and Cyn sign in, then tell me to wait in the common room. I park at a table and distract myself by sending a couple of particularly naughty texts to Zoey in response to the butt picture. She doesn't answer right away, so I'm left to stare around at the lifeless room.

After a few minutes Rick and Cyn come back, pushing Mrs. Gunderson in a wheelchair. She looks like it hurts to smile, but she's grinning from ear to ear anyway.

"Mrs. Gunderson," says Cyn, "This is Megan Henske. Remember her?"

"You don't know what this means to me, young lady," Mrs. Gunderson says.

"Uh, it's a perfect night," I say. "There's a big pink moon."

"Oh, beautiful!"

She claps her hands together, or I imagine she tries to, but her nerve issues make it so that her arms just sort of flop around. I follow as Cyn wheels her out the door and into the night.

Rick gets behind the wheel of the senior home's excursion van, giving Cyn a break from driving. I end up on the floor in the back, next to Mrs. Gunderson's strapped-in wheelchair.

"All right, Mrs. Gunderson," Cyn says as she buckles up in the front. "Just to be clear, one more time: You know what we're doing, right?"

"Killing me," says the old lady, cheerful as a toddler at snack time. "I'm going to be a new ghost on your tour!"

"Ghosting you," says Rick. "We're calling it 'ghosting.' Megan's idea."

"It's in the *Oxford English Dictionary*," says Cyn.

Mrs. Gunderson beams. "How sophisticated!"

This has to be a prank.

Has to, has to, has to.

Mrs. Gunderson is probably in on it.

Maybe it's a test to see how I do under pressure.

I lean forward and whisper to Cyn, "You're sure she's not senile?" That seems like the kind of question they'd want me to be asking.

"Yeah, she's fine."

I look at the frail woman beside me, trying to see a glimmer in her eye that can tell me it's all a joke. All I see is that same look people give Mom when she really, really goes above and beyond and helps them through a tough time at the funeral home. Gratitude. The kind of look she used to talk about getting when she was subtly trying to persuade me to take up a career in the family business.

"They'd keep me alive in that bed for twenty more years," Mrs. Gunderson says.

"As long as they could keep making money off you," says Rick.

"I tried to starve myself, you know."

"We know," says Cyn.

"I'm too weak to cut my own wrists or hang myself. All I could think to do was starve. But I got so hungry! It takes such a long time to starve."

"They'd just hook you to an IV and pump in nutrients anyway," says Cyn.

"You can't know how much it means to me that you'd do this," Mrs. Gunderson says. "Are you sure you don't mind? Really sure?"

"Hey," says Cyn. "Every time we let fuckers like Edward Tweed tell people to jump right to supernatural explanations for things they can't explain, we're killing even more people than we are right here. Whenever some nut starts shooting people because he thinks a spirit told him to, Tweed's got blood on his hands. Putting him out of business is going to save lives."

"Well, that's overstating it," says Rick. "It's not his fault people are nuts."

"It's overstating a little," says Cyn. "But think about it. Every business relies on killing. Only reason we can afford the gas to drive the bus around is people dying for oil."

I pull out my phone and see that Zoey has sent me several messages, each more explicit than the last. I send a few non-committal "mmm" and "oooh" messages. Enough to keep it going without really getting involved.

Rick turns back to Mrs. Gunderson when we get to a red light.

"Now, you understand," he says, "that we might have to scare you a bit to make sure the ghost thing works, right? We think it'll work better if you're scared when it happens."

"I understand. But it will all be quick and painless?"

"Totally," says Cyn.

"I've updated my will," says Mrs. Gunderson. "It says I want the funeral at the home you suggested."

Cyn smiles back at me, silently telling me what funeral home she means. Then she tilts her head at me and says, "You okay? You look worried."

"Well," I say, "I assume you've covered all the bases to make sure we won't get in trouble, right? Assisted suicide isn't legal."

"This would be legal in Oregon, if we were doctors," says Cyn. "That's close enough for me."

"Yeah," says Rick. "Even if there's an autopsy, it'll just look like an aneurysm."

And he pulls the van into the little parking area behind the Chicago History Museum, right near the Couch tomb.

"Thank you so much," says Mrs. Gunderson. "You really can't know what it means to me, to die on a lovely October night beneath a beautiful pink moon."

October.

She said it was October.

It's June.

As Cyn unloads the wheelchair, I feel like I've solved the puzzle. This isn't real. It's a test. And I'm going to pass.

I text Zoey that I'll be back in a few while I wait for Cyn to push Mrs. Gunderson out of earshot.

"She said it was October," I say to Rick.

"You lose track of time when you're in the home," he says.

"Is that the clue I'm supposed to pick up on? The proof that she's not lucid enough to make a decision like this, so we shouldn't be doing it?"

"Aw, she's fine," says Rick. "She's been begging and begging for this. Now, this part is your job."

He picks up a plastic bag from the floor of the van and hands it over to me. I open it up and see a gorilla mask.

A gorilla mask.

"What . . . in the boneless gummy hell?"

"It's a gorilla mask," he says.

"I can see that, Ricardo, but what is it for?"

"Hey, we're not just taking care of her as a favor. We're also trying to get her to haunt the place, so it'll help if she's scared when she dies."

I stare down at the mask. It smells like Halloween and new school supplies.

"This is supposed to scare her?"

"Hey, gorillas are some of the fiercest killers in the animal kingdom," says Rick. "Don't be fooled by those cute ones who learn sign language."

This can't be real. It has to be a test.

Cyn comes back to the van, having left Mrs. Gunderson sitting on the grass near the Couch tomb, where any imprint she might leave would be right where our customers would see it. "All set with the mask?"

"Look," I say, putting it down. "She said it was October, and it's June. It makes me worry that she's not as coherent as you said. I'm fine with assisted suicide for chronic elderly patients, but they have to be, you know, of sound mind."

"Well, go talk to her a bit if you want," says Cyn. "Make sure."

"I will."

And I hop out of the van and march up to the tomb, where Mrs. Gunderson is waiting, slumped down in her wheelchair, looking peaceful and calm in the moonlight.

"It's June, Mrs. Gunderson," I say. "Not October. Was that the clue I was supposed to notice? This is all a test, right?"

She doesn't respond, so I step closer.

Her eyes are closed, but she seems to be smiling. I wonder for a second if old people are like babies, that when she smiles it's just gas.

But her smile stays frozen as I move alongside her.

"Mrs. Gunderson?"

Her head slumps down onto her shoulder.

I wobble her wheelchair a bit, waiting for her to start laughing and admit it was all a joke, but her arms fall limp at her sides.

Oh, for the love of . . .

The right *OED* synonym for "shit" just won't come into my brain. For the love of something.

This can't be happening.

I touch her face, swear out loud, and put my finger to her wrist. No pulse. I don't know enough about CPR to know if I'm doing it correctly, but I've been around enough corpses to know one when I see one, and I'm seeing one now.

I look back at the van, where Rick and Cyn are standing by the passenger side, watching.

"Uh, minor problem!" I call out.

I motion them forward, and they walk across the grass, toward the tomb.

"What's wrong?" asks Cyn.

"She's already dead."

"What?" asks Rick, his eyes suddenly as wide as saucers. "Are you fucking kidding me?"

ADAM SELZER

"Nope. She's dead."

"This was just a hazing prank!" says Rick. "She wasn't supposed to die for real!"

"Yeah," says Cyn. "She was in on it. There's no way she's dead."

"Storven," I say. "Unquick. Bypast. Off to join the choir invisible. This is an ex-geezer."

"This is no time to make jokes," says Rick as he rushes toward me. "Have some respect, padawan."

"Let me check her," says Cyn. She comes over and takes Mrs. Gunderson's pulse, then tries some basic CPR stuff, and when she doesn't respond at all, Cyn confirms it. Mrs. Gunderson is gone.

"Well, shit," says Rick. "Should we try some chest compressions?"

"She's got a Do Not Resuscitate tag," says Cyn, stepping backward and looking down at her. "This is what she wanted. No extraordinary measures in the event of an emergency."

I look down at Mrs. Gunderson. It's seriously cliché to say "she looks so peaceful," but she totally does. She's even still smiling. Like she died in the middle of playing a prank. Not a bad way to go, if you've gotta go.

Both her hair and Cyn's blow in the breeze.

"Well, what do we do now?" asks Rick.

"We hurry," says Cyn, all business. "Let's get her back in her bed."

"Not call the police?" asks Rick.

"If they find her in her bed, everyone will think she just died of natural causes in her sleep. If we take her back and say she died, we'll be drowning in paperwork for years. The insurance company might sue us, or worse. And I sure as hell don't want to have to explain the gorilla mask."

Rick is looking pale now. "I swear this was a prank," he tells me. "You think she just died of too much excitement?"

"Must have," says Cyn. "But we can worry about that later. Let's just get her back in the room. Quick, before rigor mortis starts in."

We load Mrs. Gunderson and her wheelchair into the van and drive back to the home, wheeling her right past Shanita and hoisting her onto her bed. She really does look like she just passed away in her sleep.

I'm not freaking out, really, but I feel like I *should* be, and the fact that I'm *not* sort of disturbs me. What does it say about me that I don't really mind having just sort of participated in ending someone's life? I should feel upset about this. Guilty. Scared. I don't know.

But I feel calm.

Everybody dies, and Mrs. Gunderson probably couldn't have asked for a better way to do it at this point.

Even though I feel like there's at least a fifty percent chance that this was no coincidence, and Cyn really did punch Mrs. Gunderson in the brain while Rick was showing me the gorilla mask.

I send Zoey a text begging her to tell me I'm not a psychopath. She's seen enough of my stories to know my dark side. She sends a picture of a couple of cartoon characters hugging with a message:

ZOEY BABY:

If you are, then you're MY psychopath, sweetie.

I guess that anytime I've fantasized about making a getaway after committing a crime, I've imagined rambling through dark cobblestone alleys and through networks of winding tunnels under the ground. Our trip away from the nursing home is nothing that dramatic. It isn't even as dramatic as running away from tagging walls with a pencil. We just sit in traffic, mostly. I guess it beats running through the sewers.

At one point we get held up so badly that Cyn has time to run into a cupcake shop on Clark, just below Diversey Parkway. "If the traffic unfreezes, go around the block and pick me up," she says, as Rick takes the wheel. "You guys want anything?"

"I'm good," I say.

She bolts from the bus and into Molly's Cupcakes, and I move into the front row, right behind the driver's seat.

"You can drive the bus too?" I ask.

He nods. "I have my CDL. I'm actually going to be the driver for your first few solo tours, so I can jump in if I have to."

"So, how much of that was real?" I ask Rick. "Did

Marjorie Kay Stone really write about creating ghosts by punching brains?"

"Yeah, that part was real," he says. "So was Mrs. Gunderson wanting to die. That prayer the other day wasn't an act, it was what she did before every meal. There aren't gonna be any sad faces at the funeral. Which I think actually is at your place."

"Does the brain punch actually work?"

"Marjorie Kay Stone sure thought it did. I don't know if she ever tried it, though. She probably did. She was pretty fucked up by the time we met her. But this. This was a prank, not an experiment. Didn't Cyn tell you I was the biggest prankster in Magwitch Park?"

She didn't, but I'm not surprised. Now, while we wait for Cyn to get out of the cupcake shop, he tells me stories about filling the school toilets with Jell-O mix, so the water turned to gelatin, and something about smearing the floor of the gym with bowling lane oil.

Cyn comes running back with a box of cupcakes just before the cars ahead of us start moving, and by the time we get through the light she's already wolfing one down.

"You're really gonna eat that now?" asks Rick. "You just touched a corpse."

"She was pretty clean," Cyn says, spraying frosting from her mouth. "Death's not contagious."

"It just seems unhygienic."

Cyn turns back to me and says, "Is it, like, inherently less hygienic to touch a dead person than a living one?"

"Depends on what they died of and how long they've been dead, I guess."

She offers us each a cupcake, but we both pass.

I thought she didn't mind the basement at the house because she was a badass, but now I think maybe she's just the sort of person who has no "squick" reflex whatsoever. Which itself is kind of badass.

Eventually we make it back to Halsted Street and into a lot by the river where the bus is parked between tours. This is more like the sort of hideaway I pictured: an overgrown lot, not too unlike the one at the body dump. If it weren't for the city skyline visible over the tree line, you could pretend you were in the middle of nowhere. A few other tour buses are parked there, including both of the DarkSide ones.

"Watch out for the rats," says Cyn, as we get off the bus. "And the spiders. We have to sweep them off the bus before the tours lately."

Rick walks over to the bushes by the river to pee, and for a second Cyn and I stand there, looking at the skyline. The John Hancock Center would make a great castle for a villain. All it needs is a forest of thorns growing up around the bottom forty or fifty floors.

"So, tell me the truth," I say. "Did you punch her in the brain?"

"Hey, old people just die," says Cyn. "Happens all the time."

I notice she hasn't really answered my question.

"Hey, I'm not judging," I say. "I'm just glad I didn't have to jump out at her with that gorilla mask."

Then she cracks a smile and says, "That was Rick's idea. I wish I could've seen the look on your face."

"'Fiercest killer in the animal kingdom,' he said."

"That's my crazy bathroom."

Meanwhile, Cyn's crazy bathroom is singing "I am the Very Model of a Modern Major General" while he pisses in the bushes. When he's done he shakes his ass at us a bit, zips up, and comes back toward us.

Cyn nudges me and points to a chain-link fence, where something that looks like a dog is watching us. Only it's not a dog.

"Is that a wolf?" I ask.

"Coyote. We see him now and then. Wasn't that many decades ago we had wolves here, though. Back in the old days they used to have one day a year when they'd close all the businesses and chase all the wolves out of the woods and onto the ice on the lake. This space was all wilderness back then."

We climb into Cyn's truck, and they start driving me to the Blue Line stop.

"So, here's what we didn't tell you before your initiation," says Rick. "We're in talks with a TV producer who might want to make a show about us."

"Seriously?"

"Yeah," says Cyn. "And you look more camera-ready than either of us, so having you on the team will make it more likely for us to get the show off the ground."

I'm touched that she'd think this about me. I've never thought of myself as exactly TV-star material, visually, but I'm not bad-looking or anything. My face is kind of pear-shaped and awkward, but with the right outfit it looks okay.

"The big issue is really just making sure he won't make us look like jackasses," says Rick. "And that'll be tough. You can't really beat the system on those reality shows. No matter what you say, they can edit it to make it look like you're saying whatever they want."

"This guy seems decent enough," says Cyn. "And even if he makes us look as nutty as the idiots on *Ghost Encounters*, it'll be good for the business. We're getting buried by Tweed. Who is also talking to the same producer."

"It probably won't happen," says Rick. "Most producers are full of shit, and I'm not totally sure it's the way I want to break into entertainment, being a ghost guy. But we need someone who can fill in for us anyway, so the show was a good motivator to find a third."

I think this over a bit.

I imagine us doing like we did at the cemetery the other day, just wandering around telling stories and cracking jokes, on television.

I'd have people writing bad comments about me online, probably.

I'd have to be even more careful about Zoey.

But the idea that Cyn thought of me for it, and that it could actually happen . . . it's hard to resist getting excited.

On the train ride home, between chatting and fooling around with Zoey, I google the phrase "brain punch" and don't find anything relevant. Either they made the whole thing up, or they found a closely guarded secret buried in the memoirs of Marjorie Kay Stone.

I'm not sure which seems more likely.

MEGAN:

Good morning, you.

ZOEY BABY:

I love it when message alerts from you wake me up.

ZOEY BABY:

What's up?

MEGAN:

When the OED says "see: windfucker," you do it.

ZOEY BABY:

Uhhhh . . .

ADAM SELZER

MEGAN:

Looking up swear words again. Buried in the
F-bomb entry there's the word "fuckwind," and the
entry just says "see windfucker."

ZOEY BABY:

LOL. So what's a windfucker?

MEGAN:

A type of bird, according to Thomas Nashe. (Yay,
Thomas Nashe!)

MEGAN:

Also, a word one of Shakespeare's friends used for
obnoxious people.

ZOEY BABY:

Hehe. Look up a good new word I can call you. A
pet name.

MEGAN:

Welllllll . . .

MEGAN:

Some OED words for "sweetheart" include: Pow-
sowdie. Suckler. Heartikin. Flitter-mouse.

ZOEY BABY:

Awww . . . you're my flitter-mouse.

ZOEY BABY:

How's the new story coming?

MEGAN:

LOL. It's great. It's the Emperor and the Evil
Queen. Kind of a joke story.

MEGAN:

They're going at it inside the Couch tomb. But the
story all takes place outside, with people seeing
flashing lights coming from under the crack in the
door and thinking it's haunted. The story is all the
crowd's conversation.

ZOEY BABY:
LOL.

MEGAN:

Then someone will slide their phone under the door
to get a photo of what's happening in there. . . .

MEGAN:

The picture will just show a wrinkly ass, and the

ADAM SELZER

people will all run away screaming.

ZOEY BABY:

LOLOL! I can't wait to read it.

ZOEY BABY:

Still thinking about last night. Mmmm.

MEGAN:

It is safe to say I will never forget last night as long
as I live.

Chapter Eight

Later that morning, after an hour of working on my Evil Queen/Emperor story, I decide to head for a coffee shop, where I can post it from a public ISP that no one can trace to me. I've always been careful about this sort of thing. Paranoid, even. Especially now that I might just possibly be getting a TV show.

When I step outside, Mom is trimming bushes in a long dress. Formal wear, practically. Dressing up all the time is a funeral home thing. Her dad used to mow the lawn in suits.

She tilts her head up and gives me a hard look.

"You have some explaining to do."

My blood runs cold for a second.

Mom and I get along pretty well, but I'm always scared that one day she's going to find out just what kind of person her daughter really is. She wouldn't learn anything new about me if I told her I had a girlfriend, but what if she actually read what went on in some of my e-mails and texts to Zoey?

Or, worse, if she pokes around on my laptop and sees what I write in my stories? There are some so messed up that I never even post them, and if she saw those, she'd probably haul me off to some old-school asylum where they still have electro-shock machines and a yard full of unmarked graves. I think part of the reason I got the lip ring was to ease her into knowing her daughter is a bit of a freak. Like, maybe it'll be less of a shock if she ever hacks my phone.

And now there's the new fear that Zoey has turned out to be twelve and the cops have been called.

Not to mention the fact that I just participated in the death of another person last night. It's weird how that's about the *last* thing that occurs to me in the split second before I respond.

I pick up an old brown leaf that's still on the ground from last fall and act like I'm distracted by it.

"What's up?" I ask.

"Cynthia Fargon called a few minutes ago."

The leaf trembles in my hands.

"Oh yeah?"

"She was arranging a funeral for someone at a nursing home she's working at," she says. "But in the process, she men-tioned that she just gave you a job as a ghost-tour guide."

There's some anger in her voice, but if that's all she's found out, I'm relieved. I knew I'd have to talk to her about the job sooner or later. I toss the leaf aside and sit down on the porch. The wood is hot against my thighs. I hate wearing shorts.

"She and her friend Ricardo started a historical ghost-tour company," I say, emphasizing the word "historical." "They offered me a job as a guide, and I've been, sort of, you know . . . training."

Mom sighs and takes off the gloves she'd been wearing.

"First of all, you've obviously been lying about being out with Kacey. Here I was all happy for you that you seemed to be seeing someone."

"This is actually better. Kacey has a parole officer, you know."

"And did you even stop to think about what it could do for the business here if people think you're going to be hovering over their dearly departed mother with a proton pack, or whatever they use?"

"I'm not going to do that," I say. "The tour is mostly history stuff, not, like, telling people that a temperature drop means there's an invisible dead person floating around. And I'm sure no one uses those backpack-size proton packs from the 1980s anymore. There's probably an app for that now."

She would normally have laughed at that, but today the jokes aren't scoring me any points.

"It doesn't matter what you *really* do. People are going to *think* you're like those idiots who pretend to hunt for ghosts on TV. They're going to picture you poking around the basement trying to catch people's souls in some kind of pseudo-sciencey . . . net."

"Your potential customers won't even know about it," I say. "I use Dad's last name, not the one on the sign."

She tosses her gloves on the ground and shakes her head.

"Come on," she says. "If we're gonna fight, let's fight inside. It's too hot for this shit."

"Agreed."

Upstairs, Clarice, our cosmetologist, is sitting at the kitchen table, wearing too much lipstick and reading the paper through her enormous red glasses. She already knows, apparently.

"Morning, Megan," she says. "Catch any ghosts last night?"

"Just one, but it was catch and release, so we let it go back to its grave."

"This isn't a joke, Megan," says Mom.

She sits at the table and motions for me to do the same. I take my seat and get ready.

"Look, my lip ring didn't scare people away from the business," I say. "And everyone who knows me knows I like girls. That didn't hurt business any, either."

"I know that," says Mom. "You know I've tried very hard to let you be yourself, and let you be a normal teenager, and all of that. If anyone doesn't want me embalming their aunt because of who you are, they can bury her themselves. But I can only afford to be so picky with customers, Megan. We haven't had a funeral here in more than a week."

"Stupid internet," I say. "Everyone just watches videos on how to DIY an embalming now."

Clarice smiles, but Mom doesn't.

"This is different," says Mom. "I can't blame people if they don't want their loved ones' remains being ghost-hunted."

I get up and pour myself a bowl of cereal (a mix of Cocoa Puffs and Peanut Butter Cap'n Crunch) while I try to think up a response to that one.

The hell of it, the worst part, is that I totally understand Mom's point of view. Worrying about ghost hunters is way outside of what funeral-home customers should be expected to accept.

Then Mom makes an argument in my favor.

"On the other hand," she says, "when Cyn called, she was setting up a funeral for a nursing-home resident who died overnight."

"Right," I say, jumping onto this new thread. "Working with her might bring in more business than it scares away. And besides that, I'm sure I can keep anyone who comes on the tours from finding out where I live. If anyone asks, I'll say I live in Pilsen or Logan Square or something."

"Hipster," says Clarice.

Mom pours herself a cup of coffee while she mutters to herself. She doesn't like to talk about it, but the business isn't in great shape. It's gotten bad enough that she never really talks about me taking over when I grow up anymore, which she used to at least hint at now and then. It was never a rule that I had to follow in her footsteps, and she didn't try to push me too hard, but she used to find all these excuses to tell me what a purposeful, satisfying job it is, trying to subtly make me want to grow up to be the fourth-generation owner of the Raskin Family Funeral Home (Raskin was her maiden name).

Now she never brings it up at all, like it's just an unspoken fact that the business won't last long enough for me to make a career out of it. We'll be lucky if it lasts until Mom is ready to retire.

I hate to think of her having to go to work for some other home if ours goes under. She always tells horror stories about what rackets some corporate funeral homes are. But she doesn't really have any other skills that I know of. This is her life. The life she was raised for.

"I bet we could work something out with the home," I say. "People die there all the time. That's what people do in nursing homes. Die, and watch *The Lawrence Welk Show*."

Mom adds more sugar to her coffee.

"You're also going into the city by yourself for this job," Mom says. "I'm not sure how I feel about that."

"The only time I'm ever alone is between the Blue Line stop at Clark and Lake and the Rock and Roll McDonald's," I say. "The whole strip is well-lit and there are always lots of people. If anyone asks me to join a gang or take drugs, I'll say 'no' and tell them about the Lord."

She smiles a tiny bit.

I have her at nearly every turn. I'm winning. And she knows it.

"You're still in trouble for lying about being at a movie with Kacey."

"I'll accept any punishment that doesn't interfere with work."

"And you'll keep your job at the grocery store for now."

"But I can take the gig with Mysterious Chicago?"

"We'll call it a trial period," she says.

I hug Mom so hard she nearly chokes.

In the afternoon I hit the coffee shop to post the story I'd planned to post earlier, then hit the vintage stores on Harrison Street, looking for something "goth casual" that doesn't look like a corny costume, but makes me look the part of a modern-day murdermonger.

Two days later I help Mom set up for Mrs. Gunderson's funeral, decorating the entryway downstairs with some pictures of her that the home sent over. Most of them are group shots from when she was younger: smiling family and friends on the beach, groups of women in their USO outfits from the war, and one beautiful shot of her and a man—her husband, probably—walking down State Street decades ago.

Everyone else in the pictures with her is probably dead now. None of her friends or family are coming to the funeral. People from the home are all she had left.

After the short service, I get into Cyn's truck and ride with her and Rick out to Mount Carmel Cemetery for the graveside service, talking about life, the afterlife, and all of that. None of us are huge believers in Heaven or anything.

"I didn't notice not being alive before I was born," Cyn says. "Probably won't notice it after I kick it, either."

"I hope there's no afterlife," I say.

"Really?" asks Rick.

"Think of the longest time you can think of. If you thought of a number so big it took your whole life just to think of it, that number still wouldn't even be a drop in the ocean of eternity. We can't even conceive of infinity. Mrs. Gunderson was bored with life after ninety years. Who's not gonna be bored sitting through eternity?"

"I hear ya," says Cyn. "Ain't nobody got time for that shit."

"I just hope you still get to dream, if you go someplace," says Rick. "It wouldn't be Heaven if you can't wake up thinking you're about to be baked into a pie by a walrus now and then."

"When I was a kid I used to be afraid I could still think, but not leave my grave," I say. "So I'd have nothing to do forever but stare at the inside of my casket and let my brain run crazy while I wait for people to visit me."

"You think you'd notice people visiting?" asks Cyn.

"Maybe. I'd notice more if they robbed my grave."

"Just give yourself to a medical school and cut the middleman," says Cyn.

"That's what my mom wants. Me too, probably. As long as

someone builds, like, a giant golden statue of me someplace. Or a pyramid. Whatever. I'm not gonna tell my worshippers how to do their job."

"I don't want a tombstone at all," says Rick. "When I croak, I want someone to prop my body up on the backseat of a cross-country bus. You, Megan, if you're the one in a position to do it. Good to get someone younger in on this."

"Uh . . . okay."

"He goes on about this all the time," says Cyn. "Since he was twelve. He's obsessed."

"I am not," says Rick. "I just . . . I want to see how far I get before the driver figures out that the smelly guy in the back is a corpse. I'll bet I make it clear to the coast."

"Noted," I say.

"He wants to be an urban myth," Cyn teases. "He wants people fifty years after he died to be telling the story of Ricardo Torre, the famous comedian, being buried in a shallow grave by the bus company."

"Hey, there are stars, and there are legends," says Rick. "I'm gonna be a legend."

Cyn shakes her head and says, "Doinkus," in the most affectionate possible way.

And we drive through the gates of the cemetery to bury Mrs. Gunderson.

In my research I found a neat quote about Mount Carmel Cemetery: when one of the Genna Brothers gang was bur-

ADAM SELZER

ied there, some guy at the service pointed out the graves of a bunch of his rivals and said, "When Judgement Day comes and them tombs open up, there's gonna be hell to pay in this cemetery." And that was *before* Al Capone was buried there. Lots of local Catholic big shots, too—cardinals and whatnot. Probably not a good one for me. My dad's a Catholic, so I could probably get in if I wanted to, but even without believing in the afterlife, I still sometimes imagine spending eternity in whatever cemetery they put me in, hanging out with all the other dead people there. Watching the gangsters argue with the cardinals would be okay and all, but Graceland would be better.

Mount Carmel is a neat old cemetery, though. Besides all the old-time gangsters, there's a statue of a woman in a bridal gown, and a photograph of her wearing it in her coffin. The stone says it was taken six years after she died, and she was in good shape. And there's a statue of a family that rotates when you push it.

And now Mrs. Gunderson will be here too.

She's being buried next to her husband; her name and birth year have been carved into the stone for years, so they just had to add the death year. She was one of those people who wanders the earth with a tombstone already in place. If she remarried she might have ended up with two of them; the old one, still with its blank space, and a new one beside the other husband. That seems like the sort of thing that would inspire a ghost story.

We watch as her casket is lowered into the ground, beside her husband, and then she's gone forever.

Unless some little bit of her is still hovering around in Lincoln Park, near the Couch tomb.

For the tour the next night, I do some eyeliner tricks to look a bit older, and I wear a long, breezy black dress that I picked up. It'll be easier to look the way I really like to when it cools down and I can wear my long black jacket; I never like how I look without it. This outfit is an improvement over my grocery store uniform, at least.

On Clark Street a party trolley full of drunks catcalls as they pass me. The bum standing beside me says, "Ah, don't mind them. Dumb bunch of white assholes."

"Thanks," I say.

"You got a dollar for the Jack Daniels Foundation?"

I give him two.

Rick and Cyn are waiting for me at the bus.

"Our tour's a weird one tonight," says Rick. "Just one private party from downstate. A family or something. Rented out the whole bus. We'll sort of cater the tour to whatever they're into."

"You want me to tell any stories?"

"Feel free to jump in at any time."

We drive to the Greyhound station to pick the family up, and find out right away that what they're into is goofing off.

They're a bunch of hicks, really. Lubbers (a word first recorded in 1362). Hob-clunches (1578). Jobbernowls (1592). The kind of people who wear camouflage even though they aren't anywhere near a forest, and who say the word "shit" in front of their seven-year-old kids (whereas my mom waited until I was eleven, because she's a *lady*).

They seem a bit restless when Rick tries to tell a historical story, but they love messing with passersby. Rick cuts the stories way down and focuses on the jokes, and they love him for it.

These people are sort of idiots, but I guess they're fun idiots, at least. As long as I drop all sense of propriety and decency, I can have a good time with them. When we get stuck in traffic next to a Mexican restaurant and they start making burrito/bathroom jokes, Rick tells them about various diners (he is an expert on local grubby diners), and which ones make you need a bathroom the soonest, which ones you should only order a pizza puff from (a pizza puff is like those frozen pizza rolls, only instead of eight of them you get one big one—they come frozen so they're the same everywhere), and which ones have salsa so hot you'll be asking for toilet paper from the freezer, and all of that. They laugh so hard they almost choke.

I get into the spirit too. I pull up the *OED* on my phone and fill time at a long traffic light by looking up words for "bathroom" and "toilet." My favorite is still "gingerbread-office," but there are a ton of good ones, like "gong" (first recorded circa

1000), "crapping case" (1800s), and "shit-pot," which actually meant both "a chamber pot" and "a despicable person" in the 1840s. The example the *OED* gives is from the *New York Daily Globe*, 1849: "He called me a dirty shit-pot, and I will have the honor of being the first shit-pot to give him a cow-hiding."

That just slays them. Reading from the list of words gave me a good chance to practice my timing, waiting for a laugh to die down just enough before saying the next one, the way Rick times his jokes in his stand-up routines.

Outside of Hull House, when they're taking pictures in the courtyard, one of them says, "Hey! I got one of those orb things!"

Rick normally ignores it when people get all excited about orbs, but this time he says, "Zoom in on it. Sometimes there's a face in the middle of them."

The guy looks at his picture and zooms in, then nods. "Think I got one here."

"Awesome," says Rick. "Now, most of the time orbs, even the ones with faces, turn out to be something other than a dead person, but the face ones are cool. At one place, we used to get the same face over and over again. It looked like the dude on the Quaker Oats box."

"Sweet," says the guy. "This one look like anyone you recognize?"

Rick looks, then shrugs. "We know a bunch of people died in this house. Melicent Hull in 1860. Her son in '66.

A bunch of people in the 1870s when this was an old folks' home. But we don't have pictures of any of them."

"Bet this is one of them," says the guy.

"No way to prove it, but it's interesting to imagine," says Rick. "There's no such thing as good ghost evidence, but there's cool ghost evidence."

As we all walk back to the bus, I slide in beside Ricardo and say, "Seriously? The guy on the Quaker Oats box?"

He shrugs. "It's a private group. If they want orbs, I'm just gonna let 'em have fun with it. That's all. No one signs up to get a lecture about what an idiot they are."

Fair enough. He isn't telling them it was really a spirit. He was just telling them it's a cool picture. That it's *interesting to imagine*.

Toward the end of the night, as we're all wandering back to the bus from the Couch tomb, the same customer comes over to me. "I think I got another one here," he says.

He shows me his orb picture, and I watch as he zooms in.

There's a face in the little ball of light, all right.

And maybe it's mostly my imagination, but it looks exactly like Mrs. Gunderson.

Smiling.

Chapter Nine

"The earth keeps some vibration going
There in your heart, and that is you."
—EDGAR LEE MASTERS, "FIDDLER JONES"

O ver the rest of June, I run more tours and get more comfortable with the route, the stops, and the moves of the city.

I spend nearly every night staying up late, texting with Zoey while I trace ghost stories and murder stories through the *Tribune* online archives, looking for more stories I can tell on the tours.

The city becomes my office. My own.

After just a few tours I pretty much know what I should be saying at every turn, no matter what the traffic is like. I know how to recraft the Resurrection Mary story based on how many lights ahead of us are red when I start and how many are green. I know where the laugh lines and gasp lines are. I learn to sense which crowds I can say the words "ass" and "shit" in front of, and which ones I should change it to "butt" and "crap" for (even though, as Rick points out, "ass" and "shit" are always, always funnier).

I get to know all the peddlers, hustlers, and bums who circulate around River North—Rick calls them "urban jawas." The guy who hustles tourists into posing for caricatures is named Terrence (Cyn calls him Vincent Van Go Home). The giant-nosed necklace peddler is named Pierre (or says he is). One evening he gives me a whole lesson in why gold necklaces are easier to sell than fancy colognes, which was his old racket. I learn a lot from Pierre.

Pretty soon the stretch of Clark Street around the Rock and Roll McDonald's is a place where everybody knows my name. When I show up at the tour bus parking zone, the Al Capone tour guys tip their fedoras. The double-decker-bus sightseeing-tour guy will say, "Ghost girl!" Even Edward Tweed and Aaron Saltis get to be fairly friendly with me; when I run into them on Clark Street, we nod and say hi and chat a bit.

One time I challenge Saltis to work the word "mucocarneous" into his tour.

"What's it mean?"

"A mass composed of mucus and flesh."

He makes a face, but nods. "Shouldn't be too hard."

"Give me one."

He thinks for a second, like he's doing a really hard algebra problem in his head, then says "prestidigitation."

Easy. That's a word for "sleight of hand." Midtour I tell people that most of the ghosts people think they see on other tours are just the result of prestidigitation.

I make about three times as much money per hour as I make bagging groceries. If we get the TV show, it'll be even more.

And I love almost every minute of it. I get annoyed by some of the people who just talk all through the tour, and the weirdos who want me to confirm that their photo of a flash bouncing off a window validates all their views on obscure points of Catholic dogma, but I can ignore them, for the most part.

It's a fine life, rolling with the rotters.

For most of the first tours I run, it's just me and Rick; having him ready to jump in helps a lot before I get totally comfortable.

And he jumps in plenty. He can't resist grabbing the mic now and then, or messing with passersby. Soon we have a routine and a dynamic similar to the one he has with Cyn, only he and Cyn are like an old married couple, and he and I are like brother and sister. We tell people that he's the big brother I never had, and I'm the little sister he never wanted. I don't tell him *all* about my stories, but I tell him a lot. He says he's bi too, and we bond over that, even though I'm rooting for him to end up with Cynthia.

After work sometimes we'll go to one of the diners he loves so much, or over to a little jazz club on Hubbard. I'll sit at the bar having water while he downs a beer and gives me advice about Zoey. I pay more attention to the jazz band than to his romantic advice, but when he talks about comedy and comic timing and stuff, I listen.

My attempts to look a few years older apparently work. One night they even let me into the Signature Room, a bar on the 93rd floor of the Hancock Center, without carding me. The view is spectacular.

"I feel like I can see clear to Arizona from here," I say. "Like I could actually see Zoey."

"Maybe if she stood on a chair," says Rick.

He and Cyn both tell me to move on and find another person to date, but Zoey's still the first one I want to talk to after every tour.

And there's so much to tell her. So many things happen on tours that I can't wait to tell her about. Even if they didn't pay me, it would be worth doing the job just for the stories I get about what happens during tours.

Rick and I have a lot of games we play to help get passengers loosened up. Like, when we get to a long traffic light, we'll tell them that we can all try a psychic experiment where we pool our mental energy and focus on the color green, and that'll make the light change within a minute or two. Works every time.

In the Gold Coast we have them play "What Do They Have," which is played by looking out the window of the bus and into the windows of the mansions to see what people have.

They have some nice shit in the Gold Coast. Libraries, working gaslights, statues, grand pianos.

One time a naked guy stands at a window. We see what *he* has.

The game I tell Zoey the most about is one called "Let's Mess with Cars." This is where we pull up next to cars at red lights, open the door, and mess with them. Rick believes that a large bus that says GHOST TOURS on it is the single greatest instrument ever created for the purpose of messing with people, and tells me that having access to such a vehicle gives you a sacred duty to use it.

One gag he taught me was to ask the driver in the next car over at a red light if he wants to drag race.

"We can get this machine up to nearly forty miles per hour," I'll say, while Rick revs our engine. "Two cylinders of raw, whining power, baby."

Most people laugh. One guy just takes off right through the red light, leaving us in the dust. "Well, I guess he certainly showed us," says Rick.

Some nights we'll tell the person in the next car that the Popeye's Chicken they're stuck in traffic next to is haunted by the ghost of a one-legged stripper who lost her leg in a shuffleboard accident before buying a chicken franchise, where she died after falling into the deep fryer. They always think it's funny, but Rick worries that even though the story is pretty obviously a joke, it might end up getting repeated as fact on

ADAM SELZER

Ghost Encounters someday. He swears it's happened before.

But he lets me tell people that random statues we pass are of Captain Hezekiah Crunch, who sailed under General Mills in the Spanish-American War and inspired the cereal mascot. At least one person believes that every time. Cap'n Crunch is comedy gold. Sometimes I ask people in cars if they've accepted Cap'n Crunch as their lord and savior yet.

Most of the people on the street or in cars that we mess with are happy to play along. Now and then, though, we have a person who isn't amused. Once, during the Resurrection Mary story, we open the door to shout, "She died *right on this spot*," and there's an Amish couple standing there. The guy gives us a look that would do any pissed-off grocery-store customer proud.

"Oh, crap," says Rick. "He looked like he was gonna pitchfork my ass!"

"Yeah!" I say. "He was like, 'I'm-a poke thee, sinner!'"

And we laugh so hard that I can't even tell the rest of the story.

Then, just as we're calming down, I look up better words I could have used besides "sinner." "Fornicatress" comes up, and that starts us laughing all over again.

By the time we calm down enough to talk, we're at the spot where we start telling the story of the Haymarket Riot. Resurrection Mary is a famous enough ghost that we have to talk about her, though, so Rick veers off the route and goes by Harpo Studios, where Oprah used to film her show. One hundred years ago that building was the Second Regiment Armory, where the bodies of the victims of the Eastland Disaster were laid out to be identified.

"It's definitely said to be haunted in there," he says. "They've never allowed anyone to investigate it formally, but a lot of employees tell stories about it. One thing I hear a lot is that there's one bathroom that they usually keep locked, but they're always hearing the sound of a crying woman coming from inside of it. I like to call her Moaning Myrtle."

When no one but me seems to get the Harry Potter reference, he moves right along, saying, "Now, here's the thing: five of the victims here were named Mary and ended up buried at Resurrection Cemetery, so it could be that one of them became the ghost we call Resurrection Mary, whom Megan will now tell you all about while we head out to the next stop."

Smooth.

The laughs are addictive. The gasps are addictive.

Within a couple of weeks, I look forward to tours like a smoker looks forward to the next smoke break.

In mid-July, Brandon, the guy who is thinking of putting the TV show together, asks if we can meet him for dinner and take him on a tour.

Mom comes along with me the night of the meeting, partly because she still hasn't actually gone on a tour yet, and partly because she'll be one more person in the seats. We want to impress Brandon, so the more people we have, the better. Of course, Mom is also planning to make sure I'm not getting taken advantage of or roped into anything that could reflect poorly on her. I'm a little annoyed that she thinks I can't take care of myself, but I *do* want her to see a tour. I'm proud of the work I'm doing.

Brandon's production company is picking up the bill, so Cyn arranges to meet at some trendy foodie place (even though Rick lobbies hard for one of his beloved grubby diners). Mom and I get to the neighborhood early and wander around a bit, admiring the gorgeous old Victorian townhouses in the Armitage-Halsted historic district.

Near the restaurant, we pass a little life insurance office that's really going for the hard sell. In the window they have a sign saying

YOU JUST DIED.

YOUR FAMILY WILL BE HERE IN 15 MINUTES.

WHAT WOULD YOU LIKE ME TO TELL THEM?

Mom reads it and laughs. "Megan," she says. "If you're in this woman's office fifteen minutes after I die, I want her to tell you that you're under arrest."

"You insured for much cash?" I ask.

"Don't get any ideas."

As we walk along I tell her all about Rick's plan to have his mortal remains propped up on a bus, and she approves. She wants a simple funeral herself—I think most funeral directors do. When the time comes, I'm supposed to ship her off to a medical college and throw a little memorial party. That's what I want for myself too, really, though I do sort of want whatever college gets my body to send my ashes to my heirs when they're done with me, so they can be slipped under the door of the Couch tomb and future ghost-tour guides can know for sure that there's at least one dead person in there.

Zoey told me once that she wants someone to sneakily scatter hers at Disney World, but I've read that people try that all the time, and the Disney people just sweep them up and throw them out with the trash.

Cyn and Rick meet us outside the restaurant, and Brandon arrives just in time for our reservation; he's younger than I pictured, probably not much more than thirty, with long brown hair and a beard. If we passed him on the street during a tour, Rick would probably say, "Hey, there's a guy who knows a thing or two about coming back from the dead. On your right, Mr. Jesus Christ!" Brandon shakes my hand and treats me like one of the team, and I feel very grown-up, even though I brought my mom.

The menu is all fancy stuff. Colorado lamb. Israeli couscous. Stuff like that. If they served Count Chocula, it would be listed as "Pure Michigan Count Chocula." I'm eager to try some of it, but Rick rolls his eyes and says he wishes we'd gone to a diner.

"Yeah," says Cyn. "Because that's where you go to make a good impression. Filthy Al's House of Slop."

"Are there seriously people who know the difference between a Colorado lamb and one who came from Delaware?" Rick asks. "I sure as hell don't."

I turn to Mom. "We should start telling people that we use pure Massachusetts embalming fluid."

"I like it," she says. "Artisan funerals, with locally hand-crafted glues to keep the eyes shut."

"This!" says Brandon. "This is what I want. People love this stuff. Behind the scenes of the death industry. That's gonna pop."

"You're not filming at our house," says Mom. "That kind of publicity is bad for business in the long run."

"Yeah," I say. "We don't want anything in the show about me being a black-diaper baby."

"Black-diaper baby!" he says. "You can't give me a term like that and say I can't use it!"

"It'd be sort of insulting to my customers if we made a big deal of it," says Mom.

"We can obfuscate things like that pretty well, so they won't connect her to your place," says Brandon. "You wouldn't believe some of what we get away with on these things."

Ricardo fixes Brandon with a harsh look. "Sounds to me like you're pretty eager to fudge the facts."

"Aw, nothing like that, man," says Brandon. "But sometimes

we have to bend the story to tell the story. Like, I look at this group, your group, and I think: what's the story? What's the narrative, the hook? It's a ragtag group of ghost-hunting rebels trying to clean up the industry. Sweep out the bullshit. And part of what makes the story pop is that you recruited a funeral-home girl. Black-diaper baby. *Love* that. If we have to get her a day job at some other funeral home to get to tell that story, we'll do what we have to. But that is her story. It'd be bullshitting if we left it out."

He's got us there.

Brandon doesn't seem like a big-shot Hollywood producer to me. He seems like a guy whose parents gave him a production company as a graduation present or something. Still, the company has deep enough pockets to pick up a check for five people at a restaurant where the cheapest entree costs more than I earn in three hours at the grocery store. He doesn't even flinch when everyone but me orders cocktails that don't even have a price listed on the menu. One of those "If you have to ask, you can't afford it" deals. I wish I could get one; it's sort of humiliating to have to order a Shirley Temple, even one made with Washington cherries and small-batch meyer-lemon and Persian lime soda.

While Brandon talks, Mom shoots me a quick look that tells me I'm going to have a hard time getting her behind the TV show if the company decides to move forward, but I can't help being swept into the excitement. Someone thinks I am interesting enough to be on television. In fact, from the way Brandon talks, having *me* is the part that makes the Mysterious Chicago team most viable for TV. What gives them the edge over Edward Tweed.

Who wouldn't get excited by that?

And I'm eighteen; Mom can't stop me. She can just get mad.

While we eat, Brandon passes out some "ghost" photographs he's found online and printed up as eight-by-ten color glossies. Most of them aren't high enough quality to blow up well, though. They're pixelated as hell.

"Look at the leaves," he says as he passes a shot of a graveyard tree around. "If you look closely, you can see an Indian chief."

"Maybe if you look really hard and use your imagination," I say.

"That's called a simulacrum," says Rick. "Our brains are trained to look for faces and patterns in random visual noise."

"Maybe that's how ghosts choose to manifest," says Brandon. "Random visual noise."

"Why not just say they manifest as condiments and this black sea salt shaker is one of them?" I ask.

Mom looks at the picture and just laughs. "This is like the 'find the hidden pictures' in the *Highlights* magazines we keep in the office for kids."

"You keep copies of *Highlights* at the funeral home?" asks Rick.

"Yeah, sometimes people bring their kids along when they're pre-arranging and stuff."

"I always thought we should have our own special issue of it," I say. "Like how dentists' offices have their own Charlie Brown cartoons."

Mom chortles into her Israeli couscous. *"Gallant walks solemnly past the corpse, contemplating his favorite Bible verse,"* she says. *"Goofus pulls down the corpse's pants to see if it's true that they stuff the bodies' butts with cotton."*

"Do you really do that?" asks Brandon.

"Not with cotton," says Mom. "Big plastic plugs."

"They look like Nerf torpedoes," I say.

"Or really big-ass drywall anchors," says Mom.

"'Ass' being the operative word," says Rick.

"See, *this*!" says Brandon. "This is what people want to see! This kind of angle pops like a bottle rocket."

"Believe me, you do not want those plugs to pop," Mom laughs.

I'm glad to be in company where this kind of talk doesn't spoil the meal. And the meal is great. I order a bowl of Louisiana turtle soup, which is like no other food I've ever tasted, then wood oven–seared Puget Sound mussels with some kind of aioli, and fancy french fries that taste like bacon. I send pictures of every course to Zoey, hoping maybe this will lure her out to meet up in person.

I can imagine getting used to being a TV star and living like this. Buying myself an apartment in one of these Armitage Avenue townhouses, eating like royalty every night . . . How could Zoey say no to that sort of lifestyle?

Brandon tells us, again and again, that he wouldn't have us make fools of ourselves on the show, but then he shows us orb pictures and acts all disappointed when we say they aren't ghosts. I can tell Rick is unimpressed with him, and ready to chuck the whole thing and wait for another offer to come along.

Then, toward the end of the meal, Brandon mentions that he's meeting with Edward Tweed too, which we already knew, and with some group from Ghostly Journeys Inc, which I guess we didn't.

"What?" asks Rick. "Ghostly Journeys aren't even operating in town."

"Not yet," says Brandon. "But they've been looking to move into the Chicago market. I wouldn't worry about it, though. You guys are terrific. Only thing I like better about Tweed is that people really, seriously see ghosts on his tours."

"We've had more sightings lately," says Rick. "Just the other day a kid told me he saw a woman with a white thing on her head at Hull House. And I hadn't even told the story about the ghost in the rustling dress that night."

"Still not as many as Tweed gets. It's almost every tour for him."

"That's because he's lying," says Rick.

"Hard to prove."

Brandon hops in a cab after the meal to meet up with us on Clark Street—he wants to mingle with the passengers and blend in. The rest of us get on a CTA bus down Halsted to the bus lot.

"Well, that was a fucking bust," says Rick.

"I think we could make the show work," says Cyn.

"Yeah, we can do this," I say.

"Are you kidding me?" asks Rick. "I wanna be on TV too. It's been my dream since I was a toddler. But I don't want to have to act like some jackass *Ghost Encounters* moron. It's gotta be on my terms."

"Then you're never gonna get on TV," says Cyn. "And they'll give the show to Tweed or Ghostly Journeys, and then we'll go out of business altogether."

"What's Ghostly Journeys?" I ask.

"It's a big ghost-tour operation out of New Orleans," says Rick, who looks miserable now. "They've got tours in Boston, Savannah, Gettysburg, and all the other big ghost cities."

"If they move in here, we're screwed," says Cyn. "As it is, we're mostly just booking people who come to us because Tweed is sold out. If Journeys comes here, they'll steal every customer we get."

"Look," says Rick. "Being on a ghost show isn't my ideal way to break out as a comic anyway. I don't want to be 'the ghost guy' forever."

"But it's your most likely way of getting noticed," says Cyn. "And if you can be even halfway respectable, that could save lives."

"Yeah, yeah, I know. We're all killing people all the time," says Rick, like a kid being nagged by his mom. "The only reason I can afford a candied bar down at the 7-Eleven is because people die to keep the price of cocoa beans down. You've mentioned that."

"Dude, did you just say 'candied bar'?" asks Cyn. "Doinkus."

On Clark Street there's a big influx of people in town for a comic-book convention—you can spot them because they're in costume. We have a guy in full Ghostbusters regalia on the bus. Three guys in TRON outfits mill about by the Ronald McDonald statue, flirting with girls in fishnets and corsets.

There is eye candy everywhere tonight.

When I load up the passengers, there's a pale girl about my age with long red hair walking along by herself. Her mouth is just slightly too big for her small, angular face, and she's wearing a gothic-style dress with lace sides. It might be a costume, but if I were her, I'd dress like that every single day. She looks gorgeous. Like she could be one of those "Hollywood Sadcore" retro ballad singers, and all of her songs would be about murder and decay. A girl after my own heart.

She smiles at me from down the block when she sees me looking at her, and a few parts of me that don't normally beat start beating.

"Check it out," says Cyn. "It's a red-haired Morticia Addams."

"Please tell me she's with us," I say.

I work my way through the handful of reservations that we've racked up, and "Morticia" lingers at the back, then comes up to me when the coast is clear.

"Hey," she says. "Do you have any extra space tonight?"

"We sure do," I say.

"How much does it cost?"

She has dimples an inch deep, and the most perfect teeth I have ever seen in my whole entire life, and she smells like Oregon blueberries.

"Five bucks," I say.

"Really? I thought it was, like thirty or forty."

"It is, but if you don't tell the others I can cut you a deal."

We want as many people as possible on the bus with Brandon. Also, I want her on the bus. I would have paid *her* five dollars to come on the bus, probably.

Morticia pulls five impossibly crisp one-dollar bills from a little purse, then slips onto the bus, where she takes a seat in the back, three rows behind where everyone else is sitting.

Rick comes out to join me on the street as we wait for a missing party of four.

"Morticia's a step-on, right?"

"Yeah, but I only charged her a five spot."

He laughs. "Little sister's got a crush?"

I blush about as red as Morticia's hair. "You don't think there's any chance that she's Zoey, do you?"

"Not a dandy's chance in Wal-Mart, sis," he says. "But if

you're just looking for a one-night thing, she looks like she might be freaky enough for you."

I look over my shoulder at the bus, seeing where she's sitting, partly to keep him from seeing how badly I'm blushing. Rick doesn't know exactly what goes on in my fan-fic stories, but he knows enough.

Throughout the tour, "Morticia" seems sort of aloof. She doesn't always look at what we're pointing at on the road. When we get off the bus at the alley, she stays separated from most of the group. While the rest of the people are wandering around, taking pictures of the stage door and the fire escapes and themselves, she's off staring at some random brick, like she's looking at something only she can see. The only time she reacts to anyone is when Brandon tries to hit on her. She gives him a look that I think means, *Yeah, very funny, dream on, dork,* and walks over to look at a different brick.

But she's smiling the whole time. When she catches me looking in her direction, she smiles bigger.

Off the bus at Hull House, Mom walks beside me.

"I have to admit," she says, "I'm having a good time. Rick is really something."

"I know," I say. "He's gonna be a star someday."

"Are all those stories true about this place?" she asks. "Jane Addams and her partner said they saw a ghost here?"

"Her partner was sleeping, but Jane said she did, according to one of her friends," I say. "She never took it that seriously, though."

Just then I hear a voice behind me say, "So, were she and her 'partner,' like, partners?"

I turn back to see Morticia, smiling and staring up at the window of the room Jane and her staff half-jokingly called "The Haunted Room."

"We think so," I say. "I mean, she and Mary Rozet Smith were definitely, like, life partners, but we don't know for sure if they were . . . doing it."

She keeps smiling. "How could they not?"

"Relationships were different back then," I say.

She smiles a bit more and says, "Not that different," and walks off to stare at a flower.

"Is that someone you know?" Mom asks.

"Not really."

"Someone you want to know?"

I blush and say, "Shut up."

I can tell Mom is about to make some comment to embarrass me, so I take a step away, then call out, "All right, folks, we can head on back to the bus."

There's no physical sign of a lingering psychic imprint from Mrs. Gunderson at the Couch tomb tonight, but everyone agrees that it seems particularly eerie out there, which I don't think ever happened in the days before my "initiation." Even Mom says it's giving her chills. And Brandon at least seems to think it's cool when Rick demonstrates the Tomb Snooper 500.

Then, as we're passing the old Water Tower on the way

back to the McDonald's, toward the end of the tour, Morticia raises her hand.

"Hey," she says. "My hotel is right around the corner. Can I get off here?"

Cyn pulls over and Morticia stands up, says, "Great tour, by the way," and slips off the bus. I watch her vanish into the crowd and almost chase after her, but don't. I have a girlfriend already, right?

Cyn drives another block before slamming on the brakes and laughing out loud.

"What?" asks Rick.

"1830s. Water Tower. What was here? And what just happened? Tell them. It's perfect."

"Oh no," says Rick. "I'm not gonna say it. It sounds made up!"

"Oh yes, you are, doinkus," says Cyn. "Right now, or I'm turning this bus right back around."

Rick groans a bit, says that she's the doinkus, then takes a deep breath.

"This might seem cheesy," he says. "But we mentioned earlier that people who died in cities used to end up buried in crowded churchyards, so Chicago started putting land aside on the out-skirts, right? Well, the first two places they put aside, back in the 1830s, were down by Twenty-sixth Street, and right where we are now. So we just had a quirky girl in an old-fashioned dress, who hitched along for the night, disappear at an old cemetery. Our own vanishing hitcher, like Resurrection Mary!"

Everyone has a good laugh, and I open the door and look back behind us. Morticia is gone, all right. Vanished into the crowd on Michigan Avenue.

Well, what the hell. Maybe she *did* disappear into thin air.

When the tour comes to an end a few minutes later, everyone comes off the bus looking excited, and Brandon says he'll be in touch very soon. We make twenty-five bucks each in tips—a record for a night when we're splitting it three ways. Rick and I stretch out on the bus while Mom and Cyn go into the McDonald's for coffee. They've hit it off pretty well over the course of the night.

I'm really pumped up by how good the tour was, but Rick seems depressed, or maybe even embarrassed.

"Lucky that the disappearing girl happened right in front of Brandon," I say.

He lowers himself into a seat three rows back. "That looked like we staged it. All that told him is that we're willing to bullshit people."

"But we didn't."

Now he shakes his head.

"The hell of it is, that'd be the best ghost sighting ever, if she was one, but real ghosts make crappy tourist attractions. People think ghosts all look like old-timey translucent fucks. I only ever met the one real one, but she just looked like a normal person. No one who saw her would think she was a ghost."

"So, would blurry psychic imprints be better than actual spirits?"

Rick snorts. "Those imprint things aren't real. That's a goofball pseudoscience thing that Marjorie Stone was into. Real ghosts . . . they're just regular people. I almost feel like the tours are problematic because we act like they're all scary and shit. It's kind of . . . I don't know. Ableist."

"So you and Cyn *didn't* find a manuscript about punching them out of people's brains?" I asks.

"Well, we did, but you've gotta remember, Marjorie Kay Stone was out of her mind. God. This looked like a cheap stunt, and I'm afraid that's exactly what Brandon wanted. Someone who'll just go up there and bullshit people. Cyn says it'll make me famous anyway, but I say it'll just lead to think pieces about what an idiot I am."

Mom and Cyn come back, chatting about death-industry stuff, and I join in the talk with them as we drive off to the bus lot.

Rick sits silently, in the same seat where Morticia had been.

Mom teases me about Morticia all the way home.

"Shame she turned out to be a vanishing hitchhiker," says Mom. "You two would have made a cute little goth couple."

"Whatever, Mother."

I tell myself it was just a silly little one-night crush thing.

No different than getting a celebrity crush when you see a really hot person in a movie. Everyone's allowed to have a celebrity crush or two.

Still, I wonder if I would have kissed her if I'd had the chance. I'm happy with Zoey, but still. I go back and forth between thinking that what we do counts as sex and thinking it totally doesn't, and that I'm missing out on a basic part of being a human if I just settle for a life of long-distance sex.

While I wait for her to sign in online, I distract myself by looking up words for "mixed up" or "confused" on the *OED*.

My favorite is "puddled."

One example sentence is from a 1651 book called *Enthusiasmus Triumphatus* by Henry More: "As for those terrible mysterious radiations of God upon the Chaos . . . which thou wouldst fain shuffle off thy absurdities by; I say, they are but the flarings of thine own fancy, and the reeks and fumes of thy puddled brain."

Maybe that's what ghosts are. The reeks and fumes of your puddled brain, floating around in the environment.

I think this over and troll through the archives until Zoey signs on, then talk with her until it's almost dawn.

I picture her looking like Morticia all night long.

Chapter Ten

On the Fourth of July you can literally fry an egg on the sidewalk. They do it on the news.

The weather grows hotter and hotter, and the haze makes everyone and everything in Forest Park look diseased to me. The satellite dishes on the houses look like smallpox blisters.

One day, when I walk to work at the grocery store, it's so humid out that I feel like I'm swimming down the sidewalk, sweating out half of my brain cells through my pores. The air-conditioning in the store feels like heaven, but the fluorescent lights hurt my eyes and drain what little energy I have. I was up late digging through articles from the newspaper archives again, and I'm exhausted.

Plus, it's Sunday. Sunday afternoons are usually the worst days at the store—it's like everyone just got all of last week's sins forgiven at church, and they're all set to get a fresh start on this week.

Then there's the noise, noise, noise, noise, noise.

The noises in grocery stores are just awful. Not an instant goes by when there isn't a beep or a bloop or a clang from a register somewhere down the line, beating out of time with the elevator music that pipes through the speakers high above in the ceiling. Then there are louder beeps from the scissor lifts in the back room, the trucks out in the loading zone, and the cell phones in people's pockets. Beep, beep, boop. Constantly.

Most days I can tune it out. Today I can't. Every sound is like a needle pricking my inner ear.

I'm tired from staying up late researching, annoyed at even having to be here, and sick of old people giving me the evil eye for not treating their loaves of bread like priceless works of art. When I take groceries to cars it gets me away from some of the noise, but into the sweltering heat.

Bag after bag, customer after customer, beep after beep, I look up at the old people who glare down at me disapprovingly, and wonder if they'd volunteer to be punched in the brain. They sure do seem miserable.

One sees me adjusting the Band-Aid over my lip ring and says, "You shouldn't be bagging groceries with open wounds."

"Sorry, ma'am," I say. "I cut myself shaving this morning. My manager thinks my goatee is really unladylike."

She doesn't think this is very funny, but Kendra, who is running the register, cracks up. And apologizes to the woman about five thousand times.

ADAM SELZER

Before I got started with the tours, I never would have had the nerve to talk back to a customer like that. I would have thought about it, but just stood there, mute.

Things are different now.

I'm not just a grocery bagger anymore. I'm a murdermonger.

After one customer nearly runs me over driving out of the parking lot, I notice Kacey grabbing a smoke break at the picnic table by the dumpster and go to join her. The smell of nicotine and garbage wafts through the sweltering and greasy air.

"Honey, I'm home," I say.

Kacey smiles, and I sit down and text with Zoey a bit, in between looking up *OED* words. There are no synonyms for "apeshit." Even the *OED* is letting me down today.

I've only been there a minute when Doug, the manager, pokes his head around the corner.

"Megan, if you're done smoking, I need you back on the line."

I turn toward him. "I don't smoke."

"Then I need you back on the line."

"I'm taking a cigarette break; I'll be back in when I'm done."

"You just said you don't smoke."

"I've read the Fair Labor Standards Act," I lie. "If Kacey can take a break to smoke, I could probably come out here to have sex and you couldn't stop me, if I was so desperate as to do it by the dumpster."

Doug turns about nine shades of red.

"Well, except for public decency laws," says Kacey. "But we could take a make-out break and probably get away with it."

She grins suggestively, and I look at her to see if maybe she's serious. I mean, if we kiss now to prove a point, that wouldn't really be cheating on Zoey, it would just be, like, theater. It wouldn't even be a pity kiss. In fact, it'd actually be a pretty good way to have a proper, physical kiss that I'd never regret.

But Doug doesn't give us a chance.

"You could at least say something respectable, like you're studying for a test or something," he says.

Kacey grins, stands on one foot, and starts touching her nose while reciting the alphabet backward, like she's practicing for the drunk driving test. Or the version they do in cartoons, at least.

I think it's funny. Doug does not.

"Both of you," he says. "Back inside before I write you up."

Kacey stubs out her cigarette, mouths the word "loser," and giggles at me as we make our way back into the clanging, beeping hellhole.

Inside, I go through my usual routine of avoiding looking at the clock, hoping that it will make time go faster, but it never works. I write out a whole story in my head where Doug falls off a cliff into a deep chasm, lands on the mangled-but-still-living bodies of several Disney villains who've already fallen off the same cliff, and becomes their prisoner.

And just as I'm thinking that, a text comes in from Cynthia.

SWITCHBLADE CYNTHIA FARGON:
Minor emergency. Rick got food poisoning at a diner in the Gold Coast. Can you come run the 7 p.m. tour?

I'm supposed to be working until six thirty, which doesn't give me enough time to get downtown for a seven p.m. tour, but I tell her I'll see if I can get off early.

I go around asking people who are off at four or five if they'll stay late for me, but I don't get any takers, and finally I just ask Doug straight up if I can leave an hour or so early.

"It's kind of an emergency at my other job," I say.

"Other job?"

"I do have a life outside the grocery mines, you know."

He looks over a notepad and moves his head around like a worm has crawled up his nose and he's trying to help it get comfortable. "I seem to recall that when you applied you had unlimited availability," he says. "It's part of why we hired you."

"That's gonna change once classes start anyway."

I don't mention that I haven't actually registered for community college yet, and that I'm thinking I'll probably wait until at least the winter semester, when I won't be as busy with tours.

He mutters something about how this is why they shouldn't hire students, and I decide I just can't take it anymore.

Fuck it all.

I rip the Band-Aid off my lip ring as dramatically as possible, drop it on the ground, and stomp out of the store, storming through the parking lot, onto the sidewalk, and toward my house. On the way I text Cyn and tell her I'll be there in plenty of time for the tour.

Kacey sends me a text:

> WORK WIFE:
> Doug wants to know if you quit.

I tell her I did and she says she just might join me.

She won't, though. She'll be here for years, the poor unfortunate soul. Probably not as long as Doug, though. One day some funeral-parlor owner will bury him with his name tag still on.

I get home with enough time to grab a shower, do my makeup to make myself look a bit older, and put on a nice goth-casual ensemble. I'm ready to go with enough time left over to set fire to the porta-potty-blue uniform in the charcoal grill in the backyard.

I roast a hot dog off the flames and eat it on the way to the train station.

ADAM SELZER

On Clark Street, Edward Tweed and Aaron Saltis say, "Rolling with the rotters."

The Al Capone Tours guy says, "Ghost girl!"

Terrence the caricature guy bumps fists with me.

But Cyn doesn't say a thing when I first come up to the bus. She's leaning against it, twirling one cigarette in her fingers while another one hangs from her mouth. I don't normally see her smoke.

"What's wrong?" I ask.

"We've got eight people," she says. "Tweed has two full buses. Almost ten times as many people."

"We've had fewer before and gotten by."

She sighs and nods. "So far. But insurance for this thing is insane. The licenses we need are coming up for renewal soon, and they aren't cheap. Not to mention Crook County's three-percent amusement tax on top of all the other fucking taxes. God. We've got to have something happen, or we're fucked. We aren't even coming close to breaking even tonight."

I nod.

"What about the TV show?"

"Rick's still not convinced he trusts Brandon, and Brandon's still talking with Tweed, too. If Tweed gets the show or Ghostly Journeys opens a Chicago branch, we're just fucked."

"Well, shit," I say. "I hope we can hold on. I quit the grocery store today."

She exhales. "Yeah, that was probably a mistake."

I'll be screwed if the company goes under. Royally. Back to suffering through some crap job with nothing to distract me but an invisible girlfriend. Back to being completely pathetic. I realize that a good deal of my self-image, my self-esteem, is tied up in being good at this job now. What else have I got? I'm okay at acting, but not good enough to make it big or anything. You hear about people making a living writing erotic fan-fic, but I think it's a one-in-a-million shot, maximum.

I try to make it sound like I'm probably joking when I look at Cyn and say, "Think someone else at the nursing home might want to volunteer to become a ghost?"

She looks away from me, then up at the giant golden arches and the Ronald McDonald statue.

"A couple," she says. "If we want to go that route."

Just like that. She doesn't smirk or act like it was a joke, like Rick would have. She just acknowledges that making our own ghosts is an option.

I should be more shocked. But I think a part of me already knew that Mrs. Gunderson didn't just happen to die that night in Lincoln Park. And that part of me never felt guilty.

It's a good tour. But any way you cut it, we have just a few people. Tips come to six dollars.

When she slips me my three bucks, Cyn gives me a long, serious look.

"What?" I ask.

"You know what happened with Mrs. Gunderson, right?"

"I have a pretty good idea."

She stares a bit more, then looks out the windshield. "I don't want Ricardo to know. He'd freak out. And it's better if he thinks any ghosts we run into might really be ghosts from a long time ago."

"I understand."

She leans back in the seat and watches people pouring out of the DarkSide Chicago tour buses ahead of us. Edward and Aaron shake hands with customers and collect tips.

"Rick should be a star," she says. "But he's never gonna get there if he keeps being so stubborn."

"You have to be willing to make some compromises to get what you want," I say. "At least when you're starting out."

"Usually you have to sell your soul to get the kind of life he wants," says Cyn. "You have to step over everyone in your way. Make them wriggle like a worm on a hook."

"Eyes on the prize."

A trolley full of bachelorette partiers rolls past, and they all shout "Wooooo!" like they're imitating a ghost in a cartoon.

Cyn looks right at me and says, "So, you wanna go again?"

Chapter Eleven

S o, just to be clear," I say as we ride along, "Mrs. Gunderson did volunteer, right?"

"Oh, yeah. Of course. It was all thoroughly planned out between me and her. We let Rick think it was a hazing prank, but she knew she was dying and she was totally on board. I wasn't sure the imprint thing would work, but since then it's been weird enough out there that I think there must be something to it."

"Yeah."

"If we'd actually done the gorilla-mask thing it might have left a stronger imprint, but I thought if she actually died right then, Rick might get suspicious. Better to do it on the sly."

"True."

She stops at a red light, then says, "Nursing homes are full of people who are way past average life expectancy, who are never getting better and can't wait for it all to be over with. If they were dogs, people would say it's inhumane to keep them alive, but people expect other people to suffer as long as they can."

"Right."

"I was gonna take care of this guy in his bed later this week, anyway. They just found another kind of cancer in him to add to his collection. With chemo he'll make it three to six months, if he's lucky. And it'll be three to six months of hell with no light at the end of the tunnel. He tried and tried to get out of the chemo, but his family just wouldn't hear of it. Selfish bastards."

"Sure."

I'm speaking in monosyllables, just letting her talk. What else can I do? But now I start in with questions, making sure this is all . . . ethical.

"So, this guy knows what you do?"

"I told him. He thinks I'm full of shit about the ghost part, but if I modify things a bit and actually do scare him a bit right before, I think we could get a better imprint than we got before. He's not as friendly as Mrs. Gunderson, but that shouldn't make things any harder for us."

"And no one will know what happened?"

"Not a chance. They'll think it was the cancer. After some reflections they'll decide it was better that he went quietly, without suffering."

"You got the gorilla mask?"

"It's in the back."

We drive into the bus lot in silence, then transfer into Cyn's pickup truck. I ask what happened to Marjorie Kay Stone's memoir, the one that told her about the brain punch in the first place.

"Burned up. Her whole house burned after she died."

I don't ask how she died. I decide I don't want to know. She was pretty old. Old people die.

"What happened to the ghost you said was there?" I ask. "What happens to ghosts with nowhere left to haunt?"

"She just found another place to hang around. She just lives like a normal person most of the time."

"I'll have to meet her sometime."

Cyn doesn't answer.

We drive back out of the bus lot and onto Halsted in Cyn's truck without saying much more. We talk about TV shows a bit. Weather. Books. Street closings that we're going to have to work around on upcoming tours.

Everything except the fact that we're going to go kill a guy.

Ten minutes later we're in one of the bedrooms in the nursing home, and Cyn is nudging an old man's shoulder as he sleeps. He looks up with an annoyed scowl from beneath a push-broom mustache.

"What the hell?" he asks.

"Mr. Sturgeon?" she says. "Do you really want to be gone before chemo can start?"

He blinks and turns over a bit. His skin is leathery and tough, like the wrinkles have to fight for every dent they make. But they fight hard. Aaron Saltis has a misshapen face that looks like it was busted out of alignment in one quick fight with a blunt object. Mr. Sturgeon looks like he's been beaten down slowly, by degrees, for eighty years.

He looks up at Cyn, then says, "You mean that shit about making me a ghost?"

"Uh-huh."

"I'm an atheist," he says. "I don't believe in ghosts."

"Well, when we say 'ghost,' we don't mean, like, your soul," I say. "Just, like . . . energy. The reeks and fumes of your puddled brain."

He stares at me for a second, then says, "The what of my what?"

"Look," says Cyn. "Do you want a quick, painless death tonight, or what?"

"Yeah," he says. "Yeah. You're damn right I do."

"Get up and hit the bathroom first," she says. "As a favor to me. The less there is to leak out when your muscles relax, the better."

He gets out of bed and uses a cane to hobble into the en-suite bathroom.

Everything sort of seems like a dream to me at this point. Cyn and I stand awkwardly in his room, looking at his stuff; she reads the titles of the books on his shelves out loud. All nonfiction, mostly by cable-news loudmouths. I tuck a corner of his bedsheets back in, just because, and wait for the flush sound. He's old, and it takes a while. Cyn takes a book from the shelf, flips through it, and writes a response to something in the margins.

When Mr. Sturgeon is ready, we put him in a wheelchair and sign him out at the desk. Shanita smiles and says, "Thank God for you."

She totally knows what we're doing. I'm sure of it.

It's sort of reassuring that she so clearly thinks it's a good deed.

So we push Mr. Sturgeon out to the van, set him up in the back seat, and start driving him away.

"So, where are we gonna do this?" I ask. "The park again?"

"We already hit the park," Cyn says. "I'd kinda like to experiment with other places."

"The alley would be good, since it's the first stop, but we need more privacy than we'd get there."

"Yeah," she says. "There're cameras all over it, too."

"Do they ever pick up anything spooky?"

"Dunno. They never actually play the recordings back unless there's a crime in the alley or something. Even if they did, they wouldn't tell us. How about the body dump?"

"That'd work."

"Like fudge!" says Mr. Sturgeon. "I'm not dying in a body

dump. Or an alley, for that matter. Dying in alleys is for poets and hippies."

"We have a limited list of options, Mr. Sturgeon," says Cyn.

"Well, who's dying here, me or you?" he asks.

"Dude," says Cyn. "Do you want to die or don't you?"

"I do. But you're gonna have to do a little better than this. Honestly. I don't understand you millennials."

"I'm not sure I count as a millennial," I say. "I might be whatever comes after them."

"Well, I was part of the Greatest Generation," he says.

"You survived the depression, won the war, and came home to fight against integration in schools," I say. "Whoopty-do."

"Like you were even old enough to fight in that war," says Cyn. "Your whole wartime experience was probably watching those racist Bugs Bunny cartoons where he fucks with the Japanese."

"I collected tin, I'll have you know."

As we head toward downtown, Cyn suggests a new tour stop she and Rick have been experimenting with: Death Corner.

Death Corner was an intersection right in the middle of a neighborhood called Little Hell, which started out as Irish slums in the 1800s and morphed into Italian and Sicilian slums in the early twentieth century. In the 1910s, the intersection of Oak Street and Cleveland Avenue—Death Corner—

averaged about one murder per week. It seems like it ought to be haunted. Most of the deaths would have been sudden, traumatic, and so fast that the victim didn't have a chance to react much. Just the kind of death the brain punch was supposed to simulate.

The city eventually tore the whole neighborhood down, but then they put up the Cabrini-Green housing project in its place. Cabrini-Green was synonymous with crime for decades, so if there were any Death Corner ghosts, no one wanted to go looking for them. Now that Cabrini has been torn down too, and Death Corner is just four vacant lots, Cyn says we have a window of opportunity to find some ghosts there before they put up luxury townhouses.

"Fucking gentrification," she says. "Chases out the ghosts every time."

Looking at the vacant lots as we pull up, it's easy to forget we're in Chicago at all. But if you glance upward, you're staring right at the John Hancock Center, the Bloomingdale's building, and the Park Hyatt Chicago, three massive skyscrapers on Michigan Avenue, all of ten blocks away from us. To the south there are some boarded-up row houses left over from the Cabrini-Green days, all in pale brick rows with dirty wood covering the windows and doors. Behind them, you can see the antennas of the Sears Tower through the leaves on the trees. To the left you can see the Wenis Tower (which is what Rick calls the Donald Trump building).

Death Corner is a fantastic space, really. Overgrown fields surrounded by an art deco skyline.

But Mr. Sturgeon looks around and says, "Not here."

"This is gorgeous," I say. "Look at the view."

"I would totally die here," says Cyn.

"It's the old Cabrini-Green site," he says. "The projects. I am not going to die in the projects. I'm putting my foot down on this one."

So Cyn turns the van around.

Mr. Sturgeon tells us how even the cops wouldn't drive through this neighborhood thirty years ago, and when he starts getting political (by which I mean racist), Cyn gets him to switch gears and talk us through all of his aches and pains. And about how he only said yes to chemo to get his idiot children off his back. He'd always planned to find a way to die first, even before Cyn suggested anything. But no one would bring him a gun in the nursing home.

"You aren't using a gun, right?" he asks.

"No. It's a technique that sort of simulates a gunshot without the mess or the noise."

"Good. I wouldn't want my last act on earth to be giving those gun-control morons one more story to tell."

He's in pain, but still.

Mr. Sturgeon is a crusty cum-twang.

"You sure his family won't press for an autopsy?" I ask. "They sound kind of vigilant."

"The brain punch won't leave any marks," she says. "I wasn't lying when I told Rick it would show up as an aneurysm. And that's only if they keep looking once they've taken note of about four kinds of cancer."

"Five," Mr. Sturgeon says. "Just hurry up, will you?"

"Relax. You'll be naked on the slab in Megan's basement by tomorrow afternoon, Mr. Sturgeon."

"Lucky her," says the old asshole.

"For the record, I will not be going to the basement until you're safely in an urn," I say. "And if you don't shut your gingerbread trap, I'm not gonna come to your funeral at all."

"Like I'd even notice," he says.

"Gingerbread trap?" asks Cyn. "*OED*?"

"*OED*. Mouth."

"Very different from a gingerbread-office."

We share a laugh at our inside joke.

Eventually Cyn just pulls back into Lincoln Park, which I guess is our standard spot. Anything Mrs. Gunderson left behind is probably gone now anyway, so reloading isn't a bad idea.

"All right," says Cyn. "How's this?"

"I can live with this. What's the gorilla mask back here for?"

"We think it'll work better if we scare you just a bit right at the second we do it," says Cyn. "The last person was in a really nice frame of mind when she went, and there wasn't much of a ghost."

"I better not see you wearing one of these when you kill me. I didn't live this long to get killed by a teenager in a gorilla mask."

"I'm not doing the killing," I say.

"I think a dying man has the right to ask not to have a gorilla mask involved in his death."

Cyn looks at me with a tilted head and nods. He's right. If you can't ask your assisted-suicide facilitators not to wear a gorilla mask, what *can* you ask for?

But as Cyn wheels him toward the Couch tomb, I try to think of something else I could do that would scare the old man enough to get a good ghost. If I stood beside him and shouted, "Look out! Immigrants!" that'd probably do it. But what if someone heard me? They'd have no choice but to beat me up, and I wouldn't feel right about stopping them.

When he's up by the tomb, Cyn walks back to me.

"Okay," I say. "How you wanna do this?"

"I don't know. Just stand behind him and yell, I guess."

We walk out and I stand behind Mr. Sturgeon.

"Thanks," he says. "Thanks for this. Don't bungle."

"Count backwards from ten," I tell him.

He does, slowly, and I nod to Cyn, holding up four fingers. She nods, understanding. I know he'll be expecting to go when he gets to zero, so we take him by surprise. When he gets to four, I yell, "Boo!"

He jumps. And as he does, Cyn punches him in the brain.

Or, anyway, I guess she does. I'm not really watching,

and she moves very quickly. There's no scream, no blood, no thunking sound like someone getting hit, or anything else I would imagine might happen when you get brain-punched. Her arm moves so quickly I don't see what she's doing with it. And Mr. Sturgeon just sort of falls forward in the wheelchair.

Simple as that. No mess. No pain.

Cyn kneels down and takes his pulse and stuff.

"So that's it?" I ask.

"That's it. He's gone."

"I guess it worked, then."

She looks around the park at the passing cars, who would just see us standing there with an old man. "You okay?"

I shrug. "I'm a bit disturbed about the fact that I'm *not* disturbed," I say. "Tagging walls felt more like I was doing something wrong."

"You were. This was a good deed. One of our charities."

"You think he was trying to make it easier on us by being such an asshole?"

"Maybe."

"That was nice of him. . . ."

We stand there for a second, then Cyn says, "Well, now what? You want to say a few words?"

I shrug, then say, "Nitwit, blubber, oddment, tweak."

"That'll do, Dumbledore."

And she starts wheeling Mr. Sturgeon's body back to the

van. When we drive away, she puts on a Nick Cave album that seems very apropos.

Back at the home, Shanita smiles and crosses herself as we wheel Mr. Sturgeon past her and back to his room to be laid out in his bed, like he just died of cancer in the middle of the night.

The bus is almost full for my next tour, two days later, and it's a good crowd, too. They're laughing at every joke in my opening monologue, even when I stumble and screw up a little.

When we get off to walk through the Alley of Death and Mutilation, one little girl who can't be older than nine comes up to me.

"Are you doing okay?" I ask. "I know these stories get pretty gory."

She smiles so big I worry that she'll be sore in the morning. "They're awesome," she says. "I love dead people."

"Me too," I tell her.

Her mom comes up, smiling a dopey sort of grin of her own. "Ava adores this stuff," she says. "Blood, guts, gore. We think she's going to be a doctor."

"I wish I was a ghost," Ava says. "That way I could suck people's souls out of their ears."

"Oh, Ava!" says her mom, who obviously doesn't find this disturbing in the slightest.

I decide to keep an eye on Ava.

She kind of reminds me of me, in a way. But I never went so far as to fantasize about killing people, especially as openly as she is. Even now, when I write up new endings to Disney movies where I'm the villain and the villain wins, I never imagine killing the princesses or anything.

But, come to think of it, there are always skeletons in the dungeon, so even in my tamest self-insert fan fiction, I must have done some killing once upon a time.

At Hull House Ava tells me she wishes *she* was a devil baby, so she could eat people's heads. "I'd pretend I was a cute little baby, then when they tried to kiss me, I'd eat them!"

Eating people is a particular favorite thing of hers.

And when I tell her about Cyn having a headless ancestor, she gets all excited and asks her mom if she's part headless too.

Nothing on the tour scares her until we get to the Couch tomb.

When we're walking up toward it, across the field, she starts out skipping along, laughing about how she's skipping over dead bodies, but then she stops midskip.

"You okay?" I ask.

She suddenly looks terrified, her face frozen like she's just watched someone die right in front of her and realized that it wasn't as funny as she thought.

Slowly she raises her shaking arm and points toward the tomb.

"There's a . . . a . . ."

Up against the stone wall of the mausoleum is a solid, unmistakably human silhouette, small enough that it could only be the shadow of someone standing right in front of it.

It's there for a second, and then it's gone.

Well, shit.

It freaks me out a bit, but poor Ava is frightened out of her mind. She screams and starts crying and won't take another step toward the tomb.

I try to play it cool and just calm her down.

"You mean the shadow?" I ask. "Is that what you saw?"

She nods. Behind her, her mother takes pictures, oblivious.

"Oh, that's nothing," I say. "We see that a lot."

"Was that a ghost?" she asks.

"Nope. Just the shadow of a rat. A big, ugly rat with fangs," I say. "When the light from the street hits a big enough rat just right, its shadow looks like a person."

Ava stares forward, and the color gradually comes back into her face. She stops crying. A minute later she's asking if the rat eats people, then says, "I wish I was a rat, so I could eat people's heads!"

"Oh, you wouldn't want to eat a head," I say. "They're full of boogers."

"Ew!"

"A hundred years ago, 'booger' was another name for 'ghost.'"

That gets her laughing, running around, waving her arms and shouting "Wooo! I'm a booger!" She's forgotten that she was scared, and I feel like I've handled the situation extremely well, though I have to explain the whole history of the word (and it's connection to "boogeyman") to Ava's mom.

The shadow appears again for a second, and everyone on the tour sees it and goes nuts.

After that I don't even have to hop the fence or talk about the tomb much—everyone is looking for the shadow, or trying to find out if we've rigged up a projector to make it look like there's a shadow there.

I tell Ava that she and I are sharing a secret that it's just a rat, but everyone else is fired up and thinks they've seen a ghost. I don't know if it's really some of the reeks and fumes of Mr. Sturgeon's brain or if I was right about it being a rat or what.

And I decide not to dwell on it. All that matters is that after the tour, the tips are the best I've ever gotten, and in the morning Cyn texts me to say that we have three new five-star reviews online.

Chapter Twelve

"It doesn't matter how much money you make or how much power
you have or how much control you feel, when you die, you're likely
to end up naked and pooping. That's just the way it is. And that's . . .
very egalitarian, and very equalizing, and I really like it."
—CAITLIN DOUGHTY, ASK A MORTICIAN

In my research I find an interview with a "professional
subject-gatherer" (a very polite term for "one who
steals bodies to sell to medical schools") in an 1878
issue of the *Tribune*. When asked if he enjoyed the work, he
said, "Well, it wasn't very pleasant at first, of course, but anyone
gets used to it."

That's the way it is with creating psychic imprints. You get
used to it. Fast. "Ghosting" old chronic patients starts to feel
like a simple chore, like sweeping the spiders off the bus before
the tour, or filling it up with gas after the weekend.

If they ever make a movie about Mysterious Chicago, they
could probably show a whole montage of me and Cyn taking
care of volunteers throughout July. With "Poor Unfortunate
Souls" playing in the background, probably.

Sometimes we use the gorilla mask, and sometimes not.

We always offer to do things the way the volunteers want
them done. One woman asks us to learn the hymn "Nearer

My God to Thee" so we can sing it right before she shuffles off her mortal coil at the Holmes body dump. I'm not a great singer, and singing her off isn't as good for our purposes as scaring her, but it's a reasonable request, so we give it our best. And it might be my imagination, but the next night, when the tour stops at the dump, I think I hear the melody of the hymn, riding on the wind.

And I'm almost sure that I see the woman's shadow.

It could always be something else. There's always another possible explanation. But it's undeniable the dump seems infinitely spookier once we've done some charity work there.

Our "subjects" are always so grateful to us that it really feels like we're just doing a good deed, like shoveling their sidewalk or cleaning their bedpans or something. These aren't suicidal people who could have benefited from help from a mental health professional; they're terminal cases whose lives are effectively over already. We have guidelines regarding this sort of thing. They have to be chronically sick, above the age of average life expectancy, and totally and enthusiastically consenting. The one time a person seems a bit nervous about it, we cancel the whole thing and bring her back home. We don't take any "clients" who have second thoughts.

She dies two days later anyway.

And we're back at work on day three.

Cyn seems like she's determined to make ghosts real just so Rick can show them to people. He notices the uptick in ghost sightings on the tours, and his tours get even better. As far as he knows, the ghosts people are seeing really *could* be people who died there years ago. For my part, when I'm running the tour, I tell the historical stories, and when people think they see a ghost, I just let them go on thinking it's a ghost from the story I was telling. It's not being dishonest, exactly. I'm just leaving certain parts out. And hell, *I* don't know what they're really seeing, either. I'm never *totally* sure that the brain punch thing really works.

Our five-star reviews multiply quickly.

And so does our average number of customers per night.

One day at the end of July I come outside to find that we've had one of the biggest single-day drops in temperature ever recorded in Cook County. It's like summer has slipped out for a smoke, and autumn has crept in early while its back was turned. The air is crisp, the sky is gray, and it feels like heaven to me. I put on my long jacket and feel like I'm taking myself out of storage and coming back to life. A good six weeks earlier than I normally get to. It's unnatural, maybe, but I don't give a damn.

I leave Forest Park way early for the tour that night, take the Blue Line clear to Wicker Park, and spend way more than I should on the witchiest pair of boots John Fluevog makes. They're out of my price range and not really practical for standing up on moving buses, but the heels make me feel so tall and powerful that I have to have them.

On Clark Street, Terrence the caricature guy has a leather jacket on. Tourists from Florida act like they're in *Frozen*, huddling together as if temperatures in the sixties are something they've never felt.

Cyn grins at my outfit and says, "You look so goth, you'd tag walls with a fountain pen."

I smile.

"You ever think about dyeing your hair black again?" I ask.

"Not really. The old people at the home might not like it. But I do miss it."

"It made your skin look better. It was so bright next to the black hair. If you ever saw it, you would even say it glowed."

She nods, and we just make general small talk about skin care, boots, and the weather, like strangers who are chatting for the first time.

We don't once mention what we'd done the night before in the Alley of Death and Mutilation.

Not even later, when someone takes a picture there that looks almost like a full-body apparition of an old man crouching by the stage door. The kind of ghost you'd normally only see in a movie.

The cool weather holds into August. It's almost like a miracle. Like something has thrown off the natural order of things.

If the leaves were changing color, and gallon jugs of the good apple cider had started showing up, perched on top of

ADAM SELZER

haystacks outside of the grocery store and next to the pumpkins and gourds at the weekend farmers' market, it would feel just like autumn. It feels close enough as it is.

Zoey still hasn't sent a picture, but I send enough cute selfies for both of us, now that I can dress the way I like to. It's still a bit too warm for the jacket in the middle of the day, when the temperature hits its high, but it's cool enough in the mornings and the evenings.

Some people try to pretend the change in the weather isn't happening. I still see girls in short shorts and bikini tops walking around outside, even though they've got to be freezing. When we drive up Lake Shore Drive, there are still people swimming beside us along the edge of Lake Michigan.

But other people surrender, and just admit that October has come home early this year. We never put up Halloween decorations at the house—that'd be in pretty poor taste at a funeral home—so I've always relied on my neighbors. A house near mine always puts out theirs early—they usually have a bunch of little plastic skeletons that dangle from their tree and dance in the wind—and this year they start even earlier. It's not even September, and they have the skeletons out.

I love this.

I go tromping around wearing boots like Gaston.

While Cyn and I perfect our technique as charitable ghosters, Rick and I refine our two-step act on the tours we run together.

One prank that goes over particularly well is pulling up next to people at traffic lights and asking if they want to come to the body dump with us. One time we pull up at a stoplight next to a guy who's riding around with a girl and just say, "You wanna see a dead body?"

He waves and says, "I got dead bodies in the trunk, man!"

"Well, pop it, Al Capone!" says Rick. "Let's see!"

And the dude pops his trunk. I jump off the bus and start rooting around inside. Obviously there aren't any bodies in it, just a bunch of baseball equipment, but when the traffic light ahead of us changes, I slam it shut, jump back on the bus before we start moving, and pretend it was full of corpses.

"You knew to sever the arteries and everything!" I say. "You've done this before!"

"Sure have!" the guy says. "And she's next!"

He points at his girlfriend, who smiles and laughs as they drive away.

I'd say that it's kind of a fucked up joke to make, but it isn't that different from Rick's and Cyn's sense of humor as a couple, really. Cyn jokes about killing Rick pretty regularly, and now and then he'll give it right back to her.

I don't ask, but I'm pretty sure their relationship is in "on again" mode.

One night on a ten o'clock tour, when it's actually dark out, we pull into the body dump and there's a van that's a-rocking.

I can just picture the guy saying, "Come on, baby, I know the perfect little dead-end street, no one ever goes there. . . ." Then *here comes the tour bus*!

Our being there does not stop them. For a minute I think I should tap the window, just to let them know they aren't alone, but then I think of Mrs. Weyher and figure that maybe they'll help us out a little.

One *OED* synonym for having an orgasm is "die." Like, half the time they say "die" in Shakespeare, they mean it both ways.

Maybe there's more than one way to make a ghost by dying at the body dump.

We experiment a bit with new stops, especially places where Cyn and I have taken care of someone. The first time Rick steers the bus up to Death Corner, we notice something weird: snow.

One of the four vacant lots surrounding the corner is fenced off, and behind the fence is a thin layer of snow.

Snow!

The weather is colder, but not *that* much colder.

We all step out and wander up to the fence that blocks access to the lot itself. The snow starts a few feet inside, so no one can quite reach it to see if it's cold. But it's there, and there are footprints going through it, like a ghost has walked through. Or danced through, really. The footprints don't seem to go in any logical path, just all over. It's positively chilling.

But after the customers get off the bus at the end of the tour, Rick just laughs.

"It's probably just some weed killer," he says. "They're about to put up townhouses there." Then he pauses, looks up thoughtfully, and says, "I hope someone has the foresight to call their house 'the House at Death Corner.' Get kind of a goth Winnie-the-Pooh vibe going."

I don't tell him, of course, about the old woman, all skin and bones, who was punched in the brain right outside the fence two nights before.

One night, when we have two tours to run, I pull a trick on Rick.

The week before, I ordered a commemorative James Garfield spoon, just like the ones that had been stolen from his tomb, off eBay for the whopping price of ninety-nine cents. And on the seven o'clock tour, I hop the fence at the Couch tomb and slide it about halfway under the door, so the handle is sticking out.

On the ten o'clock tour, I direct Rick to take a route that I know will get us stuck in traffic, then have him tell the people all of his theories about the theft of the spoons from the James Garfield tomb.

"Now, here's the real kicker," he says. "The guy who shot Garfield was a Chicago man. Charles Guiteau. A complete nut who sort of failed his way through life. One of the things he failed at was joining a free-love cult called the Oneida Community. They kicked him out and he tried to sue them. Now, here's the thing: the Oneida Community is still around, only they stopped having free love. You know what they do now instead of having sex?"

"What?" I ask.

"They manufacture silverware," he says. "Spoons!"

He and I think this is the funniest thing ever, even though only a couple of customers laugh.

When we get to the tomb, I tell Rick I hurt my ankle hopping the fence on the seven o'clock tour and ask him to do it for me. Anytime you ask Rick to take the spotlight, he'll do it.

So he puts the bus's flashers on and leaves it by the side of the road, follows us out to the tomb, and jumps the fence. He notices the silvery glint sticking out from under the door right away.

"Hey, this is new."

He pulls the spoon out and stares for a second. Once he realizes what it is, he shakes his head for a second, then starts to laugh so hard he literally falls onto the ground.

He isn't fooled, of course. He knows right away that I planted it there. But once he gets ahold of himself enough that he can stand upright, he pats me on the shoulder and says, "Megan, I am so glad we hired you."

Cyn continues to talk about hooking me up with one of her friends. Even while we're heading up to the nursing home to pick someone up.

"You liked Morticia, right? Like, you would kiss her if you had the chance?

"She vanished. Like a breath into the wind."

Cyn adjusts her ass in the seat.

"Have you ever texted Zoey while we were doing 'charity work'?" she asks.

"Sure. I didn't say what we were doing or anything, but I talk to her basically constantly."

"She could still trace it to where you were, probably."

"It'd just look like we were out for a slice of pizza or something. And they know we're signing people out at the home. Shanita does, at least."

"True."

We pull around, back behind the excursion bus, and I take the gorilla mask out of the Rubbermaid container. We've upgraded from the plastic Target bag we had the first time. You can tell business is picking up. We carry our gorilla mask of scary death in style now.

"If she won't even send you a picture," says Cyn, changing the subject back, "you deserve a better girlfriend."

"It's an anxiety thing for her."

"And you don't worry that she knows too much about you while you know nothing about her?"

ADAM SELZER

I don't answer that.

Because I do, sometimes.

I worry that if anything ever happens with us, like if I break up with her, she'll spread the worst of my stories all over and tell everyone who I am and where I live and the name of Mom's business and everything.

If I don't want that to happen, I might be stuck with her.

But I'm okay with that. Every time something funny happens on the tour, Zoey is the first person I want to tell. I never get tired of talking to her. She knows just what to say to turn me on, and might be the only person on the planet who ever will.

If I can't be with her in person, I'm happy just to love the shadow she casts over the internet, and let it love me back.

Chapter Thirteen

I wake up one morning to a flurry of panicked texts.

    ZOEY BABY:
    ARE YOU OKAY?

Then

    ZOEY BABY:
    PLEASE ANSWER, MEGAN

Then

    ZOEY BABY:
    ARE YOU THERE? I NEED NEED NEED TO HEAR
    FROM YOU.

I roll over onto my back, rub the crud out of my eyes, and

type back, "I didn't get you pregnant last night, did I, baby?" with a couple of smiley faces.

This is the kind of "cute couple game" you do when you can't have proper tickle fights—you joke about getting each other pregnant when it's well beyond the bounds of biology for many different reasons. But she isn't in the mood to joke today; she is genuinely scared about something.

She sends back a million or so emojis, and then a link to a news story. Some maniac has shot up a shopping center in Crystal Lake, a strip-mall town up in the far north suburbs. I tell her not to worry—I've never even been to Crystal Lake—then get up out of bed.

Mom and Clarice are in the living room, watching the live news. The maniac has been cornered in the back of a store someplace, and the SWAT team is surrounding it.

"Rough morning," says Mom. "Six kids so far. More in the hospital."

Clarice smokes and exhales deeply.

"What was this guy's issue?" I ask.

"He posted something online about demons," says Mom. "But who the hell knows?"

For a second I feel like a slimeball.

He's blaming the supernatural. Aren't I just encouraging people to blame the supernatural when something happens that they don't understand right away? Even if I try not to? I've noticed that no matter how insistent I am that the "devil baby" was just a rumor that went around in 1913, people get out of the bus and ask where it was buried, or if I've ever seen its ghost.

I sit and watch the news and sneakily text with Zoey a bit, telling her what a shit-pot I feel like. She texts back that I'm the good kind of ghost-tour guide. That if my customers didn't come on my tour, they'd just go on an even less responsible one.

She's right, I guess. If I wasn't in the business, if Mysterious Chicago didn't exist, it wouldn't stop people from going on ghost tours. They'd just go on a DarkSide tour, or another one that didn't care about getting the stories right. One that actively told them to think every stray light in their photos was a dead person up and floating around.

This is why Mysterious Chicago is here. To be the honest company. We are the ragtag band of rebels sweeping out the bullshit, just like Brandon said.

I still sort of feel like an asshole, though. I'm supposed to be working tonight. How can I make all those flippant jokes about death on a night like this? I wonder if Rick and Cyn will just cancel tonight's tour.

Rick calls around ten in the morning.

"You ever hear of a guy called Vaughn Meader?" he asks.

"Nope."

"He was a JFK impersonator. Legend has it that when Kennedy was shot, Lenny Bruce had to go onstage that night. First thing he said was 'Poor Vaughn Meader.'"

"Have you ever had to run a tour on a night like this?"

"Are you kidding? People get shot up like this all the time in this country. It's worse when it's kids though."

"So what do you do?"

"Well, if you're lucky, it'll all be tourists who've been hanging out at Navy Pier all day and didn't hear the news yet."

"Right. But even so . . . the Alley of Death and Mutilation is out. I can't talk about dead kids today."

"The St. Valentine's Day Massacre site is out, too. And Death Corner. God. I might even skip the body dump, if I were you. No places with shootings or murders. No disaster sites where kids were among the victims."

"So, that basically just leaves Hull House and the Couch tomb," I say. "What do I do to fill the gaps?"

The two of us brainstorm a bit, and he tells me about some places we could go—like the block of Prairie Avenue south of the Loop, where all the millionaires used to live. "The Fort Dearborn Massacre happened right there," he says, "but even if you don't want to mention that, it's still full of mansions that look like something from *Scooby-Doo*. One of them's supposed to be haunted by the architect who designed it and died before it was built."

"Got it."

"You could even go up to Wrigley Field if you wanted to. People say that's haunted by a songwriter who tried to get his ashes scattered there. And he died of cancer, so there's no guts or gore."

"Noted."

"And how about Bughouse Square? You could do that as an off-bus stop to kill some time. Say One-Armed Charlie is rumored to haunt it."

The park they used to call Bughouse Square is a regular drive-by on the tour, but not a haunted spot, just a cool thing to point out. It's the second-oldest park in the city, and it used to be a popular place to go stand on a soapbox and make a speech; on any given night there'd be five or six people making speeches at once and hundreds of people there to heckle them. Newspaper articles make it sound like a mix between a carnival and walking through a field of audible Youtube comments. Awesome and awful, all at once. One-Armed Charlie was a regular speaker—his famous line that we repeat on tours was "If brains were bug juice, you couldn't drown a gnat."

"I can try that," I say. "*Some people say you can still hear him.* That sort of thing."

"Right. 'According to legend,' 'Some people say,' 'Rumor has it,' 'The story goes . . .' All those ways of covering your ass when you know a story probably isn't true, but you don't want to lie. It's an emergency, after all. And it's only gonna be a handful of people. You can equivocate a little more than usual."

After a while we have a basic list of non-gory sites I can go to, and a whole new route to try. It'll be a little short on ghost stories, really, but plenty of good history, and as long as everyone has a good time, they won't complain.

When I go back into the living room, Clarice tells me the Feds have caught the shooter alive. But the people who were just wounded at first keep dying all through the day, and TV stations keep flashing pictures of kids who died across the screen. Rick texts to say that a couple of our customers have canceled. But the tour is still on.

The faces on the Blue Line train are somber when I head downtown. A couple of people argue about gun control; the same six or seven lines you hear in all of those debates. On Clark Street, though, tourists skip around as usual, apparently oblivious. They pose for Terrence's caricatures. They pose for photos pretending to shoot the Al Capone Tours guy, which seems even more disturbing than usual.

Edward Tweed and Aaron Saltis both give me a "Well, shit, this is gonna be rough" look as I pass, though Tweed seems calm, like it's nothing he hasn't done a hundred times. Cyn gives me a small wave as I walk over and start checking customers in.

"Rick says you've got a new route set up?" she asks.

"Yeah. I'm a bit worried it'll run short, though, so feel free to add anything you want."

"Will do."

Then I tell her how freaked out Zoey was. I think it's sort of charming, how scared Zoey gets about me being in Chicago.

We go to Hull House first, where all the ghosts seem to be of people who died of natural causes, then down Roosevelt

Road, passing the place where Abraham Lincoln's funeral train rolled into town. Rumor has it that the ghost train shows up now and then. We stick around the south Loop to hit Prairie Avenue and look at all the old mansions; they sure *look* haunted.

I stop myself from thinking it's a good place to take a volunteer. It's just not a good night to think like that.

While we cruise up Lake Shore Drive I tell a few stories I looked up about the Congress Hotel, which we can see on Michigan Avenue, over on the other side of Grant Park. Then I throw in a few stories of ghost ships on the lake. It's not as good as my usual tours, but it works.

When we get off Lake Shore Drive, we wiggle through the Gold Coast and end up right at the Couch tomb, and from there we go down to Bughouse Square. It's a lovely little park, really. Nice to walk around in, even though it doesn't seem remotely spooky to me. The ghost of One-Armed Charlie declines to make an appearance. After trying to think of a sample speech I could give, I just decide to borrow Rick's—he won't mind, since it's an emergency and all. I jump onto a bench and improvise a little rant about how stupid my uncle was to be planning to cut off his limbs for the insurance money. "If brains were bug juice, he couldn't drown a gnat!"

When we get back on the bus, the tour is still running way short, and we're only a few blocks from being back at the McDonald's. Cyn takes the mic to help me out.

A D A M   S E L Z E R

"Hey," she says, "I don't suppose Megan told you about the ghost of Lillian Collier, did she?"

Everyone shakes their heads. Including me.

"This one's pretty obscure," she says. "The ghost isn't reported too often, but Lillian Collier was a flapper who used to hang out here in Bughouse Square back in the early 1920s. She ran a tea room on Michigan Avenue called the Wind Blew Inn, and one day when she was, like, nineteen, the cops raided the place because she was holding 'petting parties.' She had to go in front of a judge and say, 'There is no snuggle-pupping at the Wind Blew Inn.'"

"'Snuggle-pupping'?" I ask. "That's the best word I ever heard."

"Yeah, it's like a more illicit version of cuddling," says Cyn. "Anyway, the judge sentenced her to read a book of fairy tales to cure her bohemianism. According to legend, she died of tuberculosis or pneumonia or something, and now her ghost haunts Bughouse Square."

"You think she might be the vanishing flapper hitchhiker out at Waldheim?"

"No reason why she couldn't be, I guess. But I usually hear about her around here."

When we finish at Bughouse Square, we drive the bus through River North, meandering around and pointing out bars that are supposed to be haunted (just about all of them are) until we've been out just long enough to say we've done a full-length tour. Tips come to twelve bucks each. Not bad, really, all things considered.

As Cyn drives me to the Blue Line, I ask if the Lillian Collier story is true.

"Yeah," she says. "She was a real person."

"Is she really supposed to haunt Bughouse Square?"

"I certainly don't have a firsthand account of the ghost to cite," she says with a low-grade cackle. "She does disappear from the record in the mid 1920s, so she might have died when she was still a flapper. But she might have also just gotten married, changed her name, and had a few kids or something. You sort of look like her, you know. Now that I think of it."

I look Lillian Collier up on my phone during the train ride home. There are a couple of photos in the *Tribune* archives.

I really do sort of look like her. Her hair was shorter, but her face was kind of similar to mine.

That night I stay up for hours reading every vintage article I can find on Lillian Collier, the mysterious flapper of Bughouse Square.

Chapter Fourteen

From: Megan

To: Ricardo Torre, Cynthia Fargon

Date: Thursday, 1:05 a.m.

Subject: Lillian Collier: The Vanishing Flapper

Hey, guys. I am officially obsessed with Lillian Collier. I almost thought Cyn was making this story up, but I've been online all night digging up articles. Lillian's antics made the Tribune several times, and there are a bunch of articles about her from out-of-town papers too. She was national news in 1922.

Anyway, here's a basic rundown of what I've found:

In 1922, Lillian Collier (pronounced "Colly") was a young flapper who told a reporter she had come to town to convert Chicagoans to "the gospel of high art" with her tea room, The Wind Blew Inn, which was on East Ohio Street, right off Michigan Avenue, where the Under Armour store is now. Apparently she had been a circus performer before she opened the place. She was all over the media in the early 1920s; one time she made the news by climbing up a flagpole, and papers loved to talk about (well, make fun of) all the weirdos and artists who hung around the Wind Blew Inn.

Valentine's Day, 1922, the cops raided the place. Neighbors had complained about the noise from "syncopated 'blues' music" coming from the place, and parents feared that their children were taking part in "petting parties" there. Not to mention that this was during Prohibition, and they were rumored to be selling booze under the table. Several patrons were arrested, along with Lillian herself and her "aide" (girlfriend, I'll bet), Virginia Harrison.

At the hearing following the raid, a judge let all the patrons go, but set Lillian's trial for the next month and told her to remove the "obscene" nude statues that were used as decorations. She compromised by putting overalls on them.

At their trial, she and Virginia told the judge that they didn't serve anything stronger than chocolate éclairs, and that "There is no snuggle-pupping at the Wind Blew Inn." That was when the judge sentenced Lillian to read a book of fairy tales to cure her of her bohemian ideals and teach her "the value of the things of life in general."

Lillian dutifully marched into the library and posed for the press holding the book of fairy tales she'd checked out, promising to mend her ways if the stories in the book convinced her to.

A month later the Wind Blew Inn burned down.

The fairy tales obviously didn't work, though. Two years later, in 1924, Lillian was quoted in a widely-circulated article entitled "Is Today's Girl Becoming a Savage?" In it, she claimed that flappers were not "savages" at all, like stuffy society marms were saying they were, but represented a new era of freedom and opportunity for women. "Our open and honest ways are too frank for mid-Victorian critics," she said. "Women for too long have played the role of the underdog. The flapper of today is the product of a new age turning toward the light." (Article attached.)

After that article, though, Lillian vanishes from the record completely. I couldn't find anything saying she died in the 1920s, but the Social Security Death Index didn't start until the 1930s. It may just be that she got married and changed her name, and somehow the marriage isn't in the records either, but I just feel like there must be more to her story. I have found several women from 1930 and beyond named Lillian Collier who may have been her. A poet in Canada. A suffragette in Texas. A New York socialite who married an Olympic fencer (he died in a blimp crash right after the wedding). But none of these can be definitively shown to be to the same Lillian Collier who took Chicago by storm in 1922. Even many of the known stories of her have only been traced to provincial papers so far—the Chicago Tribune covered her arrest, but not her bizarre sentencing.

I'm going to solve this mystery.

—Megan

> MEGAN:
>
> I dreamed I was her last night.

ZOEY BABY:

That flapper girl?

> MEGAN:
>
> Yeah.

MEGAN:

In the dream she/I changed my name and became a silent film star in 1926. But in the dream it was the 1950s, and I was living in a hotel, singing sultry songs like "Why Don't You Do Right" and "Young and Beautiful" in the hotel bar while Cyn played piano.

MEGAN:

It was kind of cool. Like I was in hiding. No one at the hotel knew I used to be famous. Even though one of my movie posters was on the wall.

ZOEY BABY:

You think she was sending you a message about what happened?

MEGAN:

I have to admit, I woke up hoping so.

MEGAN:

God, now I really, really want to be a washed-up silent film actress living in a seedy hotel in 1955.

ZOEY BABY:

Hey, if movies have taught me one thing, it's that dreams can come true. LOL.

MEGAN:

Yes. If I work hard and set my mind to it, I CAN go

be a washed up 1920s starlet living in the 1950s. I

believe.

MEGAN:

WISSSSHHHHHHHHING

ZOEY BABY:

WISSSHHHH

Chapter Fifteen

For the first part of the summer, I was always having dreams about the Couch tomb. Like, I'd dream I found a tunnel that led into it. Or that I'd hop the fence, the door would swing open, and there would be Ira Couch, in his bathrobe and his underpants, eating some toast and saying, "What?"

Sometimes in my dreams it was full of more dead bodies than it could really hold. Recent ones. Once there were bodies, plus a bunch of cubicles where guys were doing office work, not even noticing all the bodies. It was usually bigger on the inside. Night after night, I was inside that tomb in my dreams.

But after I get into Lillian Collier, most of my dreams are of her.

Some 1920s slang words I dig up, and resolve to start working into tour stories at once:

Oil burner: a girl who chews gum (or takes drugs)

cake-eater: a playboy

crumpet-muncher: same as a "cake eater"

dool-owl: a dull, depressing person

cuddle cootie: a guy whose idea of a date is taking a girl for a bus ride

lollygagger: a young man who "pets" in the hallways

the berries: an excellent person or thing (similar to "the bee's knees" or "the cat's pajamas") (as in: "Cap'n Crunch with Crunch Berries is the berries.")

OAO: One and Only (1920s version of OTP or BAE)

I spend an afternoon strolling through Waldheim Cemetery, looking for graves that might be hers if she's the vanishing flapper who supposedly hitches rides there, even though I don't exactly believe those hitchhiking ghosts are real.

Before my next tour, I even walk over to the sportswear store on Michigan Avenue that was built over the grounds where the Wind Blew Inn used to stand and stroll around, just letting myself be impressed with the fact that Lillian probably stood right in the space where I'm standing now.

I don't talk out loud to dead people, normally. I know they can't hear me. But I find myself whispering, "Here I am, Lillian. Can you give me a clue?"

Nothing happens, though, and thinking that the site of the Wind Blew Inn is just a place selling sporting goods and stuff now starts to get depressing. There are no ghosts here. No quiet echo of the "syncopated 'blues' music" that neighbors used to complain about. No soft sound of laughter and secret make-out parties. No faint smell of spiked tea and chocolate eclairs.

Just a lot of people buying moisture-wicking underwear.

With no traces of Lillian at her old stomping grounds, I go to the McDonald's, order a coffee, and just sit there, watching the city go by. Terrence the caricature guy gives me a nod through the window.

After a minute I hear a voice beside me.

"Rolling with the rotters?"

Aaron Saltis, the other DarkSide tour guide, takes a seat next to me.

"Cruising with the corpses," I say.

He smells like gin. Or vodka, maybe. I don't really know. Embalming fluid, for sure.

"How's business?" he asks.

"We're getting by."

"October is coming."

"Yeah."

"Sixty-five percent of the business is in October, you know. Bunch of October-only tour companies are gonna sprout up.

The Segway Tours start running ghost tours. Trolley company, too. Even the fucking food tours. Death Alley's gonna be a battle zone every night. Four, five big groups crowding in at once."

"Well, we'll just have to have a rumble," I say. "We're the Sharks, you're the Jets. You have to be the racist ones."

He laughs a gross, throaty, "just crawled out of the grave" laugh.

"I assumed you must be funny if you got a gig with Rick," he says. "You know Rick tried to get me to go into business with him when he left DarkSide?"

I shrug. "I don't know all the history between you two."

"He did. I didn't think 'Mysterious Chicago' would last, though. Edward's safer. And I don't trust that Cynthia girl."

I take some offense at this.

"At least she isn't going around telling people their flash bouncing off a window in a photo is a ghost."

Aaron chuckles and grunts in a single sound, then looks off into the distance. "People just come on these things for thrills and chills," he says. "Most of them assume the stories are all fake anyway."

"They don't have to be," I say. "The real stories are good enough. We don't need to make up shit about devil babies and Indian burial grounds."

"Or people hanging themselves from the ceiling," he adds. "Ninety percent of the ghost stories that start with a suicide, it's someone hanging themselves from the ceiling. You ever notice that? Heh."

I wonder for a second if maybe getting hanged from the ceiling is similar to getting punched in the brain, physically, which would explain why there are so many ghost stories like that. Like, if you die while doing auto-erotic asphyxiation, it leaves something behind. It seems logical, in a pseudoscience sort of way. But it's probably just a folklore thing—hanging oneself from the ceiling sounds good in a ghost story. That's all.

I decide to take advantage of the fact that Aaron is admitting the stories are mostly BS.

"Yeah," I say. "And how many Indian burial grounds can there be?"

He chortles again. "And how many kids got killed in a bus on railroad tracks so their ghosts can push cars over them? Half the small towns in the world have that story."

"Pregnant nuns getting walled up inside a former nunnery."

"Ever hear of a former insane asylum that *wasn't* supposed to be haunted?"

He pulls a flask from his pocket and offers me a sip. I turn him down. If it was after the tour I might take it, but I don't want to be lightheaded at work.

"I don't really traffic much in those kinds of stories," I say. "I'm afraid I'm gonna get fact-checked."

"Look," he says as he unscrews his flask. "I know our stories are shit. But Edward's got a fan base. And when they come on a DarkSide tour, they want the Edward stories."

"Fair enough."

"And keep this on the down low, but I'm in talks with Ghostly Journeys, the company down in New Orleans, to bring them up here."

This is interesting news.

"I heard someone was."

"Sooner or later someone's gonna do like Vince McMahon did to pro wrestling in the '80s. Gather up all the best talent from the rinky-dink local markets and build an empire. You want a job? You could get more tours with me, and they're talking to that TV fucker, too. If we get you, we get the show. I'm sure that'd clinch it."

"I'm pretty loyal to Rick and Cyn."

"Yeah, but how many tours do you get to run?"

"Couple a week, usually. Sometimes three."

"What if I got you three or four more, and paid you double? Because one day Rick's gonna get a part in some B-list sitcom pilot and leave you out to dry."

I'm about to tell Aaron off when I hear a voice behind me that makes me forget all about him.

"Hey."

I turn to see a vision in black, with red hair and a giant, unbelievable smile.

Morticia.

Our vanishing hitchhiker.

I try to smile back half as alluringly as she smiles, and forget all about Aaron Saltis and Ghostly Journeys.

"Hi, you," I say. "We were starting to think you were a ghost the whole time."

She laughs. "Well, who says I'm not?"

"No one," I say. "In fact, I sort of like to imagine that you are."

Aaron breaks in and says, "I can't see through you," but she doesn't take any notice of him. She keeps looking at me as she wiggles her fingers in front of her face and says, "Boo."

Then she smiles.

Oh God. She's flirting with me.

Outrageously, even.

"I'm Megan," I say.

"I know." She laughs. "It's my last night in town, and I wanted to tell you how much fun I had on the tour. Thought you might be here."

"You want to come again tonight?" I ask. "On the house?"

She smiles, then nods. "Sure."

I excuse myself from Aaron, and Morticia and I walk out to the Ronald McDonald statue and chat a little bit.

I'd thought she was in town for the comic convention before, but she says she's been in town for the summer, working some sort of marketing internship. She says her name is Enid. No one's name is Enid. But I don't care if she's lying, really. It's better if she is, in a way. Obviously I'm not trying to cheat on Zoey with her if I don't even try to get her real name, right?

Right?

I tell her all about Lillian Collier, and all the research I'm doing, and the word "snuggle-pupping," which she thinks is the best word she's ever heard, too.

"How would you like to be known as one who snuggle-pups?" I ask.

She laughs. "I'd like it fine."

Then she demurely sips from a water bottle and looks out at the city.

"There aren't many people like me back home," she says. "If you know what I mean. I was sort of hoping I'd meet someone here. Have a little fling. Get some snuggle-pupping in."

"Yeah?"

"Hasn't happened yet, though."

And she bats her eyelashes.

At me.

Me.

I don't give my very best tour that night. I'm usually not as good when Cyn drives as I am when Rick does, and anyway, I can't focus because I'm too busy checking to see if Morticia (I still call her that in my head, not Enid) is looking at me. She usually is. I'm the tour guide, after all.

Every time she catches me looking, she smiles. Her teeth are perfect. I wish any part of me was as perfect as her teeth. I pretend not to notice when she brushes her shoulder against mine in the Alley of Death and Mutilation.

At Hull House, as customers roam through the courtyard and peer into the front windows, I walk around to the back of the house. Morticia comes around behind me. We're alone.

I know I shouldn't be doing this blatant flirting.

Not with Zoey and all.

But I'm like a moth and Morticia's like a flame.

"You know," she says, "you're really good at this job."

"Thanks."

"Lillian Collier would be proud of you, cuddle cootie."

I smile, and she moves an inch closer. I can feel her breath on my face. She is totally coming on to me.

"So this is your last night in town?" I ask.

She nods. "Going home tomorrow."

Her toes bump into mine.

I feel the hair stand up on the back of my neck, and for the first time ever, I really, really feel like there's something super-natural about Hull House.

But it probably isn't ghosts making me freak out.

"Are you going to disappear outside of the Water Tower again?" I ask.

"Do you want me to?"

"I sort of like the illusion," I say. "There was a cemetery

there once, so it's like you're our own beautiful vanishing hitchhiker."

"I can disappear again and make it part of the show," she says.

"When you go back home, you'll leave a ghost story behind in Chicago."

I feel her breath on my nose, and she wiggles her fingers in front of her face and says, "Are you scared of me?" with a teasing smile.

Every sign I can pick up tells me she wouldn't stop me from kissing her.

And I want to.

I have really been wanting to find a way to kiss someone (without technically cheating on Zoey, of course). I'm really starting to feel like I'm missing out on something as a human being by never getting a real kiss. Cyn is making too many good points. If I can get it out of the way and see that it's no big deal, not a necessary part of life, I can get her off my back. A harmless kiss with a girl who, for all practical purposes, functions as a ghost wouldn't count as cheating, right? It would just be a way to cross something off my bucket list.

Then I hit on another idea.

"So, Jane Addams and her partner shared a bed for years," I say. "But Victorians had these, like, romantic friendships. They might have been partners and girlfriends and all of that without ever getting physical. Poor unfortunate souls."

She giggles a tiny bit, then says, "Let's pretend we're them and make up for lost time," and then I feel her lips on mine.

She's kissing me.

Oh, sweet holy Christmas hell. She is kissing me. I am being kissed.

And I am kissing her back.

Kissing! I am *kissing*!

It isn't *us* kissing. As far as I'm concerned, we're acting as proxies for Jane and Mary. It's like a whole century of their romantic tension is being released in one beautiful kiss. But it feels incredible for me, too. It's perfect and I feel like I'm going to leave an imprint behind on Hull House with my brain waves.

We're still kissing a few seconds later when I hear the sound of Cyn starting the bus back up. Morticia gives me one more smile, then heads back for the bus. A DarkSide bus has pulled up, which is our cue to get going.

I feel like I could float to the body dump as the sun sets, hitting the skyline just right, so the city looks like a matte painting in an old movie, glowing and golden and beautiful against a red cloud sky.

I rely on muscle memory to get through the rest of the tour, because my brain is too busy thinking, *I've been kissed. I've been kissed. I did it. I won't die unkissed!* It makes it a bit hard to think about what I'm doing.

Like we planned, Morticia asks to be let out near the Water

Tower, and when Cyn opens the door for her, she steps off into the crowd.

This time I run off and try to follow, half-expecting her to leave a shoe behind and sort of hoping she won't, because I know I'd follow her, and then, well, things could get complicated. But I can't just let her go without a good-bye.

"Wait!"

"Didn't you want me to just disappear?" she asks.

"I don't think 'want' is the right word," I say. "Is there a word for when you want something, but you also don't?"

"'Bittersweet'?"

"Something like that."

She smiles again, then says, "Good-bye, snuggle-puppy," gives me a very quick kiss, and slips into the crowd of Michigan Avenue tourists.

I didn't even get her last name. Or probably even her real first one.

She'll always be Morticia to me.

My name and info are up on the Mysterious Chicago website now. She can find me if she wants to. Maybe I'll see her again sometime.

I make my way back onto the bus and go through the motions of saying that we're on the grounds of an 1830s cemetery, so maybe she was a vanishing hitchhiker, but my knees are shaking, and no one thinks it was seriously a ghost sighting this time. They can tell I'm just kidding about it.

But I decide that I prefer to think of her as just a ghost. A real ghost. Who somehow had a couple of weeks to come back to life and have one more chance to kiss someone, because she never did when she was alive. Now she can go back to her grave, satisfied.

And I swept her off her feet.

She was owlblasted (first recorded in 1603). Elf-stricken (1699). Puckfoisted (1890).

By me.

I look up more words on the train home, trying to find a word for what I'm feeling, a word for feeling elated that something happened, even though it can never happen again. A word for being glad Morticia disappeared but also wishing she'd stayed. The only good historical synonym for "bittersweet" is "glycipricon," first recorded in 1599. And the only time it was recorded after that was once in 1621, in *Anatomy of Melancholy* by Robert Burton. "He saith our whole life is a glycipricon, a bitter sweet passion."

It was just a kiss with a girl I'll almost certainly never see again.

And the kiss wasn't even *us*, it was us standing in as proxies for Mary and Jane (or, anyway, that was the excuse I used).

But it's good to know that I'm not going to die without knowing how it feels to kiss someone properly. That I am capable of making people want to kiss me.

A couple across from me on the train make out like they're going for the gold.

The rumble of the train sounds like a round of applause.

Chapter Sixteen

The next morning I wake up to my phone buzzing again and again. Even more than it did the day the maniac shot up Crystal Lake. I roll over and check it to see a long list of messages.

ZOEY BABY:
There's a review about your tour last night. On a blog.

ZOEY BABY:
Wake up! LOL

ZOEY BABY:
ALARM CLOCK!

She's texting so fast that more messages come while I'm trying to write out a reply.

MEGAN:

You know I don't read reviews! It's like playing

chicken with my self-esteem.

ZOEY BABY

Relax. This one's good. Really good. They loved it.

ZOEY BABY:

Why did they think your girlfriend was on the
bus, though?

Shit.

I don't normally read reviews, but I follow the link Zoey
sent, since I already know it's a good one.

And it is a good one. But right in the middle of it, there's
a random line about "our tour guide's girlfriend" disappearing
from the tour toward the end. They thought I was just joking
about her being a ghost, and thought it was very cute.

I open the *OED* online and look up some quick words to
send Zoey.

MEGAN

Puzzling.

MEGAN:

Knurry (1615).

MEGAN:

Snaggled (1896).

A minute goes by, and then she sends one of her own:

ZOEY BABY

Sussy.

I have to look that one up. It means "suspicious."

I read through the whole review, trying to figure out what I should tell Zoey, exactly, and whether it might be better just to tell the truth and lay it on the line.

But ten minutes later she sends more texts.

ZOEY BABY:

FUCK YOU. I HATE YOU. DIE.

Then she sends me a link, and it brings me to a photo-sharing page with all of the blogger's pictures from the night before. Ones that weren't on the blog post.

There is a picture in the courtyard at Hull House, and in the background you can see me kissing Morticia, with a caption saying, *Our guide and her girlfriend sneak a kiss when they think no one is looking. Awwwww.*

My vision goes blurry for a second, and I try to send Zoey a message saying we weren't kissing as ourselves, but as Mary

Rozet Smith and Jane Addams (even though I know it sounds like a stupid excuse).

There is no response.

She has signed out of every online account we use to chat. When I try to send her offline messages, I get notifications back saying the accounts have been deactivated.

The only new thing I see from her in the next hour is an anonymous comment on that blog post, saying I am a fucking two-timing lying bitch and I suck.

I read it over and over again.

My stomach ties itself in knots. The blood drains from my face. My head swims, and I nearly throw up a couple of times.

She's completely right about me.

What I did was completely unacceptable. And I hate myself for making Zoey feel the way she must feel right now.

After over an hour of trying to get in touch with her, I spend some time just looking up names for myself in the *OED*, words like "hayne," "hinderling," "whelp," and "pilgarlic."

cittern-head (1598)
pode (1528)
ketterel (1572)
scabship (as in "her royal scabship") (1589)

There aren't enough words for what I am.

There is no blood in my heart, just some goopy black crud chugging along through my arteries.

I finally post a comment of my own on the blog post.

Please text me, Zoey. I can explain.

She never does.

And I stare at my phone all day, waiting.

The Blue Line is full of old women in raincoats.

And scab-scalped men with jowls down to about their collar bones.

Scruffy winos wearing winter coats in August.

Sinister looking jag-offs whose body spray infects the train car.

None of them are smiling. Today everyone on the train looks like they're heading out to rob a grave, or going back to their home in the sewer tunnels. And I feel like I belong with them. Like one of the raincoats should open like a cocoon so I can just fold myself in, hibernate all the way to the end of the line, and crawl out as one of them when the train gets to the airport, revealed at last as a a hideous slimy old hag.

This is real villainy. Being a villain is not singing and cackling in castles and holding your arms in the air as your minions fly above you. It's hurting people. Even people you care about.

When I get to the McDonald's, Cyn is waiting with the bus.

"You okay?" she asks. "You look like shit."

I shake my head, then break down and start crying into her shoulder.

She gives me a hug without making me tell her what's wrong first, then leads me onto the bus and shuts the door, so I can spill my guts in peace. She nods along, and when I'm done she hugs me and tells me I'm not a bad person.

"Listen," she says. "You didn't do anything you didn't have every right to do."

"I didn't have any right to cheat on Zoey," I say. "I never told her she had to send a picture of herself or I'd think of myself as a free agent."

"No one would blame you if you had, though," says Cyn. "You should have. I was afraid you were gonna go through life and never kiss anyone, all for someone who's actually a sixty-two-year-old man."

I exhale and wipe my eyes. My eyeliner is a mess. Right before the tour.

"But she understood me," I say. "I told her everything about me, and she didn't get freaked out. I may never find anyone like that again. If Morticia had read my stories, she never, ever would have kissed me."

Cyn leans back in her chair a little. She looks like she's about to say something comforting, then she stops.

"Wait," she says. "You say you told Zoey everything?"

"Yeah."

"Even about . . . our charities?"

I shake my head. "I classified that next to nude pictures that showed my face. Even she didn't have that level of clearance."

Cyn relaxes, gives me a big hug, says, "Ah, bless your twisted little heart," and lets me cry a bit more.

"Can you still go on with the tour tonight?" she asks. "I mean, I could do the tour and drive at the same time if I have to."

"I can manage," I say. "I need to think about something else for a while."

While we wait on the last party of two to arrive, a drunk college-age guy in a backward baseball cap hobbles up to me.

"Whuz this?" he slurs.

"Ghost tour," I say. "We take people around to murder sites, disaster sites, body dumps, and places like that."

"For real?"

"Uh-huh."

He looks at the bus. I can look at his eyeballs and practically see the booze sloshing around.

"Fucking awesome," he says. "Do you know the guy on *Ghost Encounters*?"

"Not that well," I say, lying to imply I'd ever met him, or wanted to meet him, at all. "But we have a lot of mutual friends."

"Seriously?"

"Sure, man."

When he asks how much the tour costs, I tell him "fifty bucks." That is more than it actually is, but it's the price of how much I'm willing to take to put up with a drunk in a backward baseball cap. He fishes two wadded up twenties and two fives out of his pocket and gets on board.

I start to regret it when I start warming up the crowd.

"All right," I say. "What do you guys want to see?"

"Ghosts!" someone says.

"You taking your top off!" says the drunk.

I ignore him as well as I can and say, "Ghosts! Perfect! Did anyone bring someone we can murder?"

"The trick," says Cyn, turning around and looking right at Drunky McLoserbro, "is for us to find someone who's traveling alone, paying in cash, so no one knows where he is and no one can trace him to the tour, and who doesn't know how to behave himself with a basic amount of propriety, so no one cares if he disappears."

Most people look over at the drunk guy, but he doesn't seem to notice that Cyn is talking about plotting his murder.

I look at her with a bit of a smirk. Obviously, this guy isn't a volunteer. But just knowing that she could punch him in the brain . . . I hate to say it feels good, but it does.

I tell myself that dealing with him gives me someone to hate besides myself for a while, but before we've gone two blocks on the tour, I wish I hadn't taken him on at any price, and I wish we could seriously punch him in the brain right where we are. He's one of those guys who just has to shout out an inappropriate response to everything I say. I point out the spot where Tillie Wolf was stabbed with an umbrella stick, and he shouts, "Awwww shit!"

"Look, man," I say, interrupting my opening talk. "There are kids on the tour tonight. Please conduct yourself accordingly."

I realize that a person getting stabbed in the face should be more disturbing than the word "shit," but still.

He says he'll behave, but he's drunk enough that he sort of forgets after a minute. He cheers when I say how long it took people who were hanged in Chicago to die. When I talk about the owner of the Iroquois Theatre cutting all the corners that made the fire so deadly, he keeps shouting, "Was he retarded?"

God.

Even when he's not shouting anything particularly problematic, it's distracting, disrespectful, and infuriating. Getting interrupted in the first couple of minutes throws the whole tour out of rhythm. Even Rick says he has trouble getting the atmosphere and feeling back if someone interrupts him in the opening monologue. It's where you set the mood for the whole thing.

When I get people off the bus to check out the Alley of Death and Mutilation, he stumbles along with a stupid, shit-eating grin.

I apologize to a woman who's on the tour with her two kids.

"Not much you can do about it," she says. "I own a coffee shop in Columbus, so I know. If you try to deal with him, he'll go straight to Yelp."

She walks right up to the guy herself and asks if he would keep it down around her kids. The guy smiles sheepishly and says, "Are you a ghost?" Then he laughs like he's just said the funniest thing in the world.

When I try to tell the Resurrection Mary story, his comments start to be more about me. "Are you her?" and "I'd give you a ride." Shit like that.

At a traffic light, Cynthia leans over to me and says, "Don't worry. You ever hear the expression 'I'm going owl-hunting and you just called out '*whoo?*'"

"No."

"Well, it's an expression. I'm douche-bag hunting, and this guy just called out '*bro.*'"

Normally, Cyn just stays on the bus during stops when we have people wander around, but this time she gets off with us at Hull House, leaving the bus running, and leads the guy around to the back of the house. I don't see them at all while I pad around the grounds, answering questions and suggesting good spots for photos.

When I call everyone back to the bus, the drunk is nowhere to be seen.

Neither is Cyn, for that matter.

I assume she ran into the bathroom at the UIC student center, right behind Hull House, so I kill time by telling everyone the tale of Thomas Ward, a story I found in the *Tribune* archives. He was shot by his brother (while he was trying to stab his mother) in his house back in 1902. Sightings of his ghost on the back porch got so common that the cops had to do crowd control. That house was right about where the student-center bathroom would be now.

"I just hope he isn't spying on Cyn in there right now," I say.

A couple of minutes later, when she still hasn't come back, I talk about the funeral home that stood near the site of the bathroom, where the undertakers allegedly tried to resurrect the body of a gangster named Nicholas "The Choir Singer" Viana after he was hanged back in 1920.

When I finish the story, Cyn's finally coming back. Alone.

"All right, my friends," she says as she hops back into the driver's seat. "Our drunken companion has taken leave of us."

Everyone claps.

"Did you kick him off?" someone asks.

"I persuaded him to run off and never be seen in the vicinity again," says Cynthia. "I don't like to tell people not to talk during tours, but when you're shouting out things like that in front of little kids . . . I don't care if he gives us a bad review. Doinkus probably won't even remember what company we were anyway."

"Yeah," I say. "He'll end up giving a bad review to Dark-Side."

"Maybe even the Al Capone guys," says Cyn.

Everyone chuckles with relief, and then I get to ask what has become my favorite question of all time: "Who wants to go to the body dump?"

Then I lead them in a cheerful chant of "Bo-dy dump! Bo-dy dump! Bo-dy dump!" that echoes down South Halsted Street.

For a few minutes I can lose myself in my work and just be happy again.

When we get to the body dump and everyone gets off the bus to explore the dead-end street, I hang back and ask Cyn what she told the drunk guy.

"Nothing," she says. "He asked me where the bathroom was, and I gave him bad directions."

"So we just ditched him?"

"Yep."

"I kinda thought you might have punched him in the brain."

"That's absurd," she says. "What would I do with the body?"

Having Mr. McLoserbro gone helps the second half of the tour, but we never really quite salvage the atmosphere on the bus, and any way you cut it, we only have eight people. When they get off the bus at the end, there's nothing left to distract me from what's going on in my life. I just go back to checking my phone, making sure I have notifications turned on for every app I used to talk to Zoey with, and seeing if by some chance Morticia might have tracked me down and e-mailed me or something. It's radio silence on all fronts.

Cyn is nice enough to drive me all the way home, even though it's way out of the way for her. As she drops me off, she suggests that it might help me start fresh if I cut my hair shorter.

"You think so?" I ask.

"I can bob it for you," she says. "You'd look exactly like Lillian Collier."

Chapter Seventeen

I try to sleep, but every time I close my eyes and start to drift off, I see the drunk asshole's face. I try to forget him, but then I start to think of Zoey and what a shitty person I am again, so I go back to focusing on how much I hated the drunk guy, who is probably even shittier.

In the middle of the night I look up words for "drunk" on the *OED* to distract myself. It's a treasure trove.

Cup-shotten (first recorded in 1330).

Tap-shackled (1604).

Swilled (1637).

Muzzed (1788).

Elephant trunk (1859). (I figure this is a thing you run into now and then where slang is made up of weird rhymes, like when "pork pies" meant "lies" in London in the 1800s.)

Loaded for bears (1890). (Yeah, no idea what the

hell people were thinking there.)

I try to memorize and repeat them to get my mind off of everything. It helps a little, but not much. Maybe even that guy never cheated on anyone. But I never really do get any sleep. Just a few minutes here and there. And when I nod off at all, I wake up sweating from bad dreams that I'm grateful not to remember.

In the morning I go to the library downtown, just to give myself something to do besides think about Zoey and Morticia and Drunky and everything else. I'm going to focus on Lillian Collier instead.

I'm pretty sure I've found every single piece of information you could get about her from the old newspapers that are available online, but I know there will probably be more stories in the defunct Chicago papers that only exist on microfilm reels now. Good ones, too. Stories by reporters who were actually on the scene. Most of the stuff about her online is from out-of-town papers, really. They might be third-hand stories that no one bothered to fact-check.

The library on State Street is a thing of beauty on the outside, with high windows and a gorgeous green ornamental roof with gargoyle owls, but the microforms room on the third floor is very, very plain. Beige microfiche readers, beige walls, and beige cabinets full of microfilm reels. And three beige people using them.

The machines are not exactly intuitive, and no two of them

are quite the same. Finding the reels I want is easy enough, but I have to try four machines before I find one that I like. One has a bulb that's entirely too dim. One can't seem to rotate the pages the right way. The next just won't focus. And even when I find one that works like I need it to, finding information is a hell of a lot harder than it is on online newspaper-archive sites, where I can search using keywords.

But it's worth the trouble. Reading the papers on micro-film feels totally different from searching them online. Rather than getting individual articles, I'm scrolling through the entire actual newspapers, wading past headlines about Vice President Coolidge, the Bonus Act, the new Pope, and everything else that was going on in February of 1922, when the Wind Blew Inn was raided. I read ads for lunchrooms on State Street with cheap oyster stew, for the latest tub blouses at Marshall Field's, for Mr. Edison's newest music player, and for lectures by old men who knew Abraham Lincoln.

It feels as close as I can probably get to time travel. These are the papers Lillian read, the events she and her friends would have talked about. It's like I'm dipping into her world.

I get distracted reading articles about fights over the price of streetcar fare for a while, but eventually I find one new article in the *Chicago Daily News* from when Lillian Collier (they call her "Colley") was first hauled into court for allegedly running an immoral house. It has tons of new details about that night that I haven't seen before:

"We've been called over to that place about four times," testified the sergeant. "There was always action over at the Wind Blew Inn. . . . There was an immoral painting on the wall near the door."
"It isn't immoral," interrupted Miss Colley. "It's a futuristic painting of a silo."

The "futuristic silo" must have looked like a dick. Ha.

"We found several persons under the stairway. They may have fallen there. There are only two stories in this place, and I'm only telling one of 'em."
Then Miss Colley demanded her Wind Blew Innings.
"I deny that my place was disorderly," she declared. "The Wind Blew Inn was designed as a place where artists and writers could foregather to eat and discuss the arts. The windows were kept gray to give that cathedral interior effect to the dining room. The plumber's candles give it a low light. I tried to make it a place of artistic tone and spiritual uplift— as much like Greenwich Village as possible. But it wasn't possible because the dirt is so different in Greenwich Village. Despite these handicaps, I maintain that it was the best restaurant ever made out of a gasoline station."

ADAM SELZER

I'll bet Ricardo would have loved the place.

I'm still scrolling through the *Daily News*, looking for more on Lillian, when I notice that Edward Tweed has come into the microfilm room. He looks strange without the cowboy hat he usually wears; his hair up top is thinning.

"Doing some research?" he asks.

I nod. "Lillian Collier. Flapper who disappeared."

"I know who she was. Wind Blew Inn."

This is interesting news.

"Any chance you know what became of her?" I ask.

"Tuberculosis," he says. "Died in 1925."

I look over at him, away from the microfilm. "Where'd you find that? I've been going crazy trying to find a death record for her."

"I don't remember offhand, but I tell stories about her on the tours now and then," he says. "Where did *you* hear about her?"

"From Cynthia."

"Well, where do you think she learned about her from?" He chuckles. "I taught her story to Ricardo when he worked for me, and I guess he told it to Cynthia. I've got her death certificate in my files someplace. But if you can't find the data, neither can the customers. That's my motto."

I shake my head. "I try to stick to primary sources."

"That's noble and all," he says. "But mythology has value too. It gives the city character."

I look away, not so much to brush him off as because I'm getting wrapped up in a story about some sort of Ponzi scheme scandal in a 1922 paper.

"Listen," he says. "I hate that we're supposed to be rivals. It's foolish. We should be colleagues. Rolling with the rotters, you know? We're all in it together."

"I like to call it murdermongering," I say.

"Murdermongering!" he says. "Love it. Why don't we go have a drink?"

"I'm a bit busy now. Maybe after work sometime."

"Well, that would never do. If Cynthia Fargon saw you meeting up with me, she might kill us both and turn us into tour attractions."

I start rewinding the microfilm and try not to react to that at all.

Is Tweed working for the cops? Does someone know something?

Then his tone gets more serious. "I'm not entirely kidding there," he says. "She hasn't told you that Lillian is haunting any particular place, has she?"

"She says there's a rumor about Bughouse Square."

He nods. He probably made that rumor up himself. But he might have the 1925 thing right. He seems awfully confident about it.

"We should talk a bit," he says. "You want to go see some shrunken heads?"

I give him the oddest look I am capable of, then say, "Please tell me that wasn't a pickup line."

"No, I'm being totally literal," he says with a smile. "About a block from here is a building that has the clubhouse for the Adventurers Club on the sixth or seventh floor, and they've got the world's largest private collection of shrunken heads. My buddy's a member, so I can get us in if anyone's there."

"This sounds like the opening of a ghost story," I say. "Flimflam man meets pretty girl in a library, offers to take her to see a dead body, next thing you know I'm the new head in the collection, right?"

He laughs again. With his curly mustache, his beard, and the twinkle in his eye, he seems like a jolly old elf.

I take out my phone and pretend like I'm answering a text, but really I'm looking up the Adventurers Club. From a quick glance on Google I can see that they do have shrunken heads in their clubhouse. Real ones.

Every cell in my brain tells me that I should turn him down, but how the fuck can I say no to the chance to see the world's largest private collection of shrunken heads? I'm not *that* kind of girl.

"All right," I say. "Lead the way."

The half-block area around the library used to be called Hell's Half-Acre. At one time it was home to something like four dozen whiskey bars, three dozen pawn shops, two dozen brothels, and a couple opium dens. People could rob you here with something close to immunity because they knew you would never go to the police and admit you'd been in the neighborhood after dark in the first place.

Somewhere along the line, though, it was gentrified. Now it's mostly yuppies.

Plus a clubhouse full of shrunken heads.

And, according to some website, a preserved whale dick.

Oh, the possibilities.

"What sort of group is the Adventurers Club?" I ask.

"Guys who climb Mount Everest and go on safari and stuff."

"Bunch of lumberjack-looking white guys. Got it."

He laughs. "I know at least one Asian woman who's in it, so it's not all white guys. It's officially members-only, and I doubt you qualify, but I'll do my best to get you inside."

"Hey," I say. "I've been on Space Mountain sixteen times."

"I don't know if that counts, but I guess you do go on tours with Cyn and Ricardo. That's adventurous. I don't know how much you know about Cynthia Fargon. Where'd she find you?"

"She was my babysitter one summer when I was a kid."

We step into the lobby of a building with a bookshop on the first floor, and he hits a buzzer next to a label that says "Adventurers Club." So far, at least, his story checks out. He isn't just taking me to his lair or whatever.

There's no answer, so he hits it again. Still silence.

"Rats," he says. "Must be empty today. I don't have a key, personally."

"So no shrunken heads?" I ask.

"Sorry. But while I've got you here, I do need to talk to you about something."

"As long as it's not something in your pants."

"I'm being serious. Listen. You should really be careful of Cynthia."

I notice that the traveling-salesman glimmer in his eye is gone, and his face has fallen. This is the kind of face and tone people get when they're ready to say, "Enough small talk about how great my dead brother was. What's the absolute least I can spend on the funeral?"

"Cyn's one of the best friends I've ever had," I say.

"Did she ever say anything to you about some secret way to turn people into ghosts?"

I shake my head, telling myself it isn't lying if I don't say anything.

"Well, there's a technique that about six people know, and I think Cynthia is one of them."

"How would she know about it?" I ask.

"I don't know. That's a mystery I'm still working on, just like you're working on Lillian Collier. But I've been in the business long enough to have heard about it, and I'm afraid there may be a chance that Cynthia's not only learned it, she's planning on having you turn into Lillian's ghost."

I let that hang in the air and stare at Edward Tweed. If he's just trying to freak me out, he's doing a good job. This feels like a serious warning.

"If you died and your ghost started haunting someplace she was associated with, she could say that it was Lillian's ghost," he explains. "You'd look close enough."

When I just stare at him without saying anything, he goes on.

"I mean, your hair's not quite right, but I don't think that technique makes ghosts distinct enough to see those kinds of details."

When I can finally talk, all I say is "She wouldn't do that."

"Think about it," he says. "Did you have any experience in running tours? Public speaking? Acting? Anything like that?"

"I was in some plays in high school. She saw me in one."

"I don't want to put you down, because I know you're a great guide, but it sounds to me like she hand-picked you without caring whether you were any good or not just because she knew you had the right look."

I shrug. "She knew I could do research well and I have a good head for this kind of work. I'm a funeral-home kid."

"Ah." He chuckles a bit, hits the buzzer again, and says, "Well, I don't know how much you trust her, but I really recommend you reconsider. Keep your eyes open. Especially if she suggests you start dressing more like Lillian or something."

I can't help but think of her suggestion that I let her bob my hair.

"I trust her."

He leans back against the wall, then idly hits the buzzer yet again as he gives me a look over the top of his glasses.

"Like you probably trusted her not to tell anyone about Zoey? Or your Disney villain stories?"

The moment he says that, the whole vestibule is bathed in a flash of blue light from a police car zipping by, and I think I hear an explosion in the distance. A second or two goes by that are just lost to me. I think I stare at him. My jaw probably drops. But when those few seconds are gone I don't remember them anymore, like my brain is trying to wipe away the fact that he said that before it can turn into a memory.

It doesn't work.

My vision goes blurry, and all the sound from the street goes silent for a moment. The ding ding ding of the register in the bookstore that stands beside the entryway gets louder, and I stop caring about shrunken heads.

"Where did you hear about that?" I ask.

"Cynthia told me."

He's making eye contact, but it suddenly feels like I'm naked in front of him, and he's checking out my whole body. Like I'm beyond naked. Like he can see everything, including my internal organs. Like he can see right through me.

Cyn couldn't have told him about Zoey. She wouldn't have told him. Not Tweed. She hates him.

"You're full of shit," I say. "You must have hacked my computer or something."

"I'm hopeless with computers," he says.

"Then you got Saltis to do it for you."

"He's even worse."

"Then you've got our bus bugged. You've been spying on us."

"No. Nothing like that. Cyn told me the other night."

My stomach twists around, and even though I haven't eaten all day, I feel the bile rising up inside me.

This old man knows about my stories.

This. Old. Creep.

He knows about me. What has he pictured me doing? What is he imagining right now?

Tweed starts to say something else, but I run out of the entryway, through the tiny park next door and around into the nearest alley, where I throw up into a smelly metal dumpster.

"Purgament. Fellowred. Cunnigar."

I repeat *OED* synonyms for swear words to myself while I zombie-walk my way to a Blue Line stop, trying to calm down. It doesn't work. When a train comes, I find the least-crowded car and curl up into a ball in an empty seat. Fetal position.

Tweed knows about Zoey.

Tweed knows about my stories.

Oh, fuck.

Godemiche. Stercory. Hindwin. Nockhole. Stupid fucking Berkeley Hunt.

As the train starts to move, I wonder if maybe Tweed was Zoey the whole time, an idea that absolutely disgusts me. But that one, at least, doesn't seem plausible. I'd been with Zoey for a while before Ed had any idea who the hell I was.

Either he hacked my computer, he spied on us, or Cyn blabbed.

I don't know which theory I hate most.

If he hacked my computer, he knows everything. What goes on in my stories. Maybe even the stories Zoey didn't get to see. Not to mention that the hard drive contained pictures of me that I sure as hell didn't want him to see. No face in the worst of them, but he'd know it was me.

If Cyn told him, that would be a bit of a relief, in a way, since it meant he only knew what she'd told him about the stories, and that couldn't be too much. I never showed them to her or anything. But that would mean that she stabbed me in the back.

And that she might be planning to *literally* stab me in the back to turn me into a substitute for Lillian Collier's ghost.

The best-case scenario is that he's bugged our bus and has been spying on us.

That's it.

I tell myself that it has to be it.

I get off the train at the Medical District stop to puke again, this time into a garbage can, then wait for another train and ride straight home.

The reeks and fumes of my puddled brain probably leave a ghost behind on the Blue Line.

Chapter Eighteen

I don't leave the house again until the next day, when I have to go run back-to-back tours at seven and ten.

I don't talk to Rick or Cyn during the day; I just stay in my room, trying to get ahold of Zoey and trying to decide whether or not I hope Cyn is planning to turn me into a ghost, if it meant that Edward Tweed hasn't hacked my computer and seen my stories.

None of our "charity work" has led to a ghost so clear anyone could tell who the ghost was, but we aren't exactly using the best candidates. Cyn's always saying so. According to what she'd read in Marjorie's papers, a volunteer would leave a much weaker imprint than someone who wasn't expecting to die that day.

There are lots of X factors. Younger people would leave better imprints than older ones. People who are pregnant or on their period would leave a stronger one, and all of our volunteers are way too old for that sort of thing.

But I'm not.

In fact, I'm a perfect candidate.

So it might work. If Cyn timed things just right, she might be able to make me into a maximum-strength ghost that people could not only see clearly, but might mistake for the ghost of Lillian Collier.

More than once, I remember that she offered to bob my hair and make me look more like Lillian.

And I tell myself that I still trust her.

But I'm glad I'm working with Rick, not her, for my tours tonight.

On Clark Street every tourist seems like a clone of Drunky McLoserbro. Guys in backward baseball caps. Girls wearing Mardi Gras beads even though it's nowhere near Mardi Gras time, or the right city. All visibly drunk at six o'clock.

Rick and Aaron Saltis are singing a song together outside of the DarkSide bus:

> Ta-ra-ra boom-de-ay!
> We have no tour today!
> Our riders passed away!
> Don't look at me that way!

It doesn't seem as funny to me as it normally would.

As soon as Rick sees me, he pats Aaron on the back, tells

him to have a good tour, then puts his arm around me, leading me over toward our bus.

"How you holding up?" asks Rick. "I heard you got in some hot water with Zoey."

"You could say that."

This almost seems like ancient history today. Yesterday's problem. But it's still a thing. And now it bubbles back up to the surface.

"But you need to dish, sis. You kissed Morticia?"

I nod. "At Hull House."

"Were her lips super cold? Did her breath smell like the grave?"

I shake my head. "Super warm, and mint."

"Mint," he says. "She *planned* to kiss you."

"You think?"

"No one smells like mint unless they're planning to kiss someone."

"Maybe she just likes gum."

"Ghosts don't chew gum. Normally."

Rick gets distracted talking to Pierre the necklace guy, and I climb onto the bus and start looking over the dashboard, down in the Rubbermaid bin where we keep tools and extra mic cables and things, and everywhere else, thinking maybe I can find some gadget Ed is using to bug the bus.

But I don't find anything.

I manage to keep my shit together and put on a pretty

decent show for two tours that night. In fact, they're very good tours. I'm energetic. I'm yelling, "She splattered to a messy death right where that guy is standing!" at passersby. I'm milking every joke and every gasp line, trying to push the darkness away. They're maybe my best tours ever.

It always helps when we get cool pictures or have a spooky time at one of the stops, though. And that happens tonight. I get a real boost from several really creepy photos at Hull House. Vaguely human forms on people's pictures, better than anything we've gotten after charity work.

Cyn and I never took any volunteers to Hull House.

But it's the last place I saw Drunky alive.

That night, after trying to fall asleep in bed for hours, I sneak downstairs and sleep, or try to sleep, in one of the caskets, thinking that maybe I'll feel more at home in one of those. I used to get in them when I was a kid. They're surprisingly comfortable. Roomy, too. Even now that I'm much older than I was the last time I got in one, there's plenty of space to move around and mess with my phone.

I look online to see if there's anything about a young white guy who's gone missing in Chicago. Nothing.

She couldn't have killed him. What would she have done with the body?

Still, the last place I saw that drunken guy she "got rid of" seemed haunted tonight. Much more than it usually does.

If Cyn got rid of him, that makes it seem a lot more likely that she'd be plotting to do away with me, too. Maybe she was testing the waters, seeing if a younger person who didn't volunteer does leave a stronger imprint.

Even thinking about Zoey is better than thinking about this.

While I lay there, I send a handful of texts to Zoey, hoping she'll answer.

MEGAN:

I'm sorry.

MEGAN:

It wasn't what it looked like. You've got to at
LEAST let me explain.

MEGAN:

Please, at least come fight with me.

MEGAN:

I did some bad things this summer. Not really bad,
but . . . not legal. Some people would think they
were really bad. Like, really, really bad.

MEGAN:

I am a real fucking villain. But nothing makes me
feel as bad as what I did to you.

MEGAN:

I'm in a coffin right now and I feel like it's where

people like me belong.

MEGAN:

Please answer.

MEGAN:

I need you to say you don't hate me.

She never replies.

At three a.m., I wake up when my phone buzzes, thinking it might be her.

It's Cyn.

SWITCHBLADE CYNTHIA FARGON:

You still wanna do the hair bob? Come by around noon.

Chapter Nineteen

When you have reason to believe that someone may be plotting to murder you, it's probably not wise to go to their place, alone, for the sole purpose of having them come at your head with sharp objects.

But killing me at her apartment while bobbing my hair wouldn't do Cynthia much good in the long run. If she's going to ghost me, she'll want to do it in Bughouse Square or someplace where anything I leave behind could function as Lillian Collier's ghost. I'm probably safe anywhere as far off the tour route as Rick and Cyn's apartment in Humboldt Park.

And anyway, being at their place could be a good chance to do some detective work. Look for clues, ask her subtle questions, see if she lets anything slip.

So I decide to let Cyn cut my hair.

I take the Blue Line from Forest Park through the city, past the Loop, and into Humboldt Park, which is one of those neighborhoods that's supposed to be getting safer and fancier (gentrified), but still turns up on the news a lot for shootings and stuff. Cyn and Rick say they're in the "demilitarized zone," but nothing between the train stop and the three-flat where they live seems rough to me at all; it's full of dog walkers, old men pushing churro carts, and kids playing on scooters.

Cyn is sitting on her stoop, reading and smoking, when I walk up the sidewalk. I haven't seen her in person since Edward told me that she told him about Zoey, and it's awkward to actually have her right there in front of me.

She's smiling. Clueless about how much I've been thinking about her, obviously.

"You ready for this?" she asks.

"Ready as I'll ever be."

She leads me through the front door and up the steps to their apartment, which is the third floor of the three-flat. The stairway is made of rotting wood covered in chipped orange paint; the boards bend below Cyn's feet as she walks up. Inside, you can tell it was a nice place once upon a time—like, the crown molding is made with actual plaster, not some prefab stuff from Home Depot. But now the paint is peeling, the floor is warped, and there are a couple of spots where duct tape is covering holes in the drywall. Everything is drowning in piles of dirty laundry. I see stains I wish I hadn't.

On the couch beside the laundry there's a lanky rat-faced guy with a hairstyle that I guess would be a mohawk if it was sticking up, only it isn't. It's just lying down across his scalp. He's topless and filthy and appears to be stoned.

"This is Punk Rock James," says Cyn. "Old friend from college. Fellow archaeology student."

"Hi," I say to him, as he gives me a silent nod.

"Rick's working at the home today," Cyn says, leading me past James and into her bedroom. "Grab a seat on the desk chair; I'll get some newspapers to throw down."

Her bedroom is so small that it was probably a closet originally. Or maybe the place was actually a one-bedroom but some landlord made it into a two-bedroom by putting up a wall in the middle of the original one. There's just barely room for a desk, a mirror, and a twin-size bed, which looks too small for her and Rick to do it on. Maybe his is bigger.

To get to the desk chair, I have to wade through a regular pool of dirty laundry, cigarette ashes, junk mail, books, old fliers, and empty bottles. The walls are covered with band posters, and a bunch of headless dolls sit among the cosmetics and hygiene products on the desk. The necks on the decapitated dolls are about the only empty spaces in the whole room. They don't seem as cool to me today as they would have a week ago.

Cyn sets her phone to play some punk band, disappears for a second, then comes back with a pair of scissors, singing along with the song coming from the phone, which is about Sherlock Holmes taking drugs.

"This is Stiffs, Incorporated," she says. "Nineties punk.

Their songs were about Jack the Ripper and Edgar Allan Poe and stuff. We'd probably call them 'steampunk' now."

"Nice," I say.

"Only about six people bought their second album, but the guy from My Chemical Romance says it was their biggest influence."

"I can kind of hear the connection."

"You hear it a lot more on the second album than this one. I'll send you a link."

Cyn spins the desk chair around a couple of times, making me a bit dizzy, then runs her fingers through my hair.

"How long did it take you to grow it this long?"

"A while."

She grabs two handfuls of hair from the bottom, the red half, and starts to hold the locks up, sculpting my hair to simulate various styles.

"So what kind of bob are we talking?" she asks. She raises it up and says "Irene Castle?" Then she manipulates it around and says, "Clara Bow?" Then she moves it more. "Mary Pickford?"

"I think the first one," I say. "That's the most like Lillian. Irene Castle."

"Got it." She runs her fingers through it a few more times, petting me like a cat.

Then she snips off the first red lock in one move and goes

to work as the guy from Stiffs, Inc. shouts out, "Quick, Watson, bring the needle!" on the speakers.

"The other day Rick was asking me what you were like when you were a kid," she says.

"What did you tell him?"

"That you were pretty much the same, really. Didn't you even make up stories about villains winning and taking the princesses into their dungeons back then, too?"

Snip, snip, snip.

"Uh-huh."

"I imagine what goes on in the dungeons now is a little different, though."

"Maybe not as much as you'd think."

The Sherlock Holmes song ends, another guitar riff starts, and Cynthia keeps working. I look into her face in the mirror, looking for a hint of guilt or something, some sort of clue. She seems totally collected, as always.

Mirror, mirror, on the wall. Should I trust that face at all?

Snip, snip, snip.

All the red that made up the lower part of my hair is gone now. I'm no longer two-toned.

"Know what would be really crazy?" she asks. "If Lillian Collier were actually still alive and living at the home and wanted to die."

"There's no way she's still alive," I say. "If she was nineteen or twenty in 1922, she'd be about the oldest woman in the country by now."

"Yeah, we don't have anyone quite that old. I think our oldest person is a hundred and two."

"She'd be older than that."

"Shame," she says. "She'd be a perfect ghost to have on the tour, wouldn't she?"

I shudder involuntarily, and she screws up a snip because my head moves, clipping a part she didn't mean to.

"You shuddered."

"Sorry."

"There's an old superstition that when you shudder involuntarily, it means someone just stepped on the place that will be your grave someday."

"Yeah, I've heard that."

Punk Rock James is walking around in the living room now.

Fuck, is she going to bury me under the floor?

If so, isn't Cyn worried that she'll hear the beating of my hideous heart, interrupting right while she and Rick are doing it? Or at least that I'll stink the place up?

She snips around the mistake and covers it up.

The next Stiffs, Inc. song turns out to be a song about marrying Mary Pickford, the silent-film star. One line goes "It doesn't really matter that you're dead. . . ."

Cyn grabs the sides of my head and I nearly panic, thinking

maybe she's going to break my neck or punch my brain, but instead she just runs her fingers through my hair and shakes it out, sending strands flying.

Sitting still is hard.

She picks the scissors back up.

"How old was Marjorie Kay Stone when she died?" I ask.

"I think two hundred and thirty-six."

"Ho ho ho."

Snip, snip, snip.

"Why do you ask?"

"You didn't punch *her* in the brain, did you?"

Cyn laughs out loud, but doesn't quite deny it. Instead she says, "Everyone has secrets. That's why they call them secrets."

Then she laughs again and says that bit of nonsense was something Marjorie used to say.

Snip, snip, snip.

"Rick and I got rid of a drunk at Death Corner the other night," she says.

"Oh yeah?"

"Yeah. Way rid of him."

Snip, snip, snip.

For a second I actually feel better. Rick's not in on the brain-punching, as far as I know. I'd decided that maybe she could have hid Drunky in the bushes at Hull House, but there'd be nowhere to put a body at Death Corner.

Then I think of Punk Rock James, sitting out in the living

room. A guy with an archaeology degree, covered in dirt.

He could have helped get rid of bodies. She could have texted him while the bus was stopped at Hull House, had him hiding behind the fence at Death Corner, and then had him help take care of things. Maybe.

Snip, snip, snip.

I think about all this while Cyn works, and while the song goes into a section where the guy sings, "We're all quite sane . . . quite sane . . . quite sane . . ." again and again. It is obvious that the singer, or the character he's playing, is *not* quite sane.

"Hey," I say. "Did I tell you I heard Saltis say he's the one who's talking to Ghostly Journeys?"

"Him?" she asks. "Well, I guess we're in the clear there, then. No one's gonna meet with that doinkus and decide to go into business with him."

Snip, snip, snip.

"Hey, you wanna go do a proper ghost investigation one of these nights?" she asks. "I'm not sure anyone's ever done one in Bughouse Square."

There it is. She's luring me out to Bughouse Square.

Snip, snip, snip.

I try to stay calm.

"Maybe," I say. "I sometimes forget that I don't really believe in ghosts, you know?"

"Right." Then she laughs, like the kind of laugh you laugh when you have a secret.

As the song ends, she snips off a few more strands of hair, then leans down so her face is next to mine in the mirror, blows a few stray hairs from the back of my neck, and says, "There."

It looks good. Classic, yet stylish.

I go into the bathroom and change into a simple black dress that I brought in my backpack, and when I take out the lip ring and check myself out in the mirror, I look like a whole different person, from a whole other era.

Like I was a teenager long enough ago that I ought to be dead by now.

The next night I have a tour with Rick driving.

There's a big crowd milling around on Clark Street, and they're all looking for the DarkSide Tours bus. For every person who checks in to Mysterious Chicago, two or three come to ask us if they're in the right place for DarkSide.

"You're in the right place," we tell them, "but I don't see their bus yet. Just hang around. They'll be here."

Rick looks down in the dumps. Apparently he and Cyn were up arguing all night over whether we should still be pursuing the TV thing.

"I can see her point," he says. "It would still probably be better with us doing it than any other company. But still. I don't want to wreck all my credibility as a tour guide just to be on something that might only last one season anyway."

"Well, once it's canceled you can always go around saying

it was fake," I say. "Then you'll have more credibility to tell everyone the TV shows are all phony."

"That's better than the points Cyn was making," he says. "But they'd probably make us sign all kinds of forms saying we'll never talk, or they can sue us back to the stone age. They'd probably own our asses. And they aren't exactly going to make us rich for one season of a cable show."

A middle-aged woman with chipmunk cheeks and a T-shirt with a puppy on it checks in with five friends. Each of them has more makeup on than a corpse who died with severe jaundice at an open-casket viewing. I guess by their accents that they're a "Girls' Week Out" group from somewhere down south.

"We're the fun ones," one says.

I have already learned that this almost always means "We're the drunk ones."

"This is gonna be scary, right?" the woman in the puppy shirt asks.

"Terrifying," I assure her.

"It better be," says one of her friends. "I'm counting on wetting my pants."

Her friends all crack up in the way that only drunken middle-aged idiots can.

"Y'all are the tour guide?" the first one asks, looking me up and down. "Are y'all supposed to be scary?"

"I'm terrifying, madam," I say. "I pour the blood of Christian babies on my Cocoa Puffs."

Half of her friends laugh and half of them make grossed-out disapproving faces, but all of them step onboard.

The DarkSide customers—enough to just about fill one bus—are still waiting around when we leave. The bus is there, but there's no sign of Tweed or Saltis to check them in. Strange.

Puppy-Shirt Woman and her friends are not fun passengers. They spend the whole tour talking among themselves about how awful the city is.

"Everything is so expensive here."

"The houses don't have yards."

"The buildings are too close together."

"I haven't seen a single Wal-Mart since we've been here."

"Ugh, why would a Walgreens have a revolving door?" (I'm not sure why that offends them so much, but they all agree that it's a crime against nature.)

Mostly they just ignore the fact that there's a tour going on at all, but at one point when I get to a pause, one of them takes advantage and interrupts.

"Excuse me?" she asks. "I have a question. How come no one in this town can drive? People drive so crazy here."

"You saying I can't drive?" asks Rick, who doesn't even bother to cover up his annoyance.

"Well, if the shoe fits," the woman says. "God, Donna, look how much gas costs here!"

Rick stews at the wheel.

They aren't an uncommon kind of customer, really. I'd say

we get the "People must be crazy to live here" speech at least once a week from tourists whose main goal on their trip is to assure themselves that they're better off in their little hick town than they would be in a city. These ones in particular think they're so great because they live in a land where houses are cheap, Wal-Marts are plentiful, and all the signs are in English.

I hear them making fun of my witch boots.

What a bunch of windfuckers.

But then again, I suppose that when you stay in your small town, you are probably safe from being killed for the sake of being an attraction on a ghost tour.

So there's that.

When we get out of the bus to look around at the body dump, the Puppy-Shirt Woman notices a heavy blanket slumped against the fence, with a battered old suitcase lying beside it.

"That looks like a dead body," she says.

"It's probably some homeless guy sleeping," I say.

"No, I think it's a body," she says. "Maybe the suitcase is full of money."

I try to stop her, but she trots right up to the guy, like she has every right to wake him up, and lifts the blanket. When she does, she freezes for a second, then screams at the top of her lungs.

Rick, who's been showing a couple which part of the vacant lot the "glass-bending factory" would have been in, runs over to the blanket as the woman backs away from it. He looks under it for himself, then shouts out, "All right, folks, let's get on back on the bus."

He personally escorts Puppy-Shirt back. She's hysterical. I hang outside, wondering what the hell was under there, and he comes to join me when everyone is onboard.

"Is it a body?" I ask.

He leads me away from the bus and into the road.

"Uh, yeah," he says. "It's Aaron Saltis. From DarkSide."

Puppy-Shirt is still screaming. She says she's going to sue us.

That one woman she's with is probably wetting herself, just like she always wanted.

Chapter Twenty

The blanket-covered body lies by the side of the road, brushing against the tall grass. A rat runs out from under the blanket and scampers into the weeds. I resist the urge to throw up. It's not easy.

It takes me a minute to remember that I just told Cyn yesterday that Aaron was the one trying to bring Ghostly Journeys to Chicago. So she had a motive.

Rick and I stand outside while everyone else sits on the bus, looking at the covered body from across the road, as Rick calls the cops. When he hangs up, he says, "Well, this is a new one."

"How did he . . ."

"Suicide, it looks like. You know the sonofabitch did it at a tour stop just to fuck with me, too. Goddamn. I thought we were cool, he and I."

"Maybe he did it here as a favor, so we'd have a new ghost to look for."

"He didn't believe in ghosts. Not even a little. This could only have been to fuck with us."

I tell Rick about how Aaron Saltis had been in talks with Ghostly Journeys. "You think maybe a meeting with them went badly?"

"Who knows? Maybe."

"You sure it was a suicide?"

"There's a gun by his hand, and it looks like maybe there's a note. I'm not going near it, though."

I nod, and the police car pulls in, with an ambulance in tow, seconds later. I hope to God, or whoever is out there, that the funeral isn't at my house.

The cops talk to us first, and we tell them who we are, what we were doing on the dead-end street in a tour bus, and all of that. Basic stuff. The cop who does most of the talking, Officer Jackson, has a Clark Gable-type mustache right above his lip that leaves a lot of space under his nose. He agrees with Rick that it's probably a suicide, but he can't comment on the record.

"I didn't think he hated us that much," I say. "And he didn't seem suicidal."

"Hey," says Officer Jackson. "People kill themselves because of some embarrassing moment that happened fifty years ago. They kill themselves because they find out they're sick. Or some depression they beat years ago came back. It's like cancer, you know. Depression. You never really beat it."

"I know," says Rick. "Still . . . this. God."

"You say he was an actor, right?" asks Officer Jackson. "Drinking problem? I find that a lot of actors have one of those."

Rick nods. "I'm guessing drugs, too, in this case."

"I always got the impression he'd fried part of his brain years ago," I say.

Officer Jackson nods. "It's a shame."

After they're done with the two of us, the cops bring Puppy-Shirt off the bus to talk to her, since she was the one who found the body. I'm kind of amused when they seem more suspicious of her than they do of us—they don't seem to believe that she'd just randomly see a lumpy form under a blanket and decide to lift the blanket, even after someone in authority (me—ha!) told her not to.

After that the cops free us to go, so we drive away, but no one wants to hear any more ghost stories after that, so we just head back to the Rock and Roll McDonald's. We offer a refund to anyone who wants their money back, but only Puppy-Shirt's party takes us up on it. The rest seem to realize that we didn't personally plant a body there just to traumatize them.

For a minute, after they've all left, Rick and I just sit there on the empty bus. I'm feeling numb, like my brain just refuses to process one more bad thing. He's been holding his emotions together, but once the customers are gone, he loses it.

The blood drains from his face and he lets his head fall onto the steering wheel, like the effort not to break down in front of the customers took everything he had out of him.

"Jesus," he says. "Not two nights ago Saltis and I were standing right there on the sidewalk, chatting and joking around. He didn't seem like he was depressed."

It's dark now. The nightclub people are crowding the sidewalk. A couple of them try to sing along with "Don't Fear the Reaper" as it blasts from the outdoor speakers at the Hard Rock Cafe across the street.

Rick and I share memories of Aaron for a bit, though I don't have many, then he calls Cyn to give her the lowdown. I can't hear what she's saying, so I can't parse her words for clues.

But this doesn't look good.

Why the hell would Saltis have killed himself like that?

All of the stuff Cyn and I have done—all of the "ghosting"—was to get the company off the ground. It was a good deed for the volunteers, but our motives were, honestly, mostly selfish.

Would she have killed Aaron Saltis to protect our interests?

And maybe made him into a new ghost at the body dump while she was at it?

Rick drives me all the way home to Forest Park in the tour bus.

"Shit," he says, as we merge onto the interstate. "I'm trying not to see upsides here. The guy died. That sucks."

"Naturally."

"Of course, this probably means no Ghostly Journeys coming to town, if he was their contact. It'll set them back, at least."

"Probably."

"Won't be good for Tweed, either."

I don't even mention that he could have left behind an imprint right on our tour route, too. I won't be going to the body dump for a while. Maybe never again.

OED words fly through my head as I try to raze the troubles out of my brain to be replaced with strange words for bodily fluids and sex acts. It helps. A little.

When we get to Forest Park, we sit in the bus at the end of my block, just staring into space, looking at the funeral home.

"Well, weird day, little sis," he says.

I don't want Rick to leave. I don't want to be alone.

"Wanna go to Brown Cow, get some ice cream?" I ask. "Or a bar? I could probably get in if I'm with you."

He shakes his head. "I'd better call Edward. Offer condolences. No matter how much I can't stand the guy. He might even need me to cover a tour or two. I'll do it. Gotta put aside rivalries at times like this."

"Right."

When I get out I walk backward, watching him drive off, so I don't feel alone until the last second, when the lights disappear.

ADAM SELZER

As soon as I'm in my room, a feeling of abject dread flows over me. Envelopes me. It penetrates every pore and saturates me. I don't want to turn around because I'm afraid I'll see something behind me. I don't want to look ahead. I don't want to close my eyes.

I get into my bed and cover every inch of my body with my sheets, like I did when I was a little kid having nightmares. I would wake up from those and think that I was safe as long as no single part of me was visible to any monster or murderer or ghoul that may be in the room. If I let one toe out from under the covers, they could get me, but if I was covered I was safe.

I do the same thing now, and I wish I had five more quilts to cover me.

And late at night, when I have to pee, I notice that the toilet seat is up in the bathroom and run right back to my bed.

Mom's boyfriend hasn't been over, as far as I know. I cannot think of a single logical explanation for the seat being up.

I've never really believed in this supernatural stuff. I don't think I do now, either. At least not intellectually. Emotionally, I believe in all of it right now. I tell myself that even if Cynthia did kill Aaron Saltis in just the right way to create a ghost, those brainwaves or whatever they are should have been stuck at the body dump, not capable of following me clear back to the suburbs to mess with my toilet, right?

But maybe this is a whole different kind of ghost.

God. I'm turning into one of those people. We get people

on the tours all the time who worry about ghosts following them home, but they always seemed so nutty that I assumed they probably also went to the grocery store and were afraid that the guy from the Lucky Charms box would follow them home.

Now I'm one of them.

I still have to pee. I stay in my room, under the covers, for a long time, until I have to go too badly to ignore it any longer. I even consider using the empty paper cup I have on my desk, but I decide that that would be going too far. I can't let myself get so freaked out that I start peeing in cups. God.

I rush into the bathroom with my eyes closed. I won't look in the mirror for anything. I keep thinking of some movie I saw when I was a kid, in which a person looked in the mirror and saw some sort of ghost looking back.

I laughed at the time.

The thought of looking in the mirror scares the hell out of me now.

In the morning, after a nearly sleepless night, I get a text from a local number I don't recognize:

u believe me yet? -edward t

Chapter Twenty-One

The toilet seat is up again in the morning, and my Disney villain toys on the shelves look like they're plotting against me, but I feel a tiny bit better. Better enough to function, at least. The world doesn't seem as scary when the sun is out, and the lingering dread retreats enough that I can get up and walk to the bathroom. I can look around my room, even into mirrors. But the feeling of dread is still there.

I'm afraid the police will come for me.

I'm afraid I'll log on and find a million e-mails from people who've read stories I never wanted them to see.

I'm afraid that a woman I thought was my friend has been plotting to kill me this whole time. Maybe tonight will be the night.

A week ago I thought it was awesome that some people had already put Halloween decorations out to go with the cold wave. Now they don't seem fun anymore. The plastic skeletons dangling from the trees look like people who've been hanged and left to rot.

I lie in bed until the sun is fully out, then text Kacey to see if she wants to go on a road trip to a town called Magwitch Park.

The traffic on I-55 slows down, then speeds up, then slows, and speeds up again as I ride along in Kacey's car. Traffic moves in mysterious ways. I kind of prefer it when it's slow and the interstate is jammed; Kacey drives like a maniac when she has enough room.

I've only told her that we're looking for clues about Marjorie Kay Stone, who ran the Finders of Magwitch Park company, who had some information about the ghosts I research for the tours. I didn't let on about how high the stakes were. She's excited enough.

"I feel like I should've brought my dog and some Scooby Snacks," she says as she tailgates a guy with a John Deere bumper sticker. "Maybe a proton pack."

"I'd kind of feel better if we had a proton pack."

Then she opens the glove compartment and says, "Well, we do have a sort of Scooby Snack, I guess. Dig around in the tampon box."

The tampon box in the glove compartment seems like a normal one at first, but she tells me to take the tampons out, and there's a baggie of weed beneath them.

"I don't know," I say. "Doesn't this stuff make you paranoid?"

"Maybe a little."

"I'm paranoid enough these days."

"So let me get this shit straight," says Kacey as she passes a semi. "If 'straight' is a word I can use without, like, offending you."

"Go nuts."

"So Zoey saw a picture of you kissing a customer."

"Uh-huh."

"But she still never sent you a picture of herself at all? Or called you so you could hear her voice?"

"Nope."

"So you still don't even know for sure that she wasn't some dirty old man?"

I don't even answer. After Kacey passes a slow-moving Hyundai, she pats me on the knee and says, "Honey, she probably had at least five other long-distance girlfriends the whole time."

I let that hang in the air and try not to feel like an idiot for letting things get so far out of hand with Zoey. I fail. As usual.

"Maybe. I'm just afraid she'll start spreading my stories around. They're fucking dark, some of them."

"She couldn't do it without attracting attention to herself, and that's obviously the last thing she wants. Or he. Whatever. I'd say you're in the clear."

We finally pull off the interstate and into Magwitch Park, an hour or so from home. It's out beyond where the suburban trains go, but still considered a commuter town, I think; half the people who live there probably work in the city and spend fifteen or twenty hours per week just driving back and forth.

As we drive around toward the little downtown area, I can tell that Magwitch Park is an old town, not like the suburban strip malls towns and retail wastelands that grew out of nowhere in the late twentieth century. Not one house looks less than a hundred years old, and most of them look much older than that. Almost all of them need a new coat of paint, and quite a few have settled unevenly into their foundations, so now they're leaning a bit, ready to crumble into one another. Some have rooms and wings that were clearly added on years after the main structure was built; they jut out at odd angles like cancerous growths and goiters.

I swear, the central core of some of the houses, near the train station, even look too old to be in the Chicago area. The oldest house in Chicago proper is from the 1830s, and nothing on the outskirts is that much older. The Magwitch Park houses look too old to be real. It's like we've driven through a time warp or a portal or something, and now we're in some whole other dimension, not the edges of Chicagoland.

They *all* look haunted.

Weeds poke through the brick sidewalks, and a pale little kid with hair so blonde it looks white stands on a porch in his diaper, staring at nothing and looking creepy as fuck.

I direct Kacey to the address where Marjorie Kay Stone's house was, and we find a vacant, overgrown lot, not unlike the one at the body dump. The houses on this street are huge. This space among them where Marjorie's place used to be is like a missing tooth in a mouth full of cracked ones. Only the foundation and basement are still there, a big pit in the ground.

In the area that used to be the backyard, a dried-up pond and a bush that looks like it was maybe once trimmed to look like a dolphin are all that stand as evidence that anyone interesting had ever been there.

We hop into the pit that used to be the basement and I wander around while Kacey smokes up, but it's not much more than a pit in the ground with scorched brick walls. There aren't any manuscript pages tucked into the cracks or anything. I guess I didn't expect there to be.

There's nothing spooky about the place at all.

If Cyn punched Marjorie Kay Stone in the brain, anything she left behind is gone.

Thanks a lot, laws of thermodynamics. The only dead body around here is probably Ricardo's hamster somewhere in the backyard.

There are no answers in Magwitch Park. Only an odd

moment when I think I see Morticia looking out the window
of a house as we drive by.

On the drive back, I get some texts from Edward Tweed. He texts
like an old person—the way people always *think* teenagers do.

TWEED:

Have an idea. Good 4 all of us. Even Rick.

TWEED:

I want u 2 join my company. Tell whatever stories u
want. Say I'm an idiot n a fraud. It's fine.

TWEED:

But I need some1 fast 2 run the tours Aaron was
supposed 2 run.

TWEED:

(Hear me out here)

TWEED:

I want 2 pitch an idea 4 the TV show: it follows both
companies. U and I r da villains everyone will love
2 hate. Makes it a better show. Makes u more valu-
able alive than dead. Rick and Cyn r the good guys.
U can switch maybe in season 2.

ADAM SELZER

TWEED:

Can we meet n discuss? I can show u the inside of
the Couch tomb.

I don't reply to any of them, but I find myself thinking
about the plan.

I did always like the villains best.

Sleep comes in fits and starts, and each fit and start brings a
new dream full of horrors that I'm glad to wake up from.

I type a few responses to Tweed, but I never send them.
Maybe I don't want a TV show. I'm scared to death that if I get
famous enough that anyone knows who I am, the stories I sent
Zoey might leak. Maybe she'll post them. Maybe Tweed will, if
he has them and I don't do what he says.

If I'm not on TV, there's not much to gain from spreading
my stories around. It's safer to be anonymous. No one. A face
in the grocery store.

But even right now, I suppose it could reflect really, really
badly on Mom and the business if Edward made them known
just around Forest Park.

He could make me do anything if he has those stupid
stories.

Why do I have to be this way?

While I stir my Cocoa Puffs around, I decide not to make
any decisions today. There's no tour tonight, no reason for me

to run into Tweed or Cyn or anyone. I'll go downtown and do more Lillian research. It's the only thing I can think of that might distract me enough.

Mom comes into the kitchen with a cup of coffee just as I'm rinsing out my bowl. She doesn't mince words.

"You look like shit, Megan."

"Thanks, Mother, I'll tell that to my body-image therapist."

"Not funny."

I grab a cup from the dish rack and pour myself some coffee from the pot, leaving it black instead of adding creamer, like I usually do, then sit at the table, trying to look distracted by my phone.

"What's up lately, Megan?" Mom asks.

"Nothing."

"You got into one of the caskets the other day. You haven't done that since you were little."

"I've grown up around them," I say. "They're not, like, any more unsettling to me than a calculator would be to an insurance agent's kid."

"No one's so well adjusted that they just hang around in coffins when everything's fine, Megan."

I try to ignore her.

What could I tell her?

That I cheated on a girl who knows all my secrets?

That some old guy with a seven-dwarves beard might

be ready to tell the whole world that the girl who lives at Raskin's Funeral Home is a way bigger freak than you ever imagined?

That this job in the ghost-tour business involves a lot of killing?

That I might be next on the list, and she was totally right that me taking this job was a bad idea?

I stare at my coffee and act like I'm just too tired to converse, but she holds a thing of lipstick in my face and says, "Clarice is out sick."

If I turn down the chance to help with mortuary makeup, she'll *know* something is wrong.

I get up, force a smile, and follow her down to the basement, where an older woman is lying on the table. Her face seems familiar, and it takes a minute for me to realize why: she used to come to the grocery store. The lips I'm about to make up have personally told me I was bad at my job before.

I don't remember specifically, but I probably imagined her choking to death on her fiber cereal.

And now, well, here she is. Just like I wanted.

I didn't really want it.

Not really.

Fuck.

My hand is shaking, so I work very slowly to get the lipstick right, examining the valleys and cracks of her lips and making a plan of action. I let myself get so completely wrapped up in making sure I get everything perfect that I forget Mom has brought me down here to interrogate me.

"So, Megan," she says. "Cyn told me something about you having girlfriend troubles."

I jump and smear lipstick all down the dead woman's face before I look up at Mom.

"When did you talk to Cyn?"

"She called to arrange another funeral for one of the residents."

"And she said I had a girlfriend?"

"I was already pretty sure you did."

I try to get back to the lipstick, but I mis-aim and instead of her lips, I put the stick down on her cheek.

"Oh, fuck."

I take a step back, and Mom looks hurt. "Did you think I'd be mad, Megan? You're allowed to have a girlfriend. I'm not some, like, conservative person who's going to get upset about it."

Some noises I can't identify float through the room. Sure. Sure I'm old enough to have a girlfriend. But who in the HELL is old enough to have a mystery girlfriend who probably isn't who she says but knows all sorts of embarrassing secrets about me? To talk to someone without being able to see where she keeps her brain. I wasn't afraid she'd be mad about me having a girlfriend. I was afraid she'd be mad that I'm an idiot.

And surely she wouldn't support me being a cheater.

And this is just what I'm afraid of *without* her finding out any more details about me.

"I shouldn't be down here," I say. "This isn't legal. You need a license to do this stuff."

"You're changing the subject."

I put down the lipstick and turn to run up the stairs.

Mom tries to follow me, but she's in heels.

"Megan, wait. If you're having problems, let me help you."

"I'm fine, Mother."

"So fine you're sleeping in coffins. I've been through breakups. Let's talk."

I nearly trip over an armchair in the front reception area. I know Mom wouldn't be mad that I had a girlfriend, but a girlfriend I couldn't see? She'd be a shitty parent if she didn't lecture me about that. And now there's nothing she could say, nothing she would ever dream of telling me, that I haven't told myself.

If anything, I worry that she'd be too understanding. I want someone to tell me I was an idiot. I want someone to lock me in a crawl space with rats and skeletons.

Mom keeps following, but I lose her halfway down the block as I head for the Blue Line. I'm just getting to the station when it hits me that Cyn told Mom about Zoey.

Cyn told Mom.

If that's not a clue that she might have told *other* people, nothing is.

All the dread comes back, and now I feel just like I felt at nighttime again. In broad daylight. This crushing sense of fear overwhelms me to the point that I have to stop running and crouch down on the ground, curling up like a turtle retreating into its shell, right on the sidewalk of Oak Park Avenue. Cars hiss by and a dog walker steps right over me.

After a minute I force myself to stand and keep pressing on toward the train station. But the dread is still there. Maybe it will always be there, and I'll just have to live with it.

Everything seems scary all of a sudden.

The Victorian houses I pass all make me wonder how many people had lived in them and died years ago.

The sign over the interstate beside the train says that there have been seven hundred traffic deaths on Illinois streets this year, and I think of how all roads are connected, really. The stretch of it beside me is part of one massive tangle of concrete and blacktop covering the whole damn continent, and tens of thousands of people have died on it this year.

Even the ads with elves baking cookies next to the train line maps by the benches freak me out today. Those ads have been going on for decades, and the elves didn't look young when they started. They have to be dead by now. Or they would be, if they were real to start with.

And the people who laid the tracks on which the train pulls up are probably all dead now.

As I step aboard I look around at all the other people. They are all going to die someday. How do they just go about their business? How do they get out of bed? Don't they know that someday they are going to *die*?

Maybe this is what all those other babysitters felt like when they first saw a funeral in my house.

I am going to die too.

Maybe soon.

And I brought it on myself.

It's like . . . all the things I did this summer . . . the things I called "charities" . . . they threw off the natural order of things. They made the summer turn into fall. Fair into foul. Unnatural deeds bred unnatural troubles.

The face of the grocery-store woman on the slab this morning, with the lipstick I smeared across her cheek, haunts my brain, sticks in my head like the chorus of a song. I wished her dead and now she is.

As the train moves, the noise it makes going over the rails sounds like "you're next you're next you're next you're next."

When I see another train coming up the other side of the tracks, I keep thinking it's going to crash into us.

"Dread," meaning "terror," the feeling I can't

shake, was first recorded in print in the year 1200.

In 900 the word for it was "grure."

Later on there was also "fearlac," from 1225.

Ferd, 1330.

Gastness, 1374.

Raddour, 1440.

Mom sends me texts begging me to let her help me, and I put my phone in airplane mode so I won't get any messages. The only way anyone can contact me now is if they come and find me. But it also cuts me off from the *OED*, my only reliable source of stress relief.

I think of all the people Cyn and I have taken care of. It was what they wanted but I wish we hadn't done it. All of the stock "villain at the end of her rope" lines rush through my head.

It wasn't supposed to be like this.

Only now, at the end, do I understand.

We are not so different, you and I.

I'll get you for this, if it's the last thing I do.

What a world. What a world.

There are things so much worse than death.

My beautiful wickedness.

Hell is murky.

When the train goes underground, the darkness is almost

more than I can take, even with the lights in the train on. It's a huge relief to climb the stairs onto Dearborn Street and see the sunlight.

In the microforms room I set up camp at a machine where I have to turn the reel manually, because the fast-forward knob isn't working right. There are better machines, but it's worth the hassle to be at one where I can see the doorway and keep an eye out for Tweed. Or Cyn. Even though I can see everyone coming in, I keep looking over my shoulder to see if one of them has materialized behind me.

Someone drops a book and I crouch down, thinking it was a gunshot.

When I read the old papers today, I feel painfully aware of the fact that everyone in them is dead. Maybe a few of the babies in the cute baby picture contests are still alive and in the nursing home. Or maybe they were until I ghosted them over the summer.

I turn the reader to maximum brightness so I can't see my reflection in the screen. I'm a little afraid it won't be my face looking back.

And almost as afraid that it will be. I can't look at myself right now.

In an issue of the *Chicago American* I find a photo of Lillian that I haven't seen before—one from the day the Wind Blew

Inn burned. She's sitting down, wearing a round hat, a sort of blazer, and a shirt. She does look like me. If Cyn showed people this picture, and then they saw some hazy, translucent version of me in Bughouse Square, they'd totally believe I was Lillian's ghost.

The photo is pasted over a large shot of firemen hosing down the burning inn, which, itself, looks like a saloon in a western or something. Above the picture is a headline saying "Wind Blew Inn Blown Out." A caption says "Chicago's Little Bumhemia Closes Its Career in a Trail of Smoke."

The article has a big new clue for me: the reporter described Virginia as a disgruntled former employee who had threatened to get even, and was now the chief suspect for starting the fire. So if she and Lillian had been a couple at the time of the trial a few weeks before, as I've been suspecting, they must have had one hell of a falling out.

I lean back for a second, imagining there had been a big misunderstanding when Lillian kissed someone in a play or something. Maybe the day before the fire, Lillian was sending Virginia telegrams, or whatever the 1922 version of texting was, saying "Please don't hate me," but Virginia wouldn't listen.

Or maybe they were just never a couple.

Either way, I wished I could hug Lillian via microfilm.

The papers were always patronizing to Lillian, and here in the *American*'s article on the fire, they describe her as perfectly happy and gay (not that kind of gay, the old-fashioned kind), shaking her bobbed curls as the cops haul her in on suspicion of torching the place herself for insurance money. (They let her go when they found out there *was* no insurance.)

I take about twenty pictures of the photo on the screen, making sure I have the best version I can get, then move on to other reels, other papers, other articles, just trying to give my brain enough to focus on to shut everything out.

Article after article goes by on the screen.

Just when I'm starting to feel dizzy and nauseous from watching them whiz by, I finally spot a clue.

Chapter Twenty-Two

WIND BLEW INN INMATES FREED ON TEA STORY

Chicago Herald-Examiner, Feb 15, 1922

To the uninitiated, The Wind Blew Inn, 116 E Ohio St, was revealed as a composite of red bandana handkerchief tablecloths, candles, Russian tea, sooners, cigarettes, and gallon and pint bottles in the Boys' court yesterday.

The thirty-nine defendants testified that the only stimulant they imbibed at the inn was tea. Fifteen girls and twenty-five young men were charged with being inmates and Miss Lillian Collier, proprietor, with being the keeper of a disorderly house. Detectives from the East Chicago Avenue station raided the place early Sunday.

"A boiler-maker must play the piano," according to Albert Otto, who maintains a rooming house at 118 E. Ohio (next door to the inn). "The noise those young upstarts make has driven away my best roomers."

Sergeant Shutz testified that when the officers made the raid, they discovered the patrons in unconventional attitudes, "cuddling up and smoking cigarettes."

Miss Collier and her mother, Mrs. Nellie Lieberman, told the court that nothing stronger than tea was served in their restaurant. The police had been called several times in the past when outsiders were known to have brought "hip liquor" with them. They became annoyed when the disturbers were found to have escaped on their arrival.

"Because of their tender years," Judge Lawrence C. Jacobs decided to drop the charges against all but Pat Sturgeon, 35, who was fined $25 and court costs, and Lillian and Virginia Collier, whose case was continued until March 24.

So, the part where the article called Virginia "Virginia Collier" was interesting. Probably just a mistake on the reporter's part, or a typo, but it could have suggested that they were considering themselves married or something. At least in February. Before whatever falling-out made Virginia a chief suspect in torching the inn two months later.

But the big clue is that it says that Lillian's mother was

named Nellie Lieberman. From that, I can assume that Lillian's real last name (or maiden name or whatever) was Lieberman.

My phone is still on airplane mode, but I walk into the computer bank outside the microfilm room and sit down with all the homeless guys who are using the out-of-date computers to search for jobs and porn. I load up a genealogy site, type in "Lillian Lieberman," and solve the mystery of what became of Lillian Collier.

Lillian Lieberman, born 1901, first appears on the record in a 1905 census of New York. By the 1910 US census, she was a girl living in Baltimore with her parents, Nellie and Meyer, and her sisters, Martha and Bertha. When she was fourteen she published a poem called "The Coming of Love" in the local newspaper.

A 1920 census form has Nellie, Meyer, Bertha, and Martha Lieberman, plus a daughter listed as "Lillian Coltie," living in Chicago. That was why I hadn't found her in the 1920 census before; there was a major typo when they transcribed it. From birth dates, I can see this is almost certainly the same family from the Baltimore census ten years before.

Now that I know her parents' names and her sisters' names, I'm able to put more pieces together pretty easily.

I find a 1919 New York marriage record of a Lillian Lieberman marrying a guy named Herbert Collier, but I'm not certain it's her. If it is, she would have only been seventeen when she got married. And Herbert was apparently out of the picture the very next year, when Lillian was in Chicago with her family.

From other records, I'm able to find that her mother's maiden name was Bensonson. And that she and Meyer came over to the States from Russia. Having Meyer's date and place of birth make it easier to sort him out from the other Meyer Liebermans—there were a lot of them—and pull up his World War II draft registration card from the early 1940s, which had a section for him to write out the name and address of someone who would always know his name and address. In that space, he wrote "Mrs. Lillian Gerard," a daughter who was living in Hollywood.

That starts me looking up "Lillian Gerard." There were more than one, but in the 1930 census, there's a Lillian Gerard living in Los Angeles with her husband, Franklin Gerard, his brother Charlie, and Mrs. Gerard's divorced mother: Nellie Bensonson.

That pretty well clinches it: this was her. Lillian Collier became Lillian Gerard and moved to California sometime in the 1920s.

Looking her up under that name opens the floodgates.

Lillian Lieberman-Collier-Gerard became a writer, publishing under the name Nellise Child ("Nellie's child"—clever). She published two mystery novels in the 1930s, plus two more serious "literary" novels and a whole bunch of plays, one of which, *Weep for the Virgins*, was produced on Broadway by the radical Group Theater, though it only lasted a week. She hung out with Irene Castle—whose hairstyle I now have—and wrote the last play she was in.

She even wrote a section for a book of Chicago murder stories. When I see that, I freak out a bit and say, "Oh, no way," right out loud, attracting a bit of attention from the rest of the people around me.

Lillian Collier became a murdermonger.

Somewhere along the line she married again, this time to a guy named Abner Rosenfeld, and by the 1960s she seems to have been going by the name of Nellise full time. According to the *Tribune* obituary for Nellise Rosenfeld, she died in Chicago in the early 1980s and was buried at a Jewish cemetery in the suburbs. The obit gives the maiden name of Lieberman, mentions a sister named Martha, gives her birth year as 1901, and says she was a member of the Dramatist's Guild. This is her, all right.

This is all fascinating, but the main thing that it drives home for me is this: Lillian Collier didn't die of tuberculosis in 1925.

Edward Tweed was lying when he said he knew for a fact that she had, and had proof somewhere in his files. He wasn't just repeating an urban legend or exaggerating a story or stretching the truth; he was outright lying to my face.

This makes it seem a lot more likely that he's lying about Cyn, too.

The lingering dread begins to retreat.

Once I've collected all the basic facts of Lillian's life, and picked up a copy of the script for *Weep for the Virgins*, I decide that I'd better leave now if I want to see her grave today, so I head back to the train. It doesn't feel as scary underground as it did a couple hours ago. The fact that I've caught Edward Tweed in a lie is an incredible relief.

I still don't know how he knew about Zoey, but I'm a lot less inclined to believe his explanation now.

As I ride along I turn my phone off airplane mode and send Mom a text saying I'm fine. She's sent me a bunch of worried ones.

Then I send Zoey a text saying I found Lillian. Even after everything, and even knowing she probably won't even read it, I still feel like I want to tell her this.

For a while I just lean back, watch the city go by through the window, and stop worrying about what Zoey might tell people about me long enough that I can just miss her. I miss talking to her. I miss her telling me how cute I am. I miss having someone to tell my stories about the tours to.

And I wish she could help me figure out what to do now.

☠ ☠ ☠

From the train station I run home through the rain. It's coming down hard when I get in the hearse and start driving. By the time I get to Arlington Heights, where Shalom Memorial Park is, it's absolutely pouring.

I know there isn't going to be a clue here. Lillian won't be sitting on her tombstone waiting to give me all the answers. But I want to see her grave, and maybe now that I've figured out *her* story, I can figure out more of my own.

The woman at the desk at the cemetery office gives me a confused look when I come in.

"I didn't think any burials were scheduled today," she says.

It takes me a second to figure out that she saw the hearse pull into the parking lot and thought I was there in some official capacity.

"No burial," I say. "I'm just looking for a grave."

"In a hearse?"

"It's my ride. I live above Raskin's funeral home."

She nods a bit and gives me a cautious look, like she thinks I'm a weirdo who's going to dig a grave up to use the skull in a love spell or something, but I give her the name of Nellise Rosenfeld, and she digs through the files, then directs me to a plot in section twelve.

"Not the best day for finding it," she says. "Might be underwater."

"I know. I just want to see it for myself."

"Relative?"

"Research topic. This woman took Chicago by storm in 1922. She's kind of my idol."

"Isn't that nice?"

Thick raindrops blotch against the windshield as I steer through the drenched grounds. I get turned around a couple of times and nearly drive into puddles deep enough to drown me—or at least mess the hearse up. When I get to section twelve and step outside, the ground is pretty well flooded. If I wasn't in my boots, I'd be getting soaked.

The marker, a simple plaque, is underwater, but I find it. I can just make out the name ROSENFELD in gold. Below that on the left, it says: NELLISE: 1901–1981. Beside that is: ABNER G: 1896–1984.

"Well, well," I say, in my best spy voice, even though I know she can't hear me. "At last we meet, Nellise Rosenfeld . . . or should I say . . . Lillian Collier?"

I stand there on her grave, letting the rain hit the both of us, for a long minute. I wonder what she looked like when she was an old woman, a few months shy of eighty. I imagine her at that age now, under the ground, laughing as I say her old name and saying, "Lillian Collier. Now that's a name I haven't heard in a long time. A long time."

I wonder if Abner even knew about her days as a flapper.

Or if she ever saw Virginia Harrison again after that fire.

When I get too soaked to do anything but shiver, I get

back into the hearse, turn on the heat (hearses have better heat than you'd guess), and think about texting Cyn.

I need to talk to her. The fact that Edward was lying about Lillian doesn't necessarily mean Cyn isn't planning to kill me, or that she didn't kill Saltis, but turning me into a ghost in a far suburban cemetery would do her no good whatsoever. I'm about as safe as I can be out here.

So I send Cyn a message.

> MEGAN:
>
> You at work?

> SWITCHBLADE CYNTHIA FARGON:
>
> Home. What's up? Your mom has called me twice.

> MEGAN:
>
> Arlington Heights. Shalom Memorial Park, Section 12. Come at once. Emergency.

> SWITCHBLADE CYNTHIA FARGON:
>
> On my way.

Then I sit in the car for a bit—it's gonna take her a while to make it this far out of the city, especially in the rain. Traffic always slows down in the rain.

I let the sound of the drops on the roof of the hearse sort

of hypnotize me, and try to meditate a bit. As usual, I can't. I calm down with the *OED*.

Some good *OED* words for sex include "meddling" (1398), "Venus exercise" (1507), "hot cockles" (1627), and "Moll Peatley's jig" (1711).

Then the word "barney-mugging" pops in my brain. It isn't in the *OED*, but googling shows that it was a flapper term for sex. For a minute I think maybe Lillian's ghost whispered it in my ear, but I must have just heard it somewhere before. Surely no one comes back from the dead just to teach people fun new words for intercourse.

But, then again, that's exactly how I'd want to spend my afterlife.

When Cyn's truck pulls up, I step into the rain and I motion her over to the grave site. She sloshes through the swampy grass.

"Who's this?" she asks. Then she looks down and reads out "Nellise. Interesting name."

"It was a pseudonym."

"What was her real name?"

"In 1922 it was Lillian Collier."

Cyn looks up at me, and her damp face lights up.

"This is her?"

I nod.

"You're sure?"

"Airtight. I found record after record. She became a mystery writer and a playwright under the name Nellise Child."

"Seriously?"

"She had a play on Broadway. It only lasted a week and papers still called her a 'girl playwright,' even though she was thirty-five, but still."

"Yeah."

"She even wrote some true crime, so she was technically a murdermonger."

"Wow." Cyn stares down at the gravestone, then smiles. "Can we talk in the car? You're gonna catch your death in this rain."

I nod and we get into the hearse. The heater is still running.

"So, you found her," says Cyn. "How did you do it?"

I run her through the stories about the mystery novels, the murdermongering, and Irene Castle. She listens intently, then says, "You could be her reincarnation, if you believe in that sort of thing."

"Or maybe I'm her ghost," I say.

She laughs. "Nah. You've aged since I was your babysitter. Ghosts don't do that. Not real ones."

She doesn't say anything or react in any way that makes me think the idea of me being, or becoming, Lillian's ghost is anything she's been plotting.

I show her all the documents I've saved to my phone. Articles where she talks about hopping freight trains from California to New York with her dog, Prince Otto, to get her play produced. The new 1920s stuff I found. I see when I'm flipping through them that there's an article in the *Tribune* archives with the name "Nellie Lieberman" too, but a missing comma made it less apparent that she was Lillian's mom.

Then, as Cyn reads through an article I found about "Lillian Gerard" from the 1940s, I just blurt out the question.

"Why did you tell my mom about Zoey?"

She looks up from the article. "I thought your mom seemed surprised when I mentioned that. She didn't know about her?"

I shake my head.

"You and your mom tell each other everything. You're like the Gilmore Goths."

"Well, I don't tell her that about, like, sexting or freaky stuff. God."

"I thought you'd at least tell her you had someone who was important to you."

"I was afraid she'd tell me how stupid I was being."

Cyn looks guilty, then gives me a hug as she apologizes and says we all do stupid things for love. "Look," she says. "Obviously I didn't tell your mom about the stories or anything. I just asked if you were okay and mentioned that I knew you were having girlfriend trouble. That's all. If I knew it was that big of a secret, I never would have said a thing."

I nod. And Cyn looks back at the phone, reading the rest of the article about Lillian from when she was a 1940s housewife who wrote novels. When she finishes, she smiles and hands me back my phone.

I stare for a second, then ask the *really* big question.

"Did you tell Edward Tweed about Zoey too?"

She gives me a surprised look, then laughs like I just asked her if she could drive me to Italy in her truck.

"Of course not," she says.

"Seriously. It's okay. Did you?"

"Megan, I would never tell that man anything personal. If I was in front of him in line at KFC, I wouldn't want him to know if I was getting original or extra crispy."

I lean back in my seat. "Okay."

I want to believe her. I desperately, desperately want to believe her. And I think I do.

"Seriously, Megan. Why would you even think I would do that?"

"He knows all about her."

"What?"

"And at least the basics about my stories. And he says you told him."

She breathes heavily for a second, then says, "Did Zoey know about Edward?"

"I guess. I told her a little about the competition and stuff."

"She probably e-mailed him herself, then. Maybe she got so pissed off when you kissed Morticia that she sent everything over to your business rival."

I swear on the grave of Lillian, the second Cyn says that, the windshield wipers in the hearse turn themselves on. If we'd been on a ghost hunt, we'd say it was a ghost sighting. The wipers clear up the windshield just as everything becomes clear in my brain.

Of *course* Zoey must have e-mailed Edward.

It was probably some sort of revenge on me. She probably offered to give him dirt on us or something. Our tour route. Pictures of the Couch tomb interior. Stuff about my Lillian obsession. Maybe even my stories.

It all makes sense.

Edward had my phone number to text me the other day, after Aaron died. Even if Cyn was telling Edward about Zoey, surely she wouldn't have given him my phone number, right? What would be the point? But if Zoey was sending him shit about me as revenge, my phone number might have been part of it.

I think the wipers are beating at the same rhythm as my heart.

"That's gotta be it," I say. "It has to be. She told him. And he's been lying to me."

"Of course he has," says Cyn. "It's what he does. The way I see it, either he got the info from Zoey herself, or he's rigged something up to bug the bus and spy on us. Maybe both."

"I thought about that. I checked for, like, walkie-talkies or whatever you'd use. Nanny cams. I didn't see any."

"I'll check some more. But I'll bet the whole dog and pony show that Zoey told him herself."

Then I look over at Cyn. Each thunk of the windshield wipers feels like another piece of the puzzle falling into place.

Thunk thunk.

"He knows about the brain-punch thing, you know," I say. "I don't know how."

"He's been in the business a while. If Marjorie found out about it, he probably could have too."

Thunk, thunk.

"He could have been killing people at his tour stops this whole time. For years," I say. "That might explain why everyone thinks his stops are haunted, even when the back story doesn't check out."

"Totally. Proper murder victims would make better imprints than what we get."

Thunk thunk.

"Maybe *he* killed Aaron Saltis," I say.

"Yeah. Maybe after he found out Saltis was talking to Ghostly Journeys."

Thunk thunk.

"Probably did it on the tour route so I'd think it was you."

Thunk thunk.

"He's trying to throw you off," says Cyn. "So you won't suspect that he's planning to kill you himself."

"You think? I think he'd rather have me alive and do the TV show with him. He's trying to recruit me."

Thunk thunk.

"He might let you live a while if you join him," she says.

"Might. But it'll just be a matter of time."

"So . . . what do we do?"

We stay in the cemetery, talking through every point of evidence, until they're about to close the gates. Then we say good-bye to Lillian and head over to a little deli nearby to warm back up. We sit there for the next hour, comparing notes.

We can't call the cops. We've done too much we don't want them looking into.

And we can't really tell Ricardo, partly because he doesn't know what we've been doing either, and partly because we both decide we don't want to deal with all of the jokes he's sure to make about Edward trying to turn me to the DarkSide.

But we make plans.

And before I go home, I call Tweed and arrange a meeting.

Chapter Twenty-Three

"Let us deprive death of its strangeness, let us frequent it, let us get used to it . . . To practice death is to practice freedom."

—MICHEL DE MONTAIGNE

The moon hangs between the antennas of the Hancock Center as I pull the hearse into the damp, gloomy bus lot. A Halloween-sized rat scurries along by the 1930s fire truck that someone keeps parked out here. The coyote is probably out there somewhere on the other side of the chain-link fence.

Edward Tweed is waiting by his car and waves at me when I roll my window down.

"Sweet ride," he says.

"Thanks."

"I think in a couple of cities they actually have ghost tours that drive people around in hearses, but I don't know how they make any money. Only so many seats to sell."

"You want to take it out to Lincoln Park?" I ask.

"We can just take my car," he says. "They all know me at the museum, so they won't run us off if I park in their lot."

My knees are shaking like hell, but I somehow manage to

walk from my car to his. It's a fancy sports car. Mr. Tweed is doing pretty well for himself.

He drives out of the lot, and I notice Cyn sitting in a car with Punk Rock James at the intersection on the other side of Halsted Street. In the rearview mirror I see them hold back a second after we pass by, then they pull onto Halsted Street to follow us at a safe distance.

My sense of lingering dread is mostly gone now, but it's been replaced by a nervousness way beyond any I've ever felt before. The only thing I can compare it to is the second before Morticia kissed me. Only that was just a second. This is a continual buzz of nervousness.

Emprise (first recorded 1500). Twitchety (1859). Spooky (1926).

I'll get through this.

It's really sort of awesome, in fact. Espionage and intrigue already, at the age of eighteen. Fuck yeah.

I keep trying to tell myself things like that. But I'm also busy trying to gauge how scared I should be. Cyn and I agree that even if he did kill Saltis, he's probably not going to kill me today. Maybe not even this year. He might really want me to do this TV show with him.

But "probably" isn't good enough. I'm in danger. But I can't let him know that I know it.

Also, there's a very good chance that this old man has

read some of the stories I wrote. That Zoey sent him the most embarrassing ones. The idea that he knows that part of me makes me nauseous.

"I found some new articles about Lillian the flapper," I say casually, as we cruise along. "Apparently Virginia Harrison, her partner, was the chief suspect when her tearoom got torched."

"Lovers' quarrel," he says. "They were a couple, you know."

"That's one theory. I think maybe Virginia liked Lillian more than Lillian liked Virginia."

"Maybe."

"Didn't find anything about her dying in 1925, though."

"Oh, she did," he says. "Tuberculosis. Got a lot of girls back then. Probably caught it out in Bughouse Square on a cold night."

There. A lie. Evidence.

Part one of the plan is confirming our suspicions, and I'm off to a good start.

"Makes sense," I say. "So, you wanna go get some food first and talk about this TV deal before we go to the tomb? I'm starving."

"I could eat."

"I know a good place," I say.

"Point the way."

I navigate him to one of Rick's favorite diners, which is a grimy hole-in-the-wall hidden in a hotel just off the Magnificent Mile. Cyn and I have staked out a spot where

ADAM SELZER

she and Punk Rock James can park the car and keep an eye on us from across the road, unseen.

The plan is working so far.

Ed's cell phone is sitting in the change tray by the gear shifter.

Mine is rigged up so that I can call Cyn with the push of a button if I get into a jam.

I've never actually been into this diner, but it seems familiar when I step inside. It takes me a moment to figure it out, but the place looks almost like the hotel bar from the dream where I was Lillian in the 1950s. Close enough to feel really fucking weird. Maybe she and Irene Castle sang along with a jukebox here twenty thousand midnights ago.

"What's good on the menu?" he asks.

"They do a good Italian beef," I say.

Ed gets one of those, and I order a pizza puff. He pulls out his card to pay, but I'm quicker on the draw and hand over cash to the clerk. A credit card would leave behind evidence that we were here. Cash won't.

I grab us a seat by the window and we sit and chat for a bit, just making small talk. Ed talks about the old days in the ghost business, and how he used to have access to places we couldn't dream of going now. Like Bachelor's Grove, the old abandoned cemetery in the southwest suburbs that is sort of a ghost-hunting theme park now. You can't legally be there at night without a filming permit anymore, but back in the day he could take tour groups out there without any trouble.

"How did you even have time to go there on a tour?" I ask. "It's an hour from downtown."

"My old tours were six hours long, every time," he says. "People had longer attention spans back then. Only trouble we had was that sometimes we'd come out there and there'd be a bunch of kids on drugs. Once they were digging up a body."

"Yeah, I saw some newspaper articles about kids doing that out there back in the seventies," I say. "I don't know how dull life must have been in the south suburbs back then."

"Pretty dull," he says. "Supposedly one of the guys was buried with a huge wad of cash. The hell of it is, they kept digging up the same guy over and over again, even though there wasn't any cash there the last time."

He laughs a cheerful old-man laugh as our food comes. Tweed is a strange person to watch. Sometimes he seems like a young hipster, with his curly mustache and the twinkle in his eye. But then he'll laugh or cough and move his face a certain way, and look a hundred years old. Like a freaking shape-shifter.

I eat slowly. My job right now is to keep him talking, drag the meal out as long as I can. Let the food do its work. Rick mentioned this place back on the tour with those hicks from downstate—this was the place where he said the Italian beef went south fast. If all goes well, Ed will need the bathroom soon.

And with any luck, he'll leave his cell phone on the table. It's in his pocket now.

"Hey," I say. "We got a great shot at Hull House the other night on the tour. Let me send it over."

I send a tour shot—one that I know damn well is fake—over to him via text, and he pulls his phone from his pocket to see.

"Looks so good, I'd be afraid they used one of those apps to fake it," he says.

"I assume they did," I say. "But I played along."

He chuckles and sets his phone down on the table, beside his plate, instead of putting it back in his pocket. Just like I hoped he would.

"Playing along is part of the job," he says. "You're new at this, but how many people have told you Al Capone had a vacation home in whatever small town they live in?"

"I lost count the first week."

He smiles. "And you can't just tell them they're wrong. You don't want to be a killjoy."

I nod, get up to order another pizza puff (which has the added benefit of needing to be fried up on demand, which will give me a few extra minutes), then sit back down to keep the small talk going.

"So, how did you find out how to get into the Couch tomb in the first place?" I ask.

He smiled. "Old girlfriend, years ago," he says. "She could find her way into anything."

I keep a poker face.

"Was she, like, a professional finder?"

"Yeah. Ran a company. She was looking for a ghost on some movie guy's nickel back when I was just starting out—he wanted to put a real one in a film. She found all kinds of stuff. Like that thing about how to kill people just right. She knew it."

"No kidding?"

"She was an older woman. I liked older women back then. Of course, at my age now, liking older women is basically just being a necrophiliac. Or at least someone who likes the elderly, whatever you call that."

"Gerontophile."

This is an interesting piece of new data: Edward apparently used to date Marjorie Kay Stone.

I keep eating and make a point of not reacting much, except to ask a few questions about this person he knew. The kind a historian would ask when she hears about a woman who was hired to find a real ghost. This line of questioning doesn't tell me anything new, but it gets me through my second pizza puff. When that's done, I order a milk shake and stall things even further.

"Now, let's talk about this TV idea," I say. "Where we team up."

"Well, if you'll pardon me for saying it, I'm a selfish old man and I want the show. And I think I would get the show, since I get more sightings, except that they have you. You're the edge."

"We've been having more sightings lately," I say. "We're trying out new sites and having good luck. Death corner. Places like that. We were thinking of Bughouse Square, where Lillian hung out."

"That'd make good TV," he says.

"I've never even really been there," I lie. "I really want to, but it keeps feeling dangerous. I don't quite believe you that Cyn's planning to kill me and make me into Lillian's ghost, but I'm not taking any chances."

"Smart," he says. "Tell you what. I'll go out there with you right now, we can scope it out as a haunted spot and figure out how to make it spooky for TV. Even if we have to make stuff up. I know it's not really your style, but that's what would make us the villains on the show."

"Yeah," I say. "I never make up stories, really, but I always identified as a villain."

"Sure," he says.

It really is a pretty decent concept. Assuming he really plans to let me live long enough to carry it out. But now he's offered to take me to Bughouse Square himself. I can imagine him making me decide right then whether or not to leave Mysterious Chicago and join him, and if I turn him down . . .

For all the chatting, I don't have enough data on him to know how scared I should be yet.

Then it happens.

He makes "the face."

"Is there a washroom here?" he asks.

"Behind you."

"Be right back, and then we'll head out."

He leaves the table, and, hallelujah, leaves his phone sitting on the table.

I immediately grab it and run outside. Cyn is waiting on a bench just outside of the door.

"You got it?" I hold up the phone.

"Hurry," she says. "Give it here."

When I hand it to her, she attaches a cable to it that runs into her laptop, then starts punching buttons. As she does, she hands me a clove cigarette and a lighter.

"Just so you have an excuse if he comes out and finds that you aren't at the table," she says. "Say you needed a cigarette."

I try to light the thing while Cyn messes with Edward's phone. Thank fuck Ed doesn't have a password lock. I'm not totally sure what she's doing as she pushes buttons, but she told me that Punk Rock James taught her some hacking tricks.

I feel like I'm in a spy movie.

"Edward used to date Marjorie Kay Stone," I say. "That's how he knows about the brain punch."

"That would explain it," she says. "They must have made a hell of a pair."

"The TV thing sounds fairly sincere," I say. "Like he'd want to keep me alive if I joined up with him."

"Until he didn't need you anymore, or decided you knew too much."

She taps a few keys on her phone, looks something over, then unplugs the phone and hands it back to me.

"Okay," she says. "I've got what I need. We're moving forward. Stall him, don't turn your back on him, and wait for texts from me."

I start to tell her that if he's got my stories, I'm not sure I want to know about it, but before I can, she sprints back to her car, leaving me alone with the phone and the clove cigarette. I take a drag and cough. Inside, I see that Ed is just coming out of the bathroom. I make sure Cyn is out of sight, then wave to him through the window. He ambles out, joins me on the sidewalk, and takes a whiff of the spicy air.

"I thought they outlawed those clove things."

"When did something being outlawed ever stop you from being able to get it in Chicago?"

He laughs and his eyes twinkle again. "True."

Then I hold up his phone. "Sorry, I reached for my phone and accidentally brought yours out."

"Any calls?"

I shake my head and hand it over to him.

"So, Bughouse Square, then the Couch tomb?" I ask.

"Sounds like a plan."

I slip back in to get my phone off the table, completing the act of having grabbed the wrong one. We get into his car and

I take out my own phone, acting like I'm not paying attention to where we're going.

I start getting more nervous. My fingers shake.

This is it. If he's planning to kill me, I've agreed to go to two perfect spots.

As we get to a traffic light, there's a series of texts from Cyn:

> SWITCHBLADE CYNTHIA FARGON:
>
> He has e-mails from Zoey. Affirmative.

> SWITCHBLADE CYNTHIA FARGON:
>
> And he didn't turn off location tracking on a few key apps.

> SWITCHBLADE CYNTHIA FARGON:
>
> So there's data showing he was at the body dump the day Aaron Saltis died.

> SWITCHBLADE CYNTHIA FARGON:
>
> Before the tours. Before you found him. He killed him all right. Good bet you're next.

> SWITCHBLADE CYNTHIA FARGON:
>
> Are you going to the tomb or bughouse?

I text back "Plan B," meaning Bughouse Square, and try to stay calm.

It's all real. I am in a car with a murderer. Who knows way too much about me and is quite likely taking me out to turn me into a ghost myself. He doesn't know that I know the truth, so I have the upper hand, but still. Shit. It's not the same dread I was feeling a couple of days earlier, but the squirrels in my stomach are doing a regular ballet.

I try to calm myself down, repeating my best historical rude words to myself in my head.

Ordure (1390).

Hinder-fallings (1561).

Pilgrim-salve (1580).

The park is sort of crowded when he pulls over next to it. If he's been planning to kill me there, he's off to a bad start. It's full of dog walkers. Witnesses.

"It'd be tough to do a ghost hunt here," I say. "So much else in the environment."

"If we get a filming permit we can kick them all out," he says.

He glances around, like he's trying to find an out-of-the-way place where he can kill me without anyone noticing. I spot a few places myself, little clusters of trees in the tiny park.

I can see him eyeing them too.

"What about Tooker Place?" he asks.

"What's that?"

He points to an alley half a block down Dearborn. "That alley. Used to lead to a hole in the wall you'd climb through to get to the Dil Pickle Club. You know about that?"

"Sure. The indoor Bughouse Square. Lillian hung out there, too."

"Why don't we go check that out? I'm not sure if the old building is still there."

I nod, even though I'm sure the building is gone, and I'm sure that he knows it.

There's only one reason he can be leading me into that alley.

This is it.

I notice Punk Rock James's car idling on the other side of the park. Cyn isn't in it. As was the plan.

My nervousness takes over my body and I have to force myself to take each step. As I text "Tooker" to Cyn, *OED* swear words race through my head. I lock in on them, letting them distract me enough from what's happening to keep me moving.

Fex. Commixtion. Coney burrow.

Gong. Tantadlin. Rutting.

I think I see Cyn moving in the shadows as we cross over Dearborn.

There isn't much to see in Tooker Place; it's just a regular alley now, all garages and garbage cans. The mansions beside it are pretty fantastic, though. It's like we've stepped into a Charles Dickens novel. There are even gaslights flickering on one of the garages.

"You know," he says, "your new haircut makes you look even more like Lillian."

"That's the idea."

Addle. Fling-dust. Croupon.

Crepitate. Nodcock.

"In fact," he says as he comes to a stop in the middle of the empty alley, "people might even say you look just like her ghost right here."

Tewel. Emiction. Mig.

Shit-breech. Shit-fire. Shit-sack.

If that's not confirmation, nothing short of actually dying will be.

"So, listen," he says. "I want to know. Do we have a deal?"

I start to step away, not turning my back until I'm out of arm's reach. Then I start to run.

"Hey," says Ed. "Where are you . . ."

His voice cuts off mid-sentence, and I stop in my tracks.

Then I hear Cyn's voice say, "Shit, that was too close. He was getting in position."

Then Punk Rock James says, "Megan, come here. We're gonna need a hand with this."

Chapter Twenty-Four

"Usually, when a man shoots a woman, he attempts his own life. When a woman shoots a man, she seems to think that's enough for one day."

—NELLISE CHILD (LILLIAN COLLIER), *CHICAGO MURDERS*

Live from the Allstate Showcase Studio in *Tribune* Tower on Michigan Avenue, you're listening to *Pretty Late with Patti Vasquez* on WGN. It's Halloween in Chicago, and after the break we'll be back with more from the crew of Mysterious Chicago Tours, as well as the group from Diciotto Pizza, the south Loop's hottest new spot."

Patti takes off her headphones and smiles. "Awesome," she says. "Have some more pizza. Please."

I take off my headphones and take a bite of the cold pizza that some new local pizzeria brought to the radio station. It's delicious. Everything is delicious. The world is delicious.

It's the end of October. The good cider is in stores, along with Franken Berry and Boo Berry, which only ever come out around Halloween. Trader Joe's has an entire section of pumpkin things. Pumpkin granola. Pumpkin crepe mix. Pumpkin popcorn.

My vocal chords feel like raw hamburger; I've run two tours a day all through October. Not always on our own bus— we've had to book extras to fill the demand, and the microphones don't always work like they should. I sound like I've been a smoker since I was two. I'm exhausted.

And I love it.

Now we're sitting in the radio station that operates out of the Tribune Tower, talking to Patti Vasquez, a whip-smart stand-up comic who has her own nightly talk show.

We start filming the TV show in December.

And according to Brandon, I'm going to be the star. The "breakout character."

Rick is fine with this. He says he'd rather be in the background, build contacts, and just be the court jester on the show. It's perfect for him.

While Patti goes to talk with Craig, the radio show's producer, for a second, one of the guys from the pizza place leans over.

"So, did you guys know Edward Tweed?"

"I used to work for him," says Rick.

"I was on one of his tours a couple years ago," says the pizza guy. "I couldn't believe it when I heard he'd disappeared. Do they really think he killed that one guy who worked for him?"

"It's complicated," says Rick. "It looked like a suicide at first. Then Tweed just disappeared a few days later, right after the cops got a tip that Tweed had been seen around the site where the guy died before the body was found."

"So, you think he's off in Mexico or something?" asks the guy.

"Probably. But some mysteries you just never get to solve."

Cyn sips a beer. Patti slips back into the booth, all smiles.

"Back in sixty seconds, one live read," says Craig.

Patti gives him a thumbs-up, then turns to us. "You guys are terrific," she says. "You mind staying for the second hour?"

"Sure," says Rick. The two of them chat about the local stand-up scene for a second, then the producer gives Patti a signal and she reads a spiel about an insurance company into the mic—a "live read," it's called. There's a minute or so of news and traffic, and then we're back.

"All right, we are back on *Pretty Late with Patti Vasquez*. We're talking to Luis, the chef at Diciotto on Eighteenth Street, who has brought us some fantastic pizza, and with the crew of Mysterious Chicago, the authentic ghost-tour company. Now, Ricardo, you're trained as a stand-up."

"Correct."

"Is being a tour guide a similar skill set?"

"Broadly, yeah," he says. "There's a different sort of research, and you have to rewrite your act based on traffic patterns and whether any ghosts show up, but it's a similar skill set to stand-up, yes. We got really lucky when we hired a new girl who turned out to be a natural. Megan is why we got the TV-show deal. I'm convinced of it."

"Nah, man," I say. "You would have gotten it without me."

I keep myself from saying, *Especially now that Tweed is gone.*

"No," says Cyn. "It's pretty obvious that you're going to be the focus of the show, Megan."

"Now, one thing I see in your online reviews," says Patti, "is that people really have been seeing a lot of ghosts on your tours. And not, like, guys in costumes, but actual ghosts."

"We see some weird stuff," says Rick. "Some things that I've really got no explanation for. It's not always like ghosts in movies, but sometimes it's pretty close."

"Shadows that shouldn't be there," I say. "We hear disembodied voices. It could all be just how our brains react to things, though."

"Yeah," says Patti. "I think that part of why we perceive things as ghosts is that our minds can never really wrap themselves around the concept of death. We look for reasons to think that life goes on."

"Exactly," I say. "And if we don't find them, our brain manufactures them."

"Or, you know, they just actually are ghosts," says Cyn. "Let's not put ourselves out of business saying they're just optical illusions."

Everyone laughs a bit. It's such a warm, friendly vibe in the studio. I could hang out here all night.

"And you really do the research on these places, so you know who they'd be the ghost of," says Patti.

"Usually we do," says Rick. "I mean, we always do the research. Like, deep research. We never take mythology at face value. But sometimes we find ourselves in a location that sure seems haunted, and we aren't sure why. Like Tooker Place."

"Tooker Place," says Patti. "I love it. Like, 'I took 'er to Tooker.' Where's that?"

"It's a little alley that used to lead to the Dil Pickle Club on the Near North Side," I say. "Which was a bar for anarchists and weirdos right near Bughouse Square, which was a park for anarchists and weirdos."

"My kind of bar," says Patti. "Anarchists and weirdos."

The woman who reads the traffic reports isn't in the room with us, but I see her on a monitor, and she chimes in with "Yay, anarchists and weirdos!"

"There's not a lot of data on the park being haunted," I say. "But it seems like it ought to be, so we've been going there now and then."

"It's a good historical story any way you cut it," says Rick.

"There's a flapper I like to talk about there named Lillian Collier," I say. "She used to have a bohemian tearoom about two blocks from here, and she hung out at the Dil."

And I tell the whole story of Lillian Collier, live on the air. Patti's face is lit up the whole time, and I feel like I'm doing a good deed, telling Lillian's story live to thirty-eight states and parts of Canada.

"So, long story short," says Rick. "We started parking the

bus on Tooker Place to tell her story sometimes. And we aren't sure why, but that alley is freaking haunted."

"You sound like you're on *Ghost Encounters*," Cyn teases. " *'That place is freaking haunted, bro!'*"

"I do not," says Rick. "And I'm being for real. We're seeing this silhouette against a garage there that just appears and disappears. There are stains on the ground that appear and won't wash away, and then they've vanished in five minutes, but they still show up in pictures. We hear footsteps. It's crazy."

"So who's haunting it?" asks Patti. "Any theories at all?"

"That's the real question," I say. "We've heard rumors of there being some cholera victims buried on the site of the Newberry Library, which is right nearby, so that's one option."

"People got killed at the park now and then, too," says Rick.

Rick, of course, has no idea what Cyn, Punk Rock James, and I did at Tooker Place two months ago. We'll never tell him. It's better all around if he just thinks the ghost sightings there are of a victim of the Great Chicago Fire of 1871 or something.

"Hang on," says Patti. "We've got a caller." She checks her screen and says, "Okay, this looks like it's actually a call for Megan. Megan, this is Zoey on the line. Zoey, what's up?"

I look at Cyn. She looks and me and shakes her head. Rick looks shocked and Cyn whispers something in his ear.

There's nothing but breathing on the line for a minute.

"Um, hi?" I say.

More breathing.

"Zoey?" asks Patti. "Are you there?"

And then a voice says, "Megan . . . help . . . ," and hangs up.

"Okay, sorry about that," says Patti, as I keep my poker face. "Craig, did she say what she wanted?"

"Just that she had a question for Megan."

Patti nods and just moves on. "We've got another one on the line who wants to talk about the ghosts here in Chicago. Dave in Orland Park, you're on the air."

Rick fields the usual questions about the Excalibur Night-club having been a morgue once (just an urban legend), while I pull up my phone. I haven't logged in to any of the services I used to use to chat with Zoey in a few weeks, and I don't see any messages now.

Cyn gives me a look, like, *We're on the air. Do it later,* and I put the phone down.

I never looked at Edward's phone records that Cyn down-loaded, but she confirmed that he'd gotten e-mails from Zoey telling him all about me.

And she says she found out exactly who Zoey was, too. All she told me was "You dodged a bullet, but trust me, you don't want to know."

Between prep for the show and how busy we ended up being in October, I've barely had time to think about Zoey. I haven't written one story about the Emperor and the Evil

Queen since summer. Or about any other villains, either.

I didn't even start taking classes like I planned to. I pulled out of the junior college. I figure I'll get to that when I have more time. Even Mom thinks college is a waste of money for most people today; and if I've got a chance at a career without it, I should take it. I'm getting more education on this job than I probably would in school, anyway.

Plus, I get to go on radio shows that broadcast out of Tribune Tower, the gothic skyscraper on Michigan Avenue. Which would make a perfect castle for a villain.

After the show wraps for the night, we take some photos with Patti, then walk out to the parking lot below the building, where Cyn's truck is parked. It's a beautiful night. Sweater weather.

"So, that was weird," I say. "Zoey."

"It can't have been her," says Cyn as she steers us out of the parking lot and onto Lower Michigan. "Trust me."

I nod and try not to worry too much as we get into the city and wind through the nightclub zone. It's way too cold for some of the outfits the girls on the street are wearing. I wouldn't want to slut-shame them or anything, but I bundle-shame them. It's cold. Get a jacket.

"Hey," says Cyn. "I've got something I want to show you. You up for a minor expedition?"

"Sure."

"Where are we going?" asks Rick.

"You, Ricardo, are going home," says Cyn. "This is a girls-only trip."

"Ah," says Rick. "You know, you can go online and see all those movies that were just for the girls in health class, so I know all about what's in them."

"Glad you've solved that mystery," says Cyn. "But this is still a top-secret girls-only mission."

"Whatever."

The interstate is empty, and in five minutes we're in Humboldt Park to drop Rick off. He waves good night, and Cyn starts turning the truck around.

"So, where are we going?" I ask.

"Magwitch Park."

"What's out there?"

"Morticia."

She pulls onto the interstate and I stare over at her. "Seriously?"

"Yeah," she says. "I sort of need to come clean about all that."

"What?"

"She's an old friend of me and Rick. I had her come on that tour so she could slip out at the old cemetery grounds and we could say she was a vanishing hitchhiker in front of Brandon. Rick thought it was the dumbest thing ever."

"Yeah, I remember he seemed kind of embarrassed."

ADAM SELZER

"Not Rick's style, but you have to fight dirty sometimes to get where he's going, and I'm the one who does the fighting."

"So you know her?"

"Yeah. She's awesome. And she won't stop asking me about you. I didn't even ask her to come that second night."

"Seriously?"

"She's basically nocturnal, too. She'll still be up."

Cyn drives along through the streets and I try to process this. I've had plenty of dreams and fantasies about Morticia. She's the crush I've focused on to get over Zoey. I keep checking my e-mail, hoping she'll track me down. The only thing is that I didn't want another long-distance relationship.

Magwitch Park isn't too far away, though.

I text Rick:

MEGAN:

YOU KNEW MORTICIA?

RICARDO "THE RASCAL" TORRE:

Ah! That's the trip! Yeah, I thought it was a lame stunt.

RICARDO "THE RASCAL" TORRE:

But yes, she's great. And I guess you're "in" enough now to know all the secrets. Tell her I said hi. Her name's Enid, by the way.

Enid. It really is Enid.

How charming and old-fashioned.

My knees start to shake, and a kaleidoscope of butterflies take up residence in my stomach. That's what you call a group of butterflies. A kaleidoscope.

I wonder why they didn't come clean on this before.

"Will she be okay with my stories?" I ask. "And . . . what goes on in them?"

"She can outdo you. Trust me. You won't freak her out."

While I'm thinking, I notice a newsletter for the nursing home on the floor and catch a stray item about their beloved receptionist, Shanita, dying.

"Wait, Shanita died?"

"Yeah," said Cyn. "Couple weeks ago. It was quite a shocker."

"You didn't tell me?"

"We've been so busy, I forgot."

Cyn steers the truck out of Humboldt Park and turns on the radio. I'm actually—and I hate to say this—sort of relieved. I liked Shanita. But she knew way too much about what we were doing. It makes me nervous that anyone knows anything.

I'm excited, but at the same time I'm feeling bad about Shanita and worried that maybe Enid will find out about my stories and stuff and decide to stay away from me. And a bit upset that Rick and Cyn tricked me and didn't let me in on the secret until just now.

So much at once. My brain is totally puddled.

But maybe I can make it all work.

Lately I feel like I can do anything.

Cyn gets off at the LaSalle Street exit, rolling right into Lincoln Park and the Gold Coast.

"This isn't the way to Magwitch Park," I say.

"I just have one thing to take care of first."

The bare branches of the ancient trees that line the street reach for the sky like chimney smoke. They rattle like bones in the night as she steers us down Dearborn. We'll be going right past Bughouse Square in a few blocks.

Some of the townhouses have gone all-out with their decorations. Orange lights and spider webs are everywhere. One house has a full-size mummy on the porch. Another has an old-fashioned coffin. It's wonderful.

The jack-o'-lanterns are in bloom, laughing at death with their glowing smiles as we drive into the Halloween night.

A BRIEF NOTE FROM THE AUTHOR

Just to clear things up a bit:

Most of the historical stories in the book are real; the main exception is the stuff about Marjorie Kay Stone and Finders of Magwitch Park (Magwitch Park isn't even a real town, and you can't really make your own ghost by punching people in the brain, so don't come running to me if you try it and get suspended or something). People and businesses mentioned in the book are a mixture of real people and fictional ones. Mysterious Chicago Tours wasn't real when I started working on the book, though it is now!

Lillian Collier was a real person in Chicago—Megan found out what became of her after 1924 a lot faster than I did. She was a mystery to me for years until I started work on this book, decided to buckle down and clear it up, and found that *Times Herald* article that gave me her maiden name, which opened up the rest.

As to whether she and Virginia Harrison were a couple, I really don't know. Lillian's son, Frank, doesn't know for sure, either, though he says they "might very well could have been." "She was never very upset when I told her I was gay!" he says.

I asked Frank to write a brief note about his mother:

My mother, Nellise Child, (pronounced Nell . . . eese, as in peace, accent on the second syllable), was born in New York. Her parents, being Russian Jews, came to New York around the turn of the century. With only a high-school education she simply read everything she could get her hands on. She knew from an early age she wanted to be a writer. She was a member of the New Dramatist's Committee, so between 1948 and 1962, we got to see nearly every play on Broadway. She published two novels, *Wolf in the Fold* in 1941 and *If I Come Home* in 1943, as well as two mystery novels in the early 1930s. Soon after that her play, *Weep for the Virgins*, was produced on Broadway, by the Group Theatre, in New York. She was a great cook and entertainer. My father and I were very lucky to have known her!

Several plays Lillian wrote are still on file at the Library of Congress, and her books can be tracked down without too much trouble. For a time she worked as a writer for the *Herald-Examiner* under the terribly patronizing byline of "Our Little Girl Reporter," but I've only ever found one of her articles; she later recalled assignments such as fainting in the street to see what happened. Efforts are underway to make more of her work available online.

As a side note, I've never found any more information on Virginia Harrison. One paper said that her real name was Jean Lawrence, which is a good clue, but both names are common enough to make her hard to trace, and it's possible that neither was her real name. As Ricardo said, "there are some mysteries you just never get to solve."

TURN THE PAGE FOR
A SNEAK PEEK AT
PLAY ME BACKWARDS.

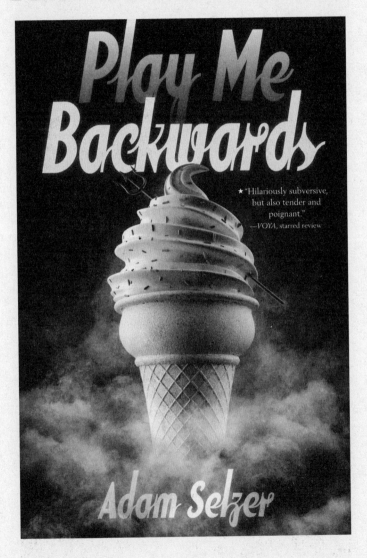

MEAT

There are times when Satan really gets on my nerves. Like, he's been saying for years that he wants to buy my soul, but every time he gets enough cash saved he decides to get his car windows tinted or something instead. He can be a real dick like that.

And on Valentine's Day, a day when I was going to really need him and his evil powers, he was late for his shift at the ice cream place where the two of us worked. I had to hold off the morning rush, such as it was, alone. He finally strolled in an hour after he was scheduled, hands in his pockets and whistling a riff from a Misfits song, like he didn't have a care in the world.

"You're late," I said.

He stopped in his tracks and walked over to me.

"Let's do the list," he said. "World Wars I and II. The Black Death. That earthquake in South America last month. *The Phantom Menace*. Algebra. The decision to make Alpha-Bits a *healthy* cereal, instead of a sugary one. All me. And you're mad at me for being late to work at an ice cream place that has three customers a day?"

"Yes," I said.

"Priorities, man," he said. "Big picture."

And he disappeared into the back room.

Dick.

I suppose most geniuses can be dicks when they feel like it. Thomas Edison once electrocuted an elephant just to prove a point.

I first met the dark lord when I was nine. My mother is a Realtor, and now and then she'd take me along on house calls when she met with people who were thinking of listing their house. My job was to play with any kids who happened to be present in order keep them out of her way. It was a living, but not an easy one. The boys often wanted me to play sports that I wasn't any good at. Girls occasionally wanted to give me makeovers. Really little kids would make me play horsey or watch *Dora the Explorer*. Real estate is a tough business.

When we showed up at this one house, there was a pointy-faced kid with glasses standing in the doorway behind his mother, eyeing me like you'd eye a piece of furniture you weren't quite sure fit in your basement.

"Hi," said Mom. "You must be Stan."

He nodded and Mom put her hand on my shoulder.

"This is Leon," she said. "He's about your age. Go play."

The kid led me into his room, and we started playing video games on a boxy old TV that got the colors wrong. His room smelled weird. Other people's rooms always do, but this one didn't smell like anything I'd ever smelled before. Years later Dustin Eddlebeck and I tried to figure out what Stan's place smelled like and ended up on "grilled cheese, old people, and freshly spray-painted ass."

"You don't have to call me Stan," he said. "My name is actually Satan. My parents just leave out the first *A* so I can go to St. Pius."

Man, I thought, *I sure meet the weirdos on this job.*

Stan/Satan didn't try to beat me up or anything, and he didn't hit the reset button on the video game every five seconds just to mess with me, like some asshole kids did, but while we played, he told me that he used to be God's favorite angel until he grew too proud and got kicked out of Heaven and became the devil. Obviously he was lying, but he wasn't chuckling or using an "evil" voice or anything. He talked about going to Hell to reign over demons as casually as other kids talked about going to Omaha to visit their aunts.

He was just telling me how he was planning to have a tornado wreck a small town that spring when some kid with a bowl cut stuck his face into the window.

"Hey, Stan."

Stan gave him a tiny nod. "Hello, Josh."

"You wanna come over?"

Stan shrugged, thought for a second, then said, "Do you have any meat at your house?"

"Got some ham in the fridge, I think," said Josh.

"How much?" asked Stan.

"About three pounds."

Stan pursed his lips, like he was considering the offer, then he shook his head and said, "Nah."

Josh didn't argue; he just nodded and took off, like it was generally known and accepted in the neighborhood that if you wanted to hang out with Stan, you needed to have an ample supply of meat at your house.

Later on I tried to make sense of the whole exchange. How could three pounds of ham not be enough? Would Stan have gone if there had been a fourth pound? Or if it was honey-roasted turkey? And what about Josh? What kind of kid even knew how many pounds of ham were in his fridge to start with? I couldn't have possibly told you what was in my own refrigerator. I only kept track of what kinds of cereal we had in stock.

Now that I know that Stan is a genius, one possessed of dark powers that have saved my ass from certain doom on occasions too numerous to mention, I realize that he might not have been planning to *eat* the meat at all. He might have had some fantastic project in mind that required at least five pounds of fresh ham. I've asked him about it, but he says he doesn't remember that day at all, and that he never even knew a kid named Josh. I'm pretty sure he's lying, but you never can tell with Stan.

He was a year ahead of me in school, and he went to St. Pius Elementary and Dowling High, the local Catholic schools (yes, I know), so I didn't see him again until my sophomore year of high school, when he and I both ended up working at Penguin Foot Creamery, one of those awful ice cream shops where the employees have to sing songs and ring bells and shit every time someone orders a large sundae. This was where I learned that he may have been a weirdo, but he was the kind of weirdo who could be destined to lead nations.

He was still going around saying he was the devil, but he didn't seem particularly evil or mean or anything. In fact he had a pretty sunny disposition for a guy who claimed to be the prince of darkness. And his skills at messing with customers made the job a lot more tolerable.

In one of his most inspired moments he got the idea that instead of up-selling drinks or T-shirts to go with people's ice cream, like we were supposed to, we could make extra money by up-selling stuff that we stole out of the manager's office. When somebody ordered a dish of ice cream and mix-ins, we'd say, "Would you like a stapler with that?" Or, "You know what would go great with that sundae? Some envelopes!" If anyone said yes, we'd grab whatever we'd just sold them out of the office and charge them an extra buck or two. We almost sold the printer once.

Half the people just thought it was part of the store's shtick, but we still got in a ton of trouble when Jane, the manager, realized she wasn't just *losing* her staplers all the time. She was ready to fire us on the spot, but Stan talked her out of it with a brilliant defense that would have done any lawyer proud. In his genius brain, he was always three moves ahead of everyone else.

Then, one afternoon, a bearded guy in a pink shirt and red pants came in to give out brochures about how you'll end up in Hell with cartoon devils poking your butt with pitchforks if you don't start praying to cartoon God. Stan took one look at the picture of Jesus on the cover and said, "Oh, I remember that guy. He came into my place one time. Said he'd just been crucified."

The man in the pink shirt looked confused.

"Your place?" he asked.

"Yeah," said Stan. "I was like, 'Welcome to Hell, my name is Satan, hand me that pitchfork' and all that, but he was all, 'Look, is there any way I can be out of here on the third day?' 'Cause I got a thing on Sunday.'"

I played along, as usual.

"What did you tell him, Mr. Satan, sir?" I asked.

"Well," said Stan, "I told him he'd be there *forever*, so there was no way he could be out that soon, but then he was like, 'Do you know who my dad is?' And well . . . you've got the brochures, man. You know."

The man stared at us some more, like he was too shocked at our insolence to say anything. Maybe he was new to this whole "evangelizing" thing, and thought everyone who saw the cover of the pamphlet would instantly become filled with love or something. His salt-and-pepper beard began to twitch.

"Oh, sorry," said Stan. "Please allow me to introduce myself. I'm the angel formerly known as Lucifer. Lord of the Flies, Father of Lies, et cetera. You can just call me Satan, though." He bowed, then pointed at me and said, "This is Leon, one of my minions."

"Pleased to meet ya," I said.

"I'll probably be putting Leon in charge of you when you get to Hell," said Stan, "so I'd tip well if I were you."

"I'm not going to Hell," the guy said.

Stan smiled and wiped down a spot on the counter.

"That ain't what God told me," he said.

That's when the guy got mad.

Now, normally when we messed with customers, they actually seemed like they could take a joke, if they realized we were messing with them at all (which was fairly rare; most of the customers were a little slow on the uptake). But this guy decided to raise a bit of Hell of his own. He threw such a fit that there was practically smoke coming out of his ears. There are probably still tiny bits of spittle and pink shirt lint in every sundae they serve at that place.

Even Stan couldn't save our jobs after that one.

But getting fired turned out to be the best thing that ever happened to us, because he got us both jobs at the Ice Cave, the B-list ice cream parlor in the old part of town, nestled away in the old Venture Street triangle near Sip Coffee and Earthways, the new age store.

The Ice Cave was nothing like Penguin Foot Creamery. For one thing, there weren't many customers to deal with. And George, the owner, wouldn't have dreamed of making us sing songs about ice cream while we worked. He'd owned the place forever, and it had never been a moneymaker on its own—honestly, I was pretty sure it was just a front that he used to launder meth money or something. He only ever stopped in to see if there was some beer in the walk-in cooler, and if he found us sitting on the couch in the back instead of mopping something, he didn't write us up. He didn't worry much about inventory, and didn't have a problem with employees wearing name tags that said SATAN and MINION, or with us helping ourselves to all the mix-in candy we could eat. After he graduated, Stan got himself promoted to manager, which meant that Satan was officially my master during my senior year of high school.

To call what we did at the Ice Cave "work" at all would be a stretch. The back room, which contained a couch, some folding chairs, and a little desk with a computer, served as the office, the storage area, and the break room. We spent most of our time at work holed up back there, listening to old-school metal and helping ourselves to the Reese's Pieces and gummy bears that were stored in big plastic barrels along the wall. Over time it became a sort of a haven for the dredges of teenage suburbia—the headbangers, the minor criminals, the stoners, and assorted lost souls and hangers-on. Some days—a lot of days—we'd get more people coming into the store just to hang around in the back than we'd get coming in for ice cream.

I felt like I had found my calling. It was the kind of job you'd think you had to sell your soul to get, and I imagined myself growing old in that back room. I mean, I could go to college, but what for? To get some crappier job that I didn't like as much? When you get a job you like, you should lock it down.

Now, that Stan is a genius cannot be restated too many times. Stories of his unholy powers are numerous and legendary. Like, for instance, there's the story of the time Dustin Eddlebeck drank enough vanilla syrup to kill a wampa.

On that day Stan, Dustin, and I were hanging around in the back room, just killing time during a slow day. There hadn't been a customer in about an hour, which was not unusual. Stan was eating Cheez Whiz right out of the spray can. At some point, Dustin noticed that the big vanilla syrup containers listed "alcohol" among the ingredients.

"Bet we could get drunk off that stuff," he said.

"I doubt it," I said. "You'd probably have to drink a ton of it."

"It's worth a shot," said Dustin. "Let me open one."

We could have easily acquired some regular booze—there was probably even some hidden in the cooler someplace. But I guess Dustin was bored and in the mood to experiment that day.

Stan got some paper cups, and we all had a swig of the thick vanilla gunk. It tasted about like maple syrup, only sweeter, and with a hint of something that tasted like engine oil. It was thicker than most maple syrup too. You literally had to choke it down.

Stan and I quit after one chug, but Dustin kept going. Over the course of the afternoon and most of the evening, in between several trips to the bathroom, he drank about half a gallon.

Let me just repeat that: The man drank *half a gallon* of vanilla syrup.

He said he was drunk, and I believe him, but I think he was too sick to enjoy it. After he drank his last shot, he wandered around looking dizzy for a minute, then collapsed on the couch in the fetal position.

"Kill me," he groaned. "Either turn down the music or kill me."

"Headache?" Stan asked.

"I feel like The Slime that Ate Cleveland is on my frontal lobe."

"Don't worry," said the dark lord. "I know how to handle this."

And he went up to the front and came back with a glass of something that he forced Dustin to drink. Dustin downed the whole glass without taking a breath, then shivered for a second before hopping up onto his feet and shouting, "Holy shit!"

"How do you feel?" Stan asked.

"Like I could pull the ears off a gundark," said Dustin. "Damn."

"What did you put in that?" I asked.

"Trade secret," said Stan. "I got the recipe from Sinatra when he came into my place."

"He went to Hell?" I asked.

"Oh, I got just about the whole Rat Pack," said Stan. "All of them except for Sammy Davis Jr. But I let him come hang out sometimes. The parties are better at my place."

Stan always makes it sound like people in hell have a pretty good time when they aren't being stabbed in the ass with pitchforks. It seems believable enough, because in addition to his mastery of hangover cures and retail managers, Stan is a bit of wizard when it comes to planning parties. He is probably the only person alive who can make a heavy metal vomit party seem authentically Christmasy.

Dustin shook his head, like he couldn't believe what had just happened, and looked over at Stan with all due reverence. "Should I, like, sacrifice a goat to you or something now?"

"Nah," said Stan. "It's cool."

"I'll be damned," said Dustin.

"Just be careful when you come to Hell," said Stan. "That last step's a doozy."

So, yeah. The guy is a genius. I don't know how I ever managed to get through life without him. Obviously, I knew *intellectually* that Stan was not really a supernatural entity, but sometimes it was hard not to believe it. Any cop at a Mothers Against Drunk Driving assembly will tell you that the only thing that can actually sober you up is time. The concoctions Stan whipped up defied all known laws of biology.

But he *did* get on my nerves from time to time, which brings us to the day he showed up late for work on Valentine's Day. A day when I really needed some help.

It wasn't that I couldn't handle what passed for a rush at the Ice Cave alone, or that I actually needed supervision from a manager, but I didn't want to be by myself if any couples came in. I couldn't deal with being around couples that day.

Also, there was a pounding in my head that I was pretty sure meant that I was hungover and needed one of his miracle cures.

The day before, February 13, had been the "unofficial" Valentine's Day at school. I had sort of hoped that having Valentine's Day fall on a Saturday would mean I'd be spared watching all the couples at school having balloons and flowers and shit sent to each other, but I guess I was just being an idiot. Girls weren't about to give up the chance to have someone deliver them a giant thing of flowers in class just because the real Valentine's Day wasn't until the next day—people just did all that crap on the thirteenth instead. Between classes you'd see girls walking around with teddy bears bigger than they were, and couples were making out everywhere you turned. Every couple was trying to outdo each other for the gold medal in PDA. I was generally happy with my life as a perpetually single retail bum, and just about content to resign myself to that sort of status for life, but watching all the happy couples rubbing it in my face just made me feel lonely as hell.

Whoever made the laws about underage drinking clearly never had to get through a high school Valentine's Day. I'd rarely had more than a sip or two even in the back room of the Cave, where drinking stuff stronger than vanilla syrup was not exactly unheard of, but on Valentine's Day eve, alone in my room, I'd broken my own drinking record by a decent margin. And now, at work, I was feeling the results.

Stan emerged from the back room wearing his apron.

"Sorry I was late," he said. "I didn't think there'd be anything you couldn't handle alone."

"There wasn't," I said. "But can you mix me up a glass of that hangover concoction of yours?"

He smiled. "Rough night last night?"

"You could say that."

"Coming up," he said.

And he got to work mixing stuff from the soda machine, the cabinets, and some mysterious Tupperware containers from his backpack.

Meanwhile, I looked down at my phone to reread the e-mail I'd gotten the night before. Far more than the Valentine's couples it was the e-mail that had pushed me over the edge and into my dad's liquor cabinet.

From: anna.brandenburg236@gmail.com

To: leon.harris50322@gmail.com

Subj: Iowa

Hey, Leon! My parents were talking about coming back to Iowa the other night; maybe even moving. Not definitely, but maybe. It'd be good to see you (and the rest of the "gifted pool" hooligans) again, so I'll keep you posted. Happy Valentine's Day.

Anna B.

Anna B. Like I'd ever think it was some *other* Anna. It was the most I'd heard from her in almost three years.

And it scared the green shit out of me.

this is
what
happens
after
happily
ever after.

The first in the companion series to the *New York Times* bestselling
MARA DYER TRILOGY

Five high school seniors.
One life-changing decision.
What future will they choose?

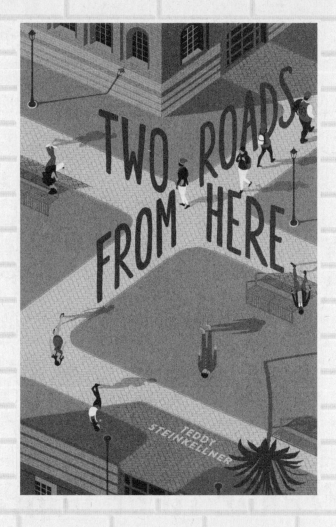